The Hitler Paradox

Andrew Dunkley

For my parents, Janice and Graham Dunkley

(Congratulations on 60 years' marriage)

Chapter 1 – Prologue

By the 2200s, the World had changed greatly in some ways and not so much in others. Most nations were the same and while some borders changed, they somehow managed to avoid a third World War despite the ongoing arguments over issues that had plagued the planet for centuries. The widening gap between rich and poor, racial issues, and the hauling in of greenhouse gases, a battle that was somehow still at the fore despite a consensus that authorities still needed to do something. Then there was the ongoing tyrannical approach of militant groups that continued to wage terror over anyone who didn't agree with them.

The biggest changes, however, were natural. The pandemic of 2111 to 2113 was thought to have been under control when it mutated into a much more lethal form. Around a billion people died over the next five years.

Medical authorities were always a step behind until it was discovered that many people had become immune to the illness, just like the milk maids of the late 1700s who were immune to smallpox because of their exposure to cowpox. These individuals all worked in Chinese wet markets and, after much negotiation between the United Nations and Chinese authorities, an agreeable compensatory deal was met to enable the antibodies of the immune to be harvested and a vaccine made available around the World. In a few short years the disease was eradicated, but the cost to the Western World was significant and gave China the absolute title of Superpower on its own.

It was also a time of great change technologically, with day-to-day life aided by artificial intelligence, robotics and supercomputing, which became available at a household level, at least for first world countries. Some say that technology was indeed the catalyst of a kind of Economic war, with China and the United States staking their claims in the artificial intelligence market, but again the Chinese proved victorious...until a breakthrough was achieved in Europe involving the fifth generation Super Collider Particle Accelerator in the Cern Nuclear facility outside Geneva, Switzerland. They managed to capture neutrinos and were able to study them, unravelling their secrets. In time physicists were able to, not only capture more of these minute particles, but produce them in great numbers and ultimately create machines that worked in ways only the imagination could give limit to.

The prize was, of course, the ability to manipulate space and time. In the year 2147, the Infinity Generator, a time machine, was created and with that, a new dilemma faced the World, what to do with it?

It was opened to global debate at the United Nations in New York where it was decided that a World authority would be formed to define the rules and regulations of time travel. The committee was represented from all corners of the Earth with most members coming from continental or oceanic regions, however, China and Russia opted to represent themselves.

The result was the International Future Directions Committee, which was something of a misnomer because the Infinity Generator or IG Machine could only send you back in time, not forward. Inevitably the machine lay dormant as debate raged about what should or shouldn't be done with it.

Over the next few decades, the committee and its subsequent sub-committees decided how the machine should be used for the betterment of humanity but as expected, the betterment of humanity differed from nation to nation and culture to culture. Rules were drawn up; a secondary IG authority was created to oversee the many checks and balances required to keep the whole project under control.

The rules were not simple, but one rule became a sticking point; any agreed change in history would not be allowed to alter the future global timeline. Astrophysicists argued that such a directive was impossible because sending back even one person could, theoretically, change the World as it was known but then, such a change would become part of history and any such knowledge that was in people's minds until that change of circumstance may simply not exist anymore.

That concept created hostile debate within the committee and the Governments of the World. No-one could agree, and it looked like the entire project would be shelved until it was suggested a test be conducted, one that could be easily monitored with no negative impact on World history.

And so, it was agreed that the Infinity Generator would send an individual back in time, one week and, once they caught up to their moment of departure, they could then report on their experience. Finding a volunteer wasn't difficult with many people within the IG faculty excited by the idea of a short trip back in time.

A young intern was selected, briefed, and, after his orientation, placed in the transfer chamber for the hop back to the same time a week earlier. He would emerge in an isolated zone away from the population area to avoid potential mishaps or terrifying people by materialising in the street. There was also a concern, despite confidence in the targeting telemetry, that materialising within a populated area could have dire consequences for anyone nearby at the time the vortex opened. They also discovered it was impossible to deposit a candidate to the interior of a building, probably due to the saturation of molecules, so an isolated outdoor area was targeted in the open.

He entered the chamber, the machine spooled up, power generators in the bowels of the building vibrating up through the floor, resulting in a brilliant white light within the transfer zone. When it dissipated, the chamber was vacant. The transfer was complete.

Almost immediately though, everyone felt strange. They were all aware that they'd tested the machine and sent someone or something back, but they couldn't recall the details. It was a weird feeling. They checked the IG machine logs and confirmed the transition was complete, but no-one knew exactly what had happened.

Further investigations revealed that those directly involved with the candidate had mixed memories of the event. They knew they sent the intern; some even recalled his name but at the same time they believed there was no such person. It didn't make sense and an enquiry was launched to try and come up with an answer.

The investigation revealed that they had indeed sent someone back in time one week. The telemetry from the Infinity Generator demonstrated as much, but no-one considered the possible creation of a time paradox.

It was ultimately proven that sending someone back to a place where they already existed caused a rift in time and the individual simply vanished from existence.

It became apparent that to succeed with such an experiment the individual would have to be sent back to a time preceding their birth and, further, not be around when they were born or a paradox would, most likely, be created. That meant anyone going back would have a one-way ticket and live out their life in two timelines, the first part of their life in the present, the second part in the past, never to cross over. The idea was both intriguing and horrifying.

To die before you were born was indeed hard to fathom but it was essentially the only way to successfully travel in time with no ill effect on the traveller.

Further experiments were carried out, this time with mice, dogs, cats and other, mostly short-lived creatures. Some were successful while others, having been clearly documented, were confusing for the physicists who conducted the experiments with the same mixed memories resulting from the paradoxical effects, the only actual proof being the machine logs. They gleaned that, in some cases, test animals sent back in time, had lived up to the time of their birth and subsequently vanished. The effect of a paradox was a solid theory and balanced against the machine logs was proof positive that the effect was real.

But how could there be evidence of these experiments when the animals had vanished from memory for most people? The physicists decided that because the events were all historical, the machine logs remained intact. Perhaps the machine, being a non-biologic, kept event records regardless of outcomes. It didn't add up but that was a problem for another time.

The paradox also seemed to apply to inanimate objects, which confirmed that any paradox could indeed be caused by the co-existence of the identical nanoparticles arriving at the same moment in time. It made sense, how could one thing be in two places at once? It ultimately couldn't.

Further experiments with inanimate objects revealed that there was a distance limit on the paradoxical effect. A coin was sent back one week but to the other side of the world and yet the coin was found and retrieved. It was thought that the Earth's magnetic field, created by the planet's molten core protected the coin, just like it protects the planet from radiation in space. So, the coin coexisted in the same time frame. Interestingly, there was one significant exception, lead. It seemed to be immune from the effects, perhaps because of its density. Sending things back in lead lined containers enabled them to co-exist in close proximity to themselves until the container was opened and then both things evaporated from existence.

The discovery did, however, give the physicists hope for a more workable approach to time travel, should there be circumstances where the risk of a potential paradox became necessary, although no-one could think of a reason why that might be the case.

A series of similar experiments showed that the paradox was also limited to a reasonably small area, a few miles or so, which meant you could co-exist within a pre-existing timeline without living in a lead shell but could never get too close to yourself or both copies would be erased.

The theory was proven with a living pot plant that was sent back one week and found in the designated location intact but as it was carried back to the IG facility, it evaporated before the scientists' eyes when it got within a few miles. It became clear that there was a protective effect of some kind, probably created by the Earth's magnetic field but it only worked until the two objects were within line of sight and the nanoparticles then destroyed each other.

With this new revelation, the International Future Directions IG Committee at Cern recommended that no human could ever be sent back to a time where they'd previously existed.

Despite the safety buffer, the risks were considered too high. Further, there were serious questions over the possibility that time travellers could make changes that might extinguish pieces of the present, including people and that the World as it was in the 2200s could be dramatically altered. Of course, any such change would be unknown to almost everyone in the present, which was a paradox. It could even result in one or more of the committee members not existing or not following a career line that saw them become members of the committee. The more they debated and discussed the ramifications, the more difficult it became.

Then one member of what became known as the IG committee, Anastasia Kuznetsov from Russia, tabled a proposal, that a volunteer from the Russian Federation be sent back in time to live out a new life, document everything they experienced and file their journals within a depository that existed then and now.

The idea was incredibly simple and would give the committee immediate feedback. The only hitch: who would want to give up life in the present and live in a past that would seem prehistoric? Kuznetsov didn't appear phased by that tiny detail.

After much more debate a series of points were agreed to that would guarantee that this person would not change history enough to disrupt the now and the committee would, once and for all know if time travel was indeed a tenable concept.

The Committee took their proposal to the United Nations and again debate raged, but after weeks of discussion the experiment was approved; zero hour 0001 hours, January 1st, 2214.

Chapter 2 – The Traveller

The vetting process had to be thorough; finding the right person to go back in time was an imperative but so was the era, a period when the World was relatively calm so the candidate would not be faced with deprivation, war, hatred or some other threat, so the post-World War 2 era was agreed upon, when life was easier than the preceding decades and better than the beginning of the 21st Century.

The committee also agreed that the individual should be female, as they would most likely be better able to observe the World independently and less likely to be influential. Their age would not be a factor as they would be long dead before 2214 regardless and thus, no paradox issues.

Jean Claude Pinet, the Infinity Generator Committee President and representative of Europe, co-chaired the vetting committee with Anastasia Kuznetsov, Gabrielle Fawcett of North America, Luciana Gonzalez from South America and Davis Brigalow of Australasia. The panel was based on their similar lifestyles and those of the candidates.

Committee members representing China, Africa, The Middle East, and the Sub-Continent did not object as they felt the experiment would have no impact on their territories but were keen to observe the process and expected to add their thoughts later.

The Russian Federation handpicked a series of candidates they felt had the attributes required, strong willed and independent women. Most were attractive, well-schooled and multilingual. They were assessed as being self-sufficient and confident. Those attributes should enable any one of them to integrate into a world that might seem totally inferior to that of the current world.

Several rules were set down that the winning candidate must adhere to, which would be discussed as a part of the interview process. Relations between the West and the Russian Federation were considered amiable in the 2200s so there were no concerns regarding ulterior motives and most agreed that a Russian woman was as good a choice as any, despite the Cold War era they were being sent back to. Clearly, they would need to be able to speak fluent English without an accent. French too.

The first candidate entered the interview room and seemed a little shocked by the gallery of interested observers in their seats behind the selection committee, "Good afternoon, Miss Tahlia Goncharov, I'm Jean Claude Pinet," and he went on to introduce the other committee members for her benefit.

"Firstly, we want to know if you understand why, you are here?"

In perfect English she replied, "Indeed I do."

She was a stunning specimen of Eastern Block femininity, a picture postcard of Russian beauty with long brunette hair, blue eyes, light, spotless skin and that perfect Russian doll face.

"Please indulge us if you will," asked Luciana Gonzalez with her Mexican accent, "We would very much like to hear you explain what you believe your role will be."

"Very well. In short, you wish to send me back in time where I will live my life freely, as I see fit and record my experiences and observations which you will study long after my death. You are wanting to see if this experiment of yours works and what might be the effect on the World of today," she explained.

Davis Brigalow spoke next, "Very good, now tell us why you would be willing to do this?"

"It's an adventure, an exciting opportunity. I would be honoured to be a part of it, and I would be making history for women everywhere. The first true time traveller? That thrills me."

Brigalow then added, "You know this is a one-way trip, you can't come back?"

"I understand that."

"You will never live to see any accolades, in fact no one will know about what you have achieved until 2214 and you cannot talk about it in the 20th Century because, well no-one would believe you and you would probably be accused of lunacy," suggested Anastasia Kuznetsov.

"I know. My duty to this World is enough to keep me motivated," Goncharov explained.

Jean Claude Pinet then asked her a question that she wasn't anticipating, "And how do you feel about living out your life alone, no marriage, no children, strictly as an observer of the past with very little money and menial jobs, jobs with no influence? Could you handle that? Because that is what we are asking."

Goncharov balked, "I don't know. I thought I would be living a normal life, perhaps as a housewife. I hadn't considered…" She didn't finish the sentence then added, "I would have to think about it."

"We understand," replied Pinet, "We will end the interview there if you don't mind."

"Of course, thank you." Tahlia Goncharov made a hasty exit.

"This might be more difficult than we thought," suggested Brigalow.

"Perhaps," agreed Kuznetsov, "but one interview doesn't mean much at this point."

"True," Brigalow said but he was dubious.

The next candidate reacted the same way, and it continued like that for a while. The information had been deliberately omitted from the initial data given to the candidates so their reactions could be considered. There was nowhere to hide if you didn't know what was coming and none of the women felt comfortable with some of the directives they would be required to meet, and the list was long. No roles of influence, no writing to the papers, no doing interviews, running for political parties, or even joining clubs; basically, nothing that could in any way alter the timeline.

The role would be live and let be, which came with a lot of baggage, and they would be giving up freedoms and equality that, while common now, were only just starting to be debated in the 20th Century.

As the day wore on, the candidates were discarded one after another, all falling flat at the revelation of their required lifestyle. Then a new candidate entered the interview hall, a plain woman of medium build. She had dishevelled hair and average features, an unremarkable candidate. She wasn't someone the committee expected, given the parameters that had been set for this task.

After the formal introductions and initial set of questions Pinet asked, "Miss Yahontov, we have asked each candidate the same questions and they have all impressed us up to this point, including you but they failed this question, all of them," and he asked her about living alone, isolated from marriage, children, influence and identity and her reaction was without hesitation,

"These things do not matter to me. I have never desired marriage or children. I am not the least interested in men, or women for that matter. I prefer to be alone; I am happiest in isolation and if I may, it would not matter to me if that was in the 23rd Century or the 20th. I require only simple things in life and so, I am not perturbed by what you ask."

"You wouldn't miss the technology or the equality," asked Gonzales.

"Not in the slightest. I love to be by myself and read. I am not someone who must be centre of attention, in fact I would rather go unnoticed."

The interview panel members and the gallery gasped with delight. She was perfect.

More questions followed and Yahontov answered them all with ease. Nothing they threw at her phased her in the slightest.

She was given a scenario and asked how she might deal with it, "You walk around a corner and witness a man running from the scene of a stabbing and clearly the victim will die if you don't do something to help. How do you react?"

"I would turn the other way, leave him to die or be saved by someone else. I cannot intervene. That could change the future. I cannot allow that," she explained.

"Not even if he pleaded with you for help," added Brigalow.

"No, not under any circumstances." She seemed almost angry that he doubted her.

Gabrielle Fawcett tried to throw her a curve ball, "What if it were a child?"

Without hesitation Yahontov replied, "Same situation, I would walk away."

"Are you sure you could?"

"Yes!" She didn't need to elaborate.

Anna Yahontov seemed cold and to a degree callous, but she was also believable. She wasn't saying what she thought they wanted to hear, she was being honest; brutally so, but that made her even more perfect for the role.

When the interview concluded it was clear that this candidate was not at all concerned about travelling back to the 20th Century, living a basic life and staying out of everything, simply observing and recording what she experienced.

More interviews followed but none of them could get past the trick questions, only Yahontov.

With further discussion, which included the observers from the committee, it was decided; Anna Yahontov would be the committee's Time Traveller.

Chapter 3 – The Test

The training for the upcoming time slip was intense. The first decision was where to send Anna Yahontov. Russia wasn't logical given the political issues of the time, so it was agreed that Western Europe may be a better option. She had to know everything about the era she was being sent to; the politics, the mindset of the people, how a woman was treated and expected to act.

France seemed a good choice, not only because she spoke the language fluently, but also because the women there were more liberated than most countries of the time and she would find it easier, psychologically. That too was tested heavily, to see if she might crack under the strain of being taken out of her 'known world' for another. She didn't.

She was also given a new identity, Phoebe Bisset. They didn't want her to sound like she was Russian and the necessary identity documentation was recreated from the archives. The chosen year was heavily scrutinised, and it was agreed that Anna, or Phoebe would be transported back to 1974.

The Vietnam war would be over, and Europe would be focussed on the World Cup. The seventies were a relatively quiet time in World history, and it would give Phoebe time to settle in and adjust to her surroundings. She would arrive at 0001 hours on January 1st, 1974.

To make certain she didn't slip up, everyone referred to her as Phoebe and a history was created to ensure she could explain herself. She moved to Paris from the Reims region after her parents died in a car crash. She sold their home and decided to get a fresh start. The story was no-frills to make it easy to sell. Besides, anything more complicated might have too many holes in it. Car accidents were common and no-one would be suspicious.

The training was always gruelling, but Phoebe never faltered. Her language skills were exemplary, and she absorbed knowledge like a sponge, memorising as much detail as she could. She was quizzed and tested regularly and never slipped up.

The committee even tried to trick her into reacting to her real name on several occasions, but she didn't flinch once; not that anyone in 1974 would ever know her identity. She was ready.

On the evening of the transfer, she dressed in 1970s clothing, smart casual attire for a European winter arrival. Being Russian, the cold wasn't a concern to Phoebe.

She was also equipped with a Globite suitcase of the era containing an array of materials she would need, more clothing, cosmetics, personal items and she had a reasonable amount of French francs to help her on her way. The IG Committee had a great deal of trouble sourcing the right notes from the era, but they managed to find enough to get her started.

Arriving on the stroke of the New Year seemed like a good idea given that most Parisians would be distracted by the party atmosphere and she could slip into the population virtually undetected. Even so, a target point was chosen that kept her well away from the major landmarks and celebration zones around the Ach de Triomphe and Eiffel Tower.

Her biggest problem may well be finding somewhere to stay that first night, but she wasn't concerned. Phoebe had not only demonstrated resilience, but she was also resourceful. No-one doubted she would make do when she arrived.

Once in Paris (1974) she would settle into a simple life and, as agreed, would never marry, never have children and never do anything that might influence the future. She was, however, allowed to have a pet.

Phoebe was moved into the transfer chamber of the Infinity Generator, an unremarkable spherical room with what appeared to be shiny metal tiles sealing its walls.

Nothing else was in there besides Phoebe and her suitcase with all the arc arrays and generators surrounding the exterior of the orb. She had been instructed to stand normally, as she would be deposited in a side street and should simply appear quietly in a flash of light.

If there was noise that might be created by her arrival, it was hoped that it would be written off as part of the New Year celebrations, but no-one could tell her what would happen with any certainty.

Every member of the Infinity Generator Committee was there to farewell her and wish her well on her historic journey. Jean Claude Pinet spoke with her before leaving the transfer room.

"How are you feeling Phoebe?"

"I'm perfectly fine."

"I can see that, you don't even look nervous," he added.

"That's because I am not."

"Good." Pinet looked her in the eye. "You are doing something incredible and very brave. I admire you for that. We will learn so much I feel. You may well be paving the way to a better world if this works."

"Perhaps, but I will never know. I will just do as I have been instructed, write my journals and deposit them as requested."

Pinet smiled, "I have no doubt." Then he kissed her on each cheek. "God speed Anna Yahontov." He deliberately used her real name for her benefit.

She smiled and nodded but didn't say another word. He left the transfer room and sealed the door.

It would only be a few minutes until the Infinity Generator was fired. Already the committee members, engineers and scientists could hear the power generators spooling up and when the power reached critical mass a simple button push would punch a brief hole in time which should, quite simply, deposit Phoebe onto a Paris street in 1974 at the dawning of a new year, 240 years ago.

Everyone felt apprehensive and quite a few had grave doubts about the test, but it was too late to stop; it was about to happen.

Sunil Patel, committee member for the Subcontinent had the ear of Zhang Jie of China,

"It's odd when you think about it. For Phoebe this will be a lifetime but for us, the results will be instant. We will know of her entire life by tomorrow."

"Yes," replied Jie, "If she survives the transfer."

"Even if she doesn't, there may be a news report in the archives to reveal what happened to her," Patel suggested.

"Unless we have a repeat of the first failure and she is simply extinguished from existence. We will only know that someone or something was sent back and nothing more," Jie explained.

Patel crossed his arms, "Hmm, that is a truly disturbing thought but that is the nature of space time is it not?"

"Indeed," said Jie.

At exactly midnight, January 1st, 2214, the Infinity Generator erupted into life. The orb within which Phoebe Bisset was standing lit with such intensity that no-one could watch it.

Those observing felt a weird combination of cold and heat all at the same time and the noise was like a jet engine hovering in the room.

Then with a blinding flash and a cataclysmic whip crack there was silence except for the wind down of the electrical turbines. The room dimmed back to normal as Jean Claude Pinet approach the transfer room. He popped the latch and opened the door. A puff of frigid air filled his lungs, and he could smell what he thought were fireworks. *Interesting* he thought. He peered at the place where Phoebe Bisset had been standing but she wasn't there.

Given that he still remembered her brought a smile to his face. He could only assume that the transfer had been a success and that Phoebe Bisset was now in Paris in 1974. He turned to the others in the room and asked out loud, "Do you remember what we just did?"

Everyone either nodded or replied yes.

"We have success," he cried and those assembled cheered and applauded.

At the stroke of midnight +1 second on January 1st, 1974, the entire populous of Paris were cheering and fireworks exploded in the skies. Every face was turned skyward as they welcomed the new year. The Arc de Triomphe and Eiffel Tower strobed in different colours as the fireworks erupted over them.

In the quiet of a dead-end street, well away from the festivities, a bright, white human sized sphere of light grew out of the gloom, flashed briefly then dissipated with a soft crackle, leaving a woman and her suitcase standing on the cobblestones.

No-one was there to witness the arrival of Phoebe Bisset. She stood for a moment, looked around and took a breath of cold Paris air, catching a whiff of firework smoke as she did so. She coughed.

She didn't move at first, except to place her Globite on the ground. She felt a wisp of cold air as a breeze blew into the street. After catching her breath, she looked herself over to make sure that everything was intact and yes, she still had all her arms and legs. She smiled with relief.

She'd been told that there was a remote chance of a glitch that might send only parts of her through, leaving her missing a limb or two.

Phoebe picked up her suitcase and walked down the street, her shoes clip clopping loudly on the cobblestones. As she emerged, she saw a young couple in a loving embrace, kissing passionately. They didn't notice her. She continued towards the city looking for a cheap hotel but doubted that there would be any vacancies.

Suddenly a group of youngsters burst around a corner giggling and chattering. They saw her and cried out, "Bonjour, bonne annee (Happy New Year)."

It took her a moment to translate in her head but then she replied in French, "Hello, Happy New Year to you too," to which they chorused "Merci," as they trotted on by, laughing as they went.

The committee was right, the reverie of the evening provided a perfect curtain behind which to hide, and she walked a few miles into the city without incident, observing the celebrations of the young and a few older residents of this magical city.

As she neared the business centre of Paris, the number of people grew. Some lingered, lovers kissed, many sat in various states of drunkenness while others wandered here and there, probably headed home. The smell of fireworks smoke was rife as it descended in the cold night air and Phoebe brushed some ash from her tunic.

She spied a hotel on a busy intersection carrying much traffic, even at this hour, and began to walk towards it when two Gendarmeries caught her eye. "Bonsoir," said one.

"Good evening," Phoebe replied in perfect French.

They then spied her suitcase.

"An odd hour to be travelling Mademoiselle?"

She had to think fast. "Perhaps, but it was the traffic you know? It took longer to get here than I expected."

"Of course. May we be of assistance?"

Surprised, she instinctively answered,

"Well, yes, I hope so, I need a hotel. I failed to book ahead."

"Hmm, that is unfortunate. I can see you are headed for the Old Grand Hotel. It will be full and is quite expensive," explained the officer while making his assessment of Phoebe's social standing.

"I see. Where might you suggest?

"The Saint Pierre. It's no palace but it is clean and cheap. And they always spare a room for late arrivals. You might be lucky."

"Oh, thank you officer, um…" she stammered, not knowing where to go.

"It's not far, just walk down there," he pointed, "about two blocks and turn left then another block and you're there. Tell the clerk that Sargent Benoir sent you."

"Sargent Benoir? I will, thank you."

"It is my pleasure Mademoiselle. Have a lovely evening," and they walked on.

Phoebe zigzagged through the traffic and made her way down the street turning where she was told and walked the next block to the Saint Pierre Hotel. It was, to say the least, a little worse for wear but she didn't care; she was tired and it was cold.

She walked through the front door to reception where the lone figure of the clerk sat reading a magazine. Clearly, he hadn't partaken in the New Year celebrations. He was unkempt, his shirt stained, and he had at least a four-day growth of stubble on his face and appeared not to care what day it was.

"Bonjour," Phoebe said.

"Hmmff," was the only reply she got.

"I have just arrived in Paris and am hopeful you have a room?"

The man just shook his head to the negative.

"Oh, um, well I was told you might, by Sargent Benoir?"

The man practically jumped out of his skin, "Why of course er?"

"Phoebe. Phoebe Bisset."

"Yes, Miss Bisset, welcome. Please, if you sign the register I will get you a key. We have a room. It's only small but it is comfortable and warm," he explained, blushing.

"Thank you. I didn't think I would find anything on a night like this." She played the damsel in distress very well, which annoyed her somewhat.

"Normally that would be true but any friend of Sargent Benoir..."

"He must be important?"

"Oh yes, he takes very good care of us here. We respect him very much," said the clerk.

"In that case I feel very fortunate." She scrawled out a signature in the register.

The clerk handed her a key, Room 107, on the first floor, "Do you need any assistance?"

"No, thank you, it's just the one bag." She had a room.

Phoebe settled in and found the room to her liking. The carpet was well worn and the bedding old, but it was warm and she quickly changed, went to bed and drifted off to sleep wondering about her new adventure.

At the Cern facility in Switzerland, the Infinity Generator Committee met for the first time after the delivery of Phoebe Bisset to Paris. They immediately scoured the digital archives for any information about their test subject but there was nothing. Well almost nothing. A small death notice in the La

Parisian newspaper, dated August 17th, 1986, indicated that a Phoebe Bisset had died and it gave an address. Probably an apartment. There were no other details. They then searched digital church records and found her funeral information, a single line in a register, name, address, which matched, age, date of burial and the plot number of her grave.

They gleaned that she had lived 12 years in Paris before her passing. She would have been 50 years old at the time, and they all wondered what might have befallen her.

They had to wait another few days to retrieve the diaries they hoped she had written. It had been agreed that she would deposit her diaries with the Banque Nagelmackers in Belgium, a bank they knew still existed in 2214 but was operating in 1974. In fact, it had been established in 1747 and was one of the oldest banking institutions ever to have existed that was still in operation.

It was hoped that she had followed the instructions and named three committee members as signatories so they could retrieve the diaries. Noone could be certain that the bank would follow the instructions or if indeed they would even know about the safety deposit boxes after all this time, but they would soon find out.

Jean Claude Pinet, Muhammad Samy Galal of the Middle East and Hamid Kanumbra of Africa journeyed to Belgium and entered the bank. They were greeted by a security guard and then a bank officer,

"Good day, how may I help you?"

Pinet explained, "This will seem a little odd, but we are here to retrieve a set of safety deposit boxes which would have been held here since the period 1974 to 1986."

The banker looked nonplussed, "Oh, that is a little out of the ordinary, but this bank has been operating for a very long time. We will be able to check on the digital register, please follow me," the young woman offered as she led them to a private office where they sat down as she woke a computer and started tapping, "Do you know what name it might have been in?"

"Yes. Phoebe Bisset," said Pinet.

"OK, let us see." She typed in the name. "Oh! Yes, we have safety deposit boxes in that name, and I can see there are four signatories listed, Phoebe Bisset, Jean Claude Pinet, Hamid Kanumbra and Muhammad Samy Galal," which she pronounced perfectly as she looked up at the men with a smile.

"Yes," answered Pinet, "that's us."

The girl's smile evaporated as she absorbed the improbability of them being named over 200 years previously, "But that is impossible."

"You might think so but here we are," Kanumbra added.

The girl blushed. "Um, yes, well I will need to bring in the manager. I'm at a loss…this isn't…" but she didn't finish the remark as she hurried off.

The trio all smiled. "Poor girl, she must be at her whits end," Galal said and they all laughed.

It took about five minutes for the girl to return and with her, a suited and distinguished man, clearly the Bank Manager who introduced himself, "Good day gentlemen, I am Lucas Peeters." He shook hands with all three.

Pinet introduced himself and his companions, "Firstly Mr Peeters, I must apologise. It must have been quite a shock to Miss…?"

"Claes," the girl said.

"Miss Claes, I apologise," reiterated Pinet. "We are from the Infinity Generator Committee; a committee of the United Nations and these deposit boxes are of the utmost importance to us. We can provide credentials." They all produced identification.

"Of course, we will have this all sorted out for you as quickly as possible," Peeters said.

With their identities verified they were escorted down a set of stairs into a large room with several caged off cells, each containing safes and rooms. They entered an antechamber where rows and rows of double locked draws filled every wall. The Manager and Miss Claes searched for the draw containing the diaries, "Here we are," called Peeters, "number 1161."

He found the correct keys and handed one to Miss Claes and she turned them for the first time in 228 years. Miss Claes struggled a little given how long they'd been inert, but it finally clacked.

Everyone watched in anticipation as the draw was pulled open. Inside were a set of diaries, all dated and all in chronological order. Pinet smiled, "Very good. She did as we had hoped. "May I," he asked Peeters and gestured to the draw.

"Of course," Peeters answered.

Pinet took a diary at the very front of the draw, dated 1986 and opened it, then flicked the pages back with his thumb until he saw handwriting. He pinched a few pages to get back to the last entry and read what Phoebe had written.

After reading it to himself he turned to Kanumbra and Galal and read it aloud to them, not caring that Peeters and Claes could hear.

This will be my last entry. I am in the final stages of breast cancer now and have chosen not to seek treatment for fear that I may interrupt the needs of someone else in this time. I am weak and tired and do not believe there is much time left. I wish to convey my thanks to the committee for choosing me for this unprecedented task, it has been a great honour. I have lived a very happy life here with my cat Rastus. Rest assured I have maintained my anonymity and was of no influence in this time. To be frank, I think you will find my entries to be quite boring. She signed the diary entry *Phoebe Bisset* and dated it 7*th* July 1986.

Pinet looked up at his colleagues, "We have been successful gentlemen," but he could already see from their smiles that they were fully aware of the achievement.

Peeters and Claes on the other hand were bewildered and at a loss for words.

Pinet, Galal and Kanumbra retrieved the diaries, all 13 of them, thanked Peeters and Claes and left without further explanation.

Chapter 4 – The New Dilemma

After the success of the Bisset experiment, further tests were commissioned, all aimed at assessing the limits to which sending people back in time could be enacted without overly influencing the existing timeline. The tests were mostly successful with two exceptions. In one instance, the candidate was murdered almost immediately after arrival. They were sent back to 1899 to witness and report on the Boer War in Africa and manifested near a village and set upon as a demon.

 The committee learned of the incident through a notation in the historical records of a Missionary who witnessed the attack.

In another instance the traveller lived only a few years before being killed while crossing the street in New York city. They'd been sent back to witness the Great Depression and report their findings. Newspaper articles describing the incident suggested the victim was drunk.

The committee was concerned there may have been an adverse effect on the driver but the trouble with historical change was that those in the "now" were oblivious to it because the reality was defined by proxy and therefore, they expunged whatever might have been written into history in the previous timeline. In simple terms the proxy was entrusted with following rules that were unpunishable if broken. It came down to intense screening of each individual and ultimately faith.

The committee members were clearly concerned with the impact of some kind of mistake or intentional alteration to the current reality, so they debated the pros and cons of testing the potential for change and eventually agreed to something subtle.

The plan would be to select something that would have no bearing on humanity at all but would be able to be documented so that after the experiment, the notes could be analysed. It was hoped that having the data sent back with the candidate before the change would mean that the original timeline evidence would be intact and thus enable a comparison.

The next problem was finding something that could be changed without any variation to life in the now. It seemed simple enough but the more they investigated, the more difficult it became to find a viable option, until David Brigalow came up with a proposal.

He suggested that a candidate be sent back to the Australian island state of Tasmania, a place of mostly wilderness, and be charged with capturing and keeping a colony of Thylacine, or Tasmanian Tigers. These creatures looked like dogs, were striped like tigers, but were in fact marsupials. They were decimated by hunting and when the authorities finally ordered they be protected it was too late and the last living specimen died at Hobart Zoo in 1933.

If someone could return and save them, it would resolve one of Man's mistakes. The committee debated the concept for weeks and eventually agreed that the human impact would be minimal. The traveller would live alone, in remote Tasmania and breed the creatures with the aim of releasing them into the wild. post 1933.

They would have to remain a recluse for much of the time, probably live a basic, or even primitive existence until the job was done. They would be given a cover story as that of a prospector which wouldn't seem unusual in the era. Tasmania was a good place for such a test. It was isolated, remote, almost untouched and contained very few people, particularly on the West Coast.

The problem was finding someone who had the qualities required. Who in 2214 could live in that era, alone, in the wild and have the necessary skills to maintain a colony of carnivorous marsupials? That proved to be much more difficult than anyone expected but eventually, they found someone. Jake Styles was already a recluse, a die-hard environmentalist who wasn't taken seriously. When he was asked how he felt about bringing back the Tassie Tiger his eyes widened and a smile erupted from ear to ear, "How?"

He hardly flinched when he was told it would mean travelling back to the early 1900s. Styles practically lived off the land as it was and that wasn't easy to do in 2214, but he preferred it. He was vetted thoroughly and passed every test, but when he was told that he couldn't do this for any other species he was angry. It went against everything he stood for and some long and frank conversations were had.

"Why just the Tiger? There are so many species gone now because of people. It seems like an awful waste of my talents and your resources to limit me to one thing," argued Styles.

Brigalow looked at him with a furrowed brow.

"Lots of people in history have dedicated themselves to the saving of one animal. You will be more effective saving the tiger rather than trying to save everything."

"To be sure but what about when I'm done? Surely, I can move on to something else?"

"Wouldn't you want to continue monitoring the tigers? You know that conservation wasn't a big deal back then and there will be trophy hunters. They'd still be a threatened species," Brigalow explained, which made Styles pause.

"That's true. They would need long term care, and I am the man for the job!"

Brigalow was almost amused by Styles' manic state, but he knew the man's heart was in the right place, "So you agree?"

Styles thought some more. "Yes...yes, I do. Oh Lordy, this is going to be great!"

And so, it was agreed. Styles studied the tiger from all the data that was known from that the time. He learned everything he needed to know about the animal, how they bred and how they lived. Thankfully, they were not territorial creatures, so keeping them in proximity wasn't going to present any problems.

Tasmania in that era was a strange place with unique animals. A former convict colony created by the British that became an island State of Australia but even by today's standards was considered wilderness. If Styles was successful, it was likely that the tigers would exist in 2214.

To ascertain the results, a dossier of information with supporting photographs and video were packaged up to be sent back with Styles. It was hoped that this information would remain unchanged when retrieved.

After extensive training and study, all was ready. Styles would be deposited on the outskirts of Hobart, make his way into the community, buy what he needed and then travel to a designated wilderness area as a prospector. His documentation was recreated from archival records, and he was given a large sum of cash to help fund the expedition.

All was ready and on August 31st, 2214, Jake Styles was transported back to save the Tasmanian Tiger.

Once again, the committee would have immediate results, when they retrieved the package which would be hidden in an area that was known to be unoccupied in 2214 and thus had not seen too many humans in almost 300 years. GPS coordinates would enable the committee to find the box, which was completely waterproof and impregnable.

Styles was sent back to 1920, between the World Wars and post the Spanish Flu pandemic. It would be a time of difficulty for the whole World with the Great Depression about to happen so it was likely Styles' activities would go unnoticed, if he was lucky.

Almost immediately the committee members realised something had changed. They had mixed memories that were, at first, very confusing. There were memories of the known extinction of the Thylacine indeed, but they also had memories of the creatures being in the here and now, living in the wild and in zoos all over the World. It didn't make sense at first but then they realized the logic of it. They knew the animal was extinct because of the mission they'd just initiated but then Styles, having succeeded in that mission had created a parallel timeline.

The committee members were the only one's privy to the mission and therefore the only ones with double memories. This wasn't anticipated and proved to be a most incredible discovery.

When Brigalow returned with the box, the contents were just as fascinating. Styles had fastidiously documented his work and sure enough, the data sent back with him, noting the extinction of the creature said as much, so they learned that data sent back before any change would remain as written and witnesses to the experiment would experience twin memories in their timeline. Truly fascinating.

A search of 2214 historical data also revealed that Styles became a folk hero for having the foresight to live with these unusual creatures and save them.

It was thought in 1933, as history ordained, that the thylacine was indeed extinct but in 1935 a party of surveyors found Styles who had set up a Tasmanian Tiger complex and were gobsmacked at what he'd achieved. His story made headlines all around the world.

As for Styles, he lived out his life in the wilderness with his beloved Tigers and died peacefully in his hut, found by welfare workers who checked on him every few months. His work however, set the agenda for the survival of, not only the Tassie Tigers but many other threatened species around the World.

Styles probably didn't know it, but he did manage to save a great many more creatures, as was his wish.

The best news for the committee was that nothing he did appeared to have had an adverse effect on the timeline, but as always, changes they weren't privy to would have been wiped from the timeline and replaced. It was an unknown quantity, but it was a good guess that this experiment worked and opened the way for more significant concepts.

The IG Committee was now at a crossroads, where to take the technology next. Building the machine and toying with the past was one thing but now that they were fully aware that things could be changed for the better, what should be the next move? This was a question that went far beyond the scope of the committee and would need to be referred to the United Nations. Only they could decide what, if anything, should be dealt with.

Making a substantial change in history would indeed change the World in the now but to what degree would depend on what might be changed. Jean Claude Pinet wrote a full report on what they had learned and achieved and delivered it to the UN in New York.

When the Secretary-General of United Nations, Blair Odette, read the report she was astonished and immediately tabled it for all the 195 delegates. The report took centre stage and was heavily debated. Many argued that the past is the past and should not be toyed with, but others argued that great mistakes could be corrected and some even considered many of humanities great failings were now able to be righted. The debate was long winded and raged for weeks, regularly seeing sessions end in stalemate until the deadlock was broken when the German Ambassador to the UN, Alexander Becker tabled a proposal from his government,

This organisation was created because of war, at a time when humanity had seen the worst of itself. The United Nations was charged with maintaining peace throughout the World, fostering good international relations, improving those relations, standards of living and human rights.

The German Government believes that this has been a haphazard task and had only variable success with some catastrophic failures. Given the history of our nation, initiating two world wars and the atrocities we were directly responsible for, we propose that the United Nations Charter be amended to include a directive to right the wrongs of the past where possible through direct intervention.

We would further propose that the first corrective measure initiated by the United Nations to be the deletion of the Nazi Holocaust, the final solution instigated by Adolf Hitler in World War 2 to create a Master Race.

We believe the fallout from this one event in the history of Mankind has been responsible for the ongoing hatred, violence, and death we have seen around the World for almost 270 years since; tens of thousands of deaths on top of the millions suffered, not only by the Jews, but the infirm and the disabled.

Even today, Neo-Nazi groups continue to run amok around the World using the Nazi swastika as a symbol of hate and white supremacy. It is the feeling of the German Chancellor, Ernst Wagner, his government with the wholehearted support of all Opposition parties that this blight on Humanity be erased.

The German Government tables this proposal for your consideration.

The immediate impact of the proposal was hardly surprising. There was uproar. But for many countries, surprisingly, the idea had some merit. Nations like the United States, France, Belgium, Poland, Russia, Australia, the United Kingdom and many others had collectively suffered millions of deaths as a direct result of WWII and their ambassadors were keen to take the idea to their respective governments for debate.

At the same time, news of the proposal made headlines globally which resulted, not surprisingly, in neo-Nazi groups resorting to violence in the streets of many countries.

It gave the UN and World governments a clear indication of how significant their presence still was, even after nearly three centuries.

The General Assembly passed the process over to the Security Council who in turn took the unprecedented step of lobbying the Governments of the 195 member states of the United Nations.

Each in turn debated the pros and cons of such a move and, over time, each gave their respective ambassadors a decision to put to the UN Security Council, who then voted on the proposal, gaining the numbers to recommend the intervention.

That recommendation was then put to the UN General Assembly for a final vote and after another lengthy debate, Resolution 423/68 was passed. It was possible that many were unaware of the implications of any historical corrections and that the World as they knew it might change. That, surprisingly, seemed to have been set aside.

When the Infinity Generator Committee received the directive from the UN, they were shocked. The logistics of such a mission were far beyond anything they'd ever considered. Most expected the UN to mothball the technology after revealing what it was capable of, not expecting they'd call for the deletion of Man's most heinous act. How would they do it?

At the next meeting of the IG committee, they discussed the directive and initially decided to refer their concerns back to the General Assembly, to make certain they were aware of what they were asking and the potential changes that the World may face. It could alter the World map or send the planet into unknown areas of tension. It didn't answer the question of the Pacific conflict in WWII.

Some argued that erasing WWII would indeed keep Japan from becoming antagonistic but that was impossible to discern.

Most notable were the concerns the committee had for the existence of individuals in the present day because of such a change.

It was almost a guarantee that many people, perhaps millions would suddenly exist that had never been born because of the War and the Holocaust and that others would cease to exist.

It could even transpire that the perceived increase in the World population might put so much pressure on resources that the planet would spiral into a period of major famine, resulting in millions of deaths anyway.

They formulated their concerns and sent them back to the UN General Assembly.

The response was succinct: *Carry out the directive as instructed.*

Chapter 5 – The Plan

With clear instructions endorsed by the United Nations General Assembly and backed by the UN Security Council, the IG Committee was tasked with changing history. They would make certain that the Nazi Holocaust never happened. The first point of order was to work out how best to enact that very idea. Once they came up with a workable concept, they could then develop the mode by which such an operation could be executed. The committee members held an initial meeting to discuss ideas.

Jean Claude Pinet opened the meeting, "Hello everyone, thank you for being here. You all know the directive and regardless of any misgivings you might have, this is not negotiable. In short, we have been charged with stopping the Nazi Holocaust." He looked around the room with a wry smile, "How do we do it?"

David Brigalow, the member for Australasia was quick to pitch his thoughts, "We send Hitler a gas bill and when he doesn't pay, we turn the gas off." As uncouth as it was, the joke got a laugh. "But seriously, we need to nip it in the bud. We can't go in and destroy the concentration camps and gas chambers after they become active. We must go in there sooner."

"Are you suggesting an armed taskforce of some kind," asked Gabrielle Fawcett, the North Americas delegate.

"Perhaps. With today's technology, it would only require a small force to overcome the German defences," added Brigalow.

Pinet responded, "I don't like the idea of sending today's tech back to that time. We would have to rely on the technology of that era I think, to avoid some unintentional advances being made, scientifically or otherwise."

Brigalow's idea was discussed and debated at length and set aside as a potential option, but Zhang Jie of China had another idea, "What if we stopped the Holocaust by stopping the Nazi Party from becoming an entity?"

"How would we do that," asked Sunil Patel of the Subcontinent.

"We assassinate Hitler," Jie suggested.

Everyone laughed. "Do you know how many attempts were made on Hitler's life," Hamid Kanumbra exclaimed, still laughing from his belly.

"Yes, I do; there were approximately 28 reasonable attempts on Hitler between 1933 and 1944 and they all failed," Jie explained.

"Exactly," said Patel. "So how do you expect our attempt would go? Not very well and even if we did succeed, we would make him a martyr, and the Nazis would no doubt follow through on his Final Solution in any case AND they'd probably win the war without him too!"

Anastasia Kuznetsov from Russia pitched an alternative idea, "Why do it when the Nazis have already come to power when we can take him out before that. When he was an unknown. We have tools that can take us back to almost anywhere at any time. We need not send a taskforce when we can send a lone assassin to kill an obscure, unknown future dictator and stop everything from happening."

The other members of the committee paused as Pinet spoke to the idea, "Do we know where he was between the wars? What was he doing? In those days I'm sure people lived in relative obscurity, so he might be hard to nail down."

"True, but we surely have the capacity to do the research and learn of his movements. There must be some records still. Then it will be as simple as installing an operative to quietly dispose of him," suggested Luciana Gonzales of the South Americas.

"Indeed," added Davis Brigalow, "I see it being the simplest approach. Track him, kill him, and wipe out the Nazi Party, World War 2 and the Holocaust in one fell swoop. I like it."

"Well, it might not wipe out the Nazi Party. Hitler didn't act alone," claimed Jean Claude Pinet.

"That's true but without Hitler, they probably wouldn't have the leadership to become the Nazi Party as we know it and would fade into history as some minor disruption in German politics," was Fawcett's assessment.

The committee discussed the idea at length and decided that the assassination of Hitler before he joined the National Socialist German Workers Party was the most prudent approach.

That would mean tracking him down between 1919 and 1933, a wide scope of time which made the probability of success quite high.

Unfortunately, the committee soon realised that Hitler's rise to power began almost immediately after World War One, in 1919 and his political connections were set accordingly. He took advantage of Germany's difficulties during the Great Depression, turning the people to his way of thinking and was ultimately appointed German Chancellor in 1933 by Paul von Hindenburg who was very much pressured into making it so. T

he ratifications of the Enabling Act increased Hitler's powers and when von Hindenburg died in 1934, Hitler merged the Chancellorship and the Presidency and declared himself Fuhrer.

This revelation complicated the committee's plan. The hope was to deal with him before he gained notoriety but gaining political attention in 1919 changed their thinking. He would have already surrounded himself with supporters and protectors which nullified the concept of the quick and quiet disposal plan.

New ideas were tabled; perhaps getting to him before the Great War broke out or even at the time of his birth. Research revealed a troubled childhood.

He was one of six children but only one of his full siblings, a sister, survived into adulthood. It was noted that Adolf's father, Alois was a temperamental man and despite giving his family a comfortable lifestyle, it was known that he took his frustrations out on his children.

Adolf's mother Klara was the opposite of her husband, a nurturing and loving person who was greatly adored by Adolf.

Hitler was an intelligent school student, praised by his teachers for his test scores. His father moved the family several times until they finally settled in Linz, Austria when Hitler was 9. It was also noted that around this time he showed leadership qualities, often taking charge during games and sports.

After Elementary school his father enrolled him into the Realschule school to study science and technology, which he hated. Then at 14 his father died, impacting him emotionally but it was December 21, 1907, that hurt him most. His mother died from breast cancer, and it rocked him to his core.

His experiences in World War 1 and the defeat of Germany combined to radicalise Hitler. He became very bitter about how Germany was treated after the war and angered by the unfair conditions imposed on Germany because of the Treaty of Versailles. He needed someone to blame.

One interesting fact that emerged from the committee's research was something called the Tandey Incident. This occurred late in WWI when a British soldier, Henry Tandey of the 5th Duke of Wellington Regiment spotted a tired German soldier who had wandered into Tandy's line of fire. The man was wounded and did not attempt to raise his gun.

Tandy decided not to fire to which the German nodded his appreciation and wandered off. While never confirmed, it is believed that it may have been Adolf Hitler. The committee soon dismissed the idea of sending someone back to be there for that moment as there was no way of determining if the German was in fact their target.

The committee was also unable to determine the catalyst that tipped Hitler over the edge, the thing that turned him towards a darkness that most cannot understand. There were hints of some trauma in Hitler's life around the 1920s but nothing could be found to ascertain what it might have been. It may well have been a major factor in forming his views and driving him on toward politics, determined to create a Superpower and cleanse the World.

"So where, or more to the point, when do we go," asked Pinet.

Gabrielle Fawcett quickly responded, "Clearly we have to get him at a time when he is vulnerable, perhaps during the time between his mother's death and the war."

"That gives us a window of seven years, right," Brigalow asked.

"Yes, that's right. Surely someone can find him in that time. We know he was in Austria then, Linz to be precise. It couldn't have been a big place, so he shouldn't be hard to track down, surely," Kuznetsoz suggested, sounding uncertain.

"It should be as simple as asking around but if it's a small place, he may hear that someone is looking for him. Might that alarm him?" Jie wondered.

Kanumbra had the same misgiving. "It would depend on his level of paranoia at the time. He would not have been affected by the war, so I imagine his state of mind might be, stable."

"Then if no-one has a better idea, that's what we do; send someone who speaks Austrian/German back to 1907 to track down Adolf Hitler and dispose of him quietly. Are we agreed," asked Pinet.

Debate continued. The idea of killing his parents before Hitler was conceived came to mind but was dismissed as they were technically innocent parties and the morality of such an approach was outside the parameters of the directive.

It was then thought that killing Hitler as an infant could resolve the problem and while everyone agreed, no-one felt right about murdering a child, even one that was to become the most despised murderer in history. On top of that, there was nothing to say that the Hitlers wouldn't have another child who could, as unlikely as it was, turn out the same. Both ideas were rejected.

Finally, after hours of discussion, everyone agreed on a plan. A time and the place were set leaving only one detail to iron out, finding an operative to transport back 308 years to not only commit a murder but to then live out their life, possibly through two World Wars, a global depression, and the Spanish Flu. It was a huge ask.

"Where do we start," Pinet asked the group.

"Easy," said Brigalow, "We ask Mossad!"

"Are you serious," came the combined voices of several committee members.

"I am. They would jump at the chance to erase such an atrocity. The Israelis to this day commemorate the Holocaust and would want to right this wrong more so than anyone else AND I don't think they would be short on volunteers," Brigalow argued.

"Yes, but where do they find a white skinned, blue-eyed operative in their ranks," Patel wondered.

"I have no doubt that they, along with every other agency like them, have personnel for all occasions, otherwise they'd find it difficult to blend in." Brigalow smiled knowingly. His claims made sense.

"But do we want to open that door? So far, we've used our own connections to find volunteers. Do we really want to approach a secret service agency," asked Muhammad Samy

Galal, the Middle East representative. "I mean, in the past many of my people have had issue with Israel, some still feel some resentment but that's not what concerns me. We'd be opening a very nasty door if we bring in espionage experts."

"I agree," Pinet said. "I think we ask the UN Security Council for guidance on this. If they're ok with it, then so am I."

So, it was agreed. The UN Security Council was consulted on the plan. They agreed that 1907 seemed the most logical approach but they felt that sending in the Israelis would indeed be a mistake.

They still felt much hatred toward the Nazis over the atrocities of WWII and that might not be the emotional approach required, regardless of their professional ability. It was decided to ask the German Government to offer up a candidate given that it was their idea in the first place.

The Germans agreed.

Chapter 6 – 1907

Elea' Gruber arrived at Linz on a very cold winter's day in early December 1907. She was 27 years old but looked much younger. Her features were nothing like those of the master race propagated in the Second World War, blonde hair, blue eyes, slim and attractive; no Elea' was a brunette with green eyes and slightly darker skin.

 The truth was that Austrians were a strange mix created through centuries of occupation by the Romans who had overwhelmed the existing Germanic tribes. Later, Slavic peoples migrated into the region.

The result was a concoction of DNA that created Austrians as they were in the early 1900s.They weren't typically beautiful but in Elea's case beauty was something she did possess. It was thought that her look would catch Hitler's eye. Her long brunette hair was tied up in a bun, and she wore the clothing of the era, including a hat, a long-sleeved pinafore style dress, covered by a long thick coat with a scarf warming her neck.

She wasn't accustomed to the frightful cold of winter in Linz in December, which was nestled in the hills of northern Austria on the Danube River. The town looked stunning with snow on the rooves and parks with the temperature around zero Celsius.

She noted the narrow cobblestones streets, the lovely old facades of the buildings and shops. Locals paid her little attention as she walked which she was relieved about. Linz was home to around 60,000 residents but Elea' cared only about one of them.

Hitler would have been 18 at this time in his life and living at home with his mother, his father already having died. It was thought that a female would be able to get close to him with ease and Elea' Gruber, an operative of the Federal German

Intelligence Service was indeed used to getting close to people in a covert sense.

This job, however, was a very different prospect. She was alone, no support teams, no modern weapons, no escape plan except for what she could create herself. This would have to be quick and dirty, which didn't bother her. Her knife skills were as good as her aim with a 2214 model G587 Glock pistol.

Elea' reached the town's main business district and was surprised by how busy it was given the cold, but the people here were used to such conditions. She would have to fake it. Her back story had to be created; a widow with no children, she was looking for a fresh start and moved to Linz from Salzburg.

In 1907, it was close enough to be visited occasionally but not be too familiar, so it shouldn't seem strange. She wouldn't seek work; she didn't expect to be "in town" that long.

Once the job was done, she would escape to England and then to the United States and live out her days in seclusion, away from the large cities. No firm location had been decided, and it was left up to her personal choice.

She was aware of the need to avoid being influential and the same rules applied to her as they did to all travellers. Elea' never wanted for children, so that wasn't a difficulty she was concerned about.

The main reason she volunteered for this role was a consequence of her last job. She had been tasked with the assassination of a much despised and influential businessman, Byron Fetterman, an Englishman who had conspired with the enemies of several Governments in the secret trade of arms.

One such deal saw the assassination of a major Government official in Berlin which forced Germany's hand. They knew who commissioned the hit and why. The official had blocked certain suspect transactions that cost the businessman millions, and he didn't take it lying down. The Federal

Intelligence Service intercepted emails showing that he had commissioned the hit with the help of his underworld connections.

That was all they needed to get a green light from the British Government and Elea was chosen for the job. The time and place were set, a fundraising event in London. Fetterman was well guarded so she would need to get close, kill him quietly, out of sight of his bodyguards, which would not be easy.

She knew about some of Fetterman's sexual *proclivities* and would use them to get him alone, whether it be a toilet or a hotel room, it didn't matter. Even so she cringed at the thought of the man's perverted desires.

On the night of the hit, he arrived, punctual as always, and mingled with friends and acquaintances. He was a rather handsome man, in his forties and did enjoy flirting with the ladies.

He never married, probably because no one woman could ever satisfy his *needs* and he did indulge his passions regularly. Elea' caught his attention, which wasn't difficult.

She looked stunning in a white, off the shoulder dress that hugged her shapely body, her hair tumbled in waves across her shoulder and tickled her ample cleavage and her piercing green eyes were highlighted by a lavender eye shadow. The dress was split to seductively reveal her legs almost all the way from ankle to groin, so it didn't take much to bring him in.

She taunted and teased him, gave him a story about her idiot husband off with friends getting drunk as usual and ignoring her.

 Fetterman was putty in her hands. He'd lost all interest in the event and offered to drive her to his hotel, which she accepted. They arrived, bodyguards at the ready, took the lift to the penthouse where he shed the guards. They enjoyed a nightcap before moving into the bedroom.

Elea' analysed the surroundings for an escape route but before she could turn around, he shoved her onto the bed. He ripped her dress off and punched her in the face, stunning her briefly. He pinned her down and even with her training, she was too groggy to fight him off at first, but as he undressed, she recovered enough to gain back her wits. He had a reputation for being tough, which she now realised she should have been better prepared for.

"I'm rather looking forward to this my dear," he said without bothering to look at her.

Elea' was angry now. She lost control and pounced on him with a fly kick that sent him across the room and into a floor to ceiling mirror which shattered, showering him in large shards of glass, one of which sliced a neat furrow into his left cheek.

He was out cold, a sitting duck but before she could bury the heel of her specially crafted stiletto shoes into his forehead, his bodyguards burst into the room, no doubt alerted by the crashing of glass. When they saw Fetterman and then the naked girl, they hesitated, giving her the moment she needed.

She disarmed one, knocking him to the floor as she snatched the handgun and shot the other before disposing of the first with two-point blank shots to the head.

She fired at Fetterman, but the gun was empty. Then she heard more men coming so she gathered up her dress and clutch purse, tucking both into her very brief underwear and bailed out of the penthouse window, scaling the balconies down the next few floors until she found an empty room, where she dressed.

She looked at herself in the bathroom mirror, her face was smeared with makeup, and she was already turning black and blue from the punch. Her dress was ripped to the point where it didn't hide much. She looked every bit a beaten woman.

She cleaned herself up as best she could, but it didn't change much. When she left the room, she used the stairs to get to the lobby and tried to slip outside unnoticed. Unfortunately, that didn't happen as more bodyguards, already downstairs, spotted her. She cursed her stupidity as she sprinted for the door and got outside looking for her team, who had followed her to the hotel. She didn't wear a wire, which would have increased the risk for this job. The team spotted her and flashed their lights.

As she ran across the street, the guards burst outside, peeling off a few shots, one grazing her shoulder. Her comrades returned fire, providing her breathing space as she dived into an open door. They drove off as a few more shots whistled into the back of the car.

At the debrief she was told that Fetterman had not only survived but had put a hefty price on her life and that her future as an agent was now compromised. Further, she would never be safe while he was alive, or dead for that matter, the job would remain open regardless; that's how he worked. It was his insurance policy.

So, when the offer of a trip back in time was brought before her, she didn't think twice. It was life in obscurity back in time or certain death, so here she was in Linz, Austria, 1907, hunting Adolf Hitler. One last mission.

Elea' saw a café and went inside. The owner looked at her and smiled. "Bitte setzen Sie sich," which she understood as "Please be seated," and she took a small table at the back of the café, away from other patrons. She looked at the menu, reading down the list: Rindsuppe (Beef soup), Tefelspitz (Boiled beef), Gulasch. She wrinkled her nose and squinted, not overly impressed by the options as the waiter came to her, "Denine Bestellung?" (Your order?)

She replied in German. While there were slight differences between how the Austrians and Germans spoke, it wasn't going to set off too many alarm bells, she hoped. "Beef soup, some bread and a Mokka please."

"Very good. You are German, yes?"

"Yes." She smiled but didn't elaborate. No need to say more than necessary and he knew to mind his business.

"Your food will be ready soon," he replied.

"Thank you," she said, relieved that she passed her first test at fitting in.

The food arrived and as it was set down on the table, she realised how very hungry she was. She ate and was astonished at how very good it was, quite unlike the prefabricated dietary offerings of her time. When she was finished, she handed over a few Krone coins and waved off accepting the change, which pleased the cashier, then asked, "Do you know of a local hotel?"

"Yes of course," the man announced. "There are many choices. Just follow the street towards the river, you will find them easily. I would suggest the Austria Linz Hotel. Quiet and comfortable."

"Thank you. I enjoyed your food," she said, and the man smiled broadly.

She found the hotel easily. It was a large building with many floors and was quite ornate. She had no trouble getting a room. She settled in and rested a while before eating supper in the hotel restaurant.

That night she formulated her plan. She knew that at this time Hitler's mother, Klara, was gravely ill and he'd returned to be by her side, having spent the previous year in Vienna, a place he would be returning to in May 1908 after settling the affairs of his soon dead mother, except none of that was going to happen now because he would most certainly not outlive her.

Next day she went to Sisters of Saint Mercy Hospital where she knew Klara Hitler had been treated for her breast cancer. She approached the front desk where she gained the attention of the duty nurse, "Yes," she barked.

"I'm hoping you can help me. I have travelled from Strasburg to see my Auntie. She is very unwell."

"Name," the nurse barked again.

"Klara Hitler."

The nurse thumbed through the patient register, "No longer here. She is at home now."

"Oh, I don't suppose you can tell me where that might be? We haven't really kept in touch, and my mother is too unwell to travel," Elea' pleaded as she let a tear trickle down one cheek. The nurse noticed and she softened a little.

"Of course, my dear, let me check." She flicked through another register. "Here it is, Humboldt Strasse 31, it is in the middle of town."

"That's right, I remember now. Thank you."

The nurse even smiled then offered, "You know she is extremely ill, only her son and daughter are with her. It may only be days. It's good that you have come."

"Thank you again," said Elea' as she excused herself and headed into Linz on foot. It involved a lot of walking but better that than leaving a trail of taxi and bus fares and she was very fit, so it proved easy and it helped keep her warm.

Heating in 1907 left much to be desired and she immediately thought of moving to Florida once the job was done.

In a short while she was standing in front of Humboldt Strasse 31, the Hitler family home. It was an unremarkable structure, three floors, oblong shaped with a sickly custard coloured façade, a sharply pitched roof to repel snow, and square white framed windows with a single, arched door at the front left of the building.

As she stood there, none of her training or professional skill could have prepared her for the man now emerging from the house. He was clearly young, had a long white face, slicked back hair parted on the right, no moustache; he wouldn't grow one until he joined the army, but it was clear to Elea' that she was looking at a very much alive Adolf Hitler. She took a sharp breath after realising she hadn't moved for almost a minute.

Hitler checked for traffic of which there was very little and crossed the street, passing Elea' without giving her a glance as he swept back some loose hair from his forehead. He strode within an arm's length of her, and she caught the scent of a cologne, something she didn't expect.

She pretended to be scrounging through her purse and dared not look at him directly, but her keen peripheral vision was enough. Her immediate thought was that the young Hitler was handsome up close, and she felt sick at the thought. He strode off with some urgency, so she followed.

He headed into the town centre, and she struggled to keep up without the occasional skip and trot, he was a fast walker. The streets were quiet; it was after lunch, so people were at home or at work. Hitler ducked up a lane and, in her haste, to keep up she didn't slow, turning straight around the corner with her head down and suddenly felt something cold and sharp pinch her abdomen.

She looked upon a knife that was embedded in her stomach just as the pain ripped into her core. She glanced up at her assailant. It was Hitler. He looked her in the eye fiercely.

"They told me you would come. They told me you would kill me. I didn't believe them at first but then I saw you. They gave me this knife and said I should not hesitate to use it if I saw you."

Elea' felt her life draining away as Hitler plucked the knife out of her body but before she could fall, he rammed it in again, piercing a lung, "You think you can kill me that easily? I think not Fraulein."

Hitler pushed her to the ground, and she watched him walk away, throwing the knife into a drain as he muttered to himself, his infamous anger surfacing.

He didn't look back as Elea' slumped against the side wall of a building in the lane hiding her from direct view of the main road.

In her dying breath she saw him stop as two men emerged and spoke to Hitler. They looked at her, smiled and then the trio moved off, leaving her there as she drowned in her own blood.

Chapter 7 – Aftermath

All members of the committee sat quietly absorbing the report of Elea's mission. The data indicated that she had been murdered in Linz only a day after arriving in the town. It was a significant setback and not expected from such a well credentialed operative.

The report was short given the lack of time the operative had been in the field. The only real record of her fate appeared in two newspapers from 1907 in Linz, the Oberdonau-Zetung and Tages-Post.

Follow up stories indicated that no-one was ever arrested and the murder went unsolved. The only theory was a robbery gone bad. The victim was unknown in town, and no relatives were ever traced.

"Does anyone have any thoughts at all? Do we know what could have gone wrong," Pinet asked with serious concern.

Zhang Jie spoke first, "I can only see a few possibilities; it was a careless robbery attempt that went wrong, which is what has been reported or she got sloppy and Hitler overcame her...or..." He was about to add to his remarks but was cut off.

"Elea' wouldn't have tried to move on Hitler so soon and I very much doubt that anyone could get the better of her," Kanumbra suggested with an accompanying frown.

"Kanumbra makes a good point," added Gonzales, "She hadn't been there for more than a day. She barely had time to change her clothes."

"And yet she was found a block from Hitler's home," Fawcett pointed out.

"It could be a coincidence. She may have been on her way there or simply walked past the house to take a quick look and got jumped by someone. We don't know," Galal said.

"Precisely. We don't know," agreed Brigalow. "But if I were a betting man, I would say it's just bad luck."

"Well, we need to make our best guess because if it's only bad luck, we can try again BUT if Hitler was responsible that could complicate things," Pinet explained then added, "Let's assume it was Hitler for a moment. We don't know what would have motivated it, but we must assume he acted out of a sense of danger. He wasn't a man who randomly murdered people on the street."

"No, he used gas chambers, torture and firing squads," Patel interrupted.

Pinet looked at him with frustration. "Of course, but that's not what we're talking about. This was an 18-year-old man, dealing with an illness in the family and under a lot of pressure personally. He couldn't have been paranoid about his own safety at the time so if he did kill Elea' it may have just been a momentary lapse of judgement due to the strain he was under or even just self-defence. He got lucky."

Kuznetsov frowned in deep thought having said nothing to this point. After reading the report and sizing up everyone's thought she chimed in, "She was there 24 hours and we assume she hadn't engaged her target, hadn't revealed herself to him and wound-up dead in a lane near his home. Nothing connects Hitler to her other than proximity to his home while he was at his mother's bedside. Klara was only days away from death and that's what Hitler was focussed on. What's the most obvious scenario? I think Elea' was unlucky. Some unknown assailant did this. Think about it, she wouldn't have made a move so soon. No way."

"I think you are right," Pinet added, "Elea' was a professional and would have taken her time to size up her target and choose her moment wisely and there is no chance he could have known who she was or why she was there. I agree with you Gabrielle."

"Ok, so I'll play Devil's advocate," said Jie, getting back to his third point. "Let's then assume that Hitler did know something was up. He would have acted to protect himself, right? We only must consider how he could have learned of her reason for being in Linz."

"And pray tell how would he have found out?" scoffed Kanumbra.

"Well let's carve it up and see what happens," Jie suggested before realising his faux pas. "Sorry, poor choice of words. How could Hitler have found out? Aside from what I said before she could have made a move when an unexpected possibility became apparent and he got the better of her; she said something that raised an alarm and he was warned or, someone else sent someone back to warn him."

"What," exclaimed Pinet as everyone gasped in unison.

"Think about it. We have a machine that can send people back in time, albeit with certain restrictions, but we haven't accounted for the likely fact that this machine may well still be in operation long after we are gone OR that it will be copied or stolen or hacked or any number of possibilities in the future. Why dismiss the concept of some future faction going back to warn him?"

"Preposterous," cried Patel.

"Really? You are so sure we will control this tech forever? I highly doubt it," added Jie.

"I think we're getting too entrenched in the unlikely," Pinet pointed out. "Let's look at it in basic terms and while I don't totally disagree with you Jie, the security surrounding the IG Machine is significant. I doubt anyone could copy it or steal the concept."

"Never say never Jean Claude," Jie suggested.

"Nevertheless, I agree with Gabrielle. It was simply bad luck I think and the only way to know for sure is to try again. I propose we repeat the exercise. Are we agreed?"

The discussion went around the table a few more times with Jie making certain his views were on the record but in the end they all agreed to send another operative to 1907.

Then Brigalow had a thought, "Why don't we send them back a bit before Elea' arrived and have them work together?"

"Brilliant," cried Pinet and all agreed.

Finding another ideal candidate was a simpler task than expected with German intelligence offering a disavowed operative who had worked with Elea' previously. He would go back to 1907 a little sooner than Elea's arrival and intercept her, explaining the way things transpired and then execute a new plan.

Liam Konig was a well-trained operator who, like Elea', was identifiable after a low-key operation went wrong and was reduced to roles in research and other non-field work.

He was an older man, late forties and had gained much respect amongst his peers, so his decision to volunteer for the operation was indeed a bonus. He had no family ties to speak of and would not be missed.

How he might adjust to life in 1907 was anyone's guess and he was warned that he may well have to serve in WW1 where conscription was a reality for many German servicemen of the era, although his age may see him avoid front line action if he was lucky.

He didn't hesitate, knowing that Elea' was in trouble and that he could help. The usual caveats were made known to him but didn't sway him from the mission.

After the final briefing and with all the necessary documentation and funds acquired, Konig was sent back to 1907 to intercept Elea. The insertion into December 1907 went perfectly and Konig found himself in a forested area outside Linz upon arrival.

Within seconds of planting he heard two loud cracks, felt a searing pain in his upper back and he fell to the ground, coughing up blood. He noticed two shadowy figures in the trees walking towards him. A third pistol crack made sure he would never reach Elea'.

The committee once again sat at their meeting table dumbfounded by the latest report, which included extracts from the newspapers of the era about a mysterious stranger who had been shot and killed in the forest outside of Linz. Again, the murder was never solved.

"Do I need to make my point again," announced Zhang Jie with some authority. "They knew he was coming. He was found almost exactly where we inserted him. That cannot have been bad luck or a coincidence. He was assassinated. Someone knew he was going to be there!"

"I fear you are right," conceded Pinet and no-one voiced any dissent this time. "So, what do we do now? Who did this?"

"If I may, I have a theory," Jie said, "We can assume it's no one in this time because we are the only ones with knowledge of this project, right? So, what if whoever it was doesn't exist yet and that sometime in the future something changes and this machine or one like it gets into the hands of a group with a different agenda. Saving Hitler," Jie claimed.

"If that's true, and I don't discount the possibility Jie, how do we stop it," Kanumbra asked, clearly devoid of his own ideas.

Kuznetsov was blunt, "If we send back another then another, they will face the same fate. We could send a small force, and it would still fail."

"That appears to be likely," Pinet agreed. "If they are disrupting us from the future, anything we do now will be known to them. They clearly have access to the logging data and can intercept us at any turn."

"Perhaps we can test Jie's theory. Is there a way of corrupting the data? Faking the insertion point so they go to the wrong place," asked Patel.

"Perhaps but it wouldn't matter I don't think," added Gonzales. "Even if we successfully inserted someone undetected, the fact that they then executed their mission would be known in the future and therefore be able to be intercepted."

"I agree in part," said Fawcett, "but if we succeed then the faction that is trying to stop us might never come into existence. So, it's worth a try, if we can corrupt the data."

"It would have to be not only altered but be irretrievable forever. A complete wipe and destruction of digital logs, a full reset of the Infinity Generator," Brigalow suggested. "We may even have to consider totally destroying the machine."

"Ridiculous," blurted Galal. "Destroy the greatest invention humanity has ever created? That's going way too far in my opinion."

"Perhaps it is, but it's clear that we are already compromised by a future we cannot control or predict. Someone knows or will know whatever we do going forward and we can only go backwards, so how do we hide it," Jie pointed out.

"The fog of War," announced Brigalow.

"What," Pinet asked with some astonishment.

"We take advantage of the war, 1914 to 1918. We insert an operative or operatives into the Western Front and fake the data so that anyone who might know we did it cannot find them. We also send them through with identities that are never recorded in our time so no-one can know who they were, not now or in the future."

Everyone looked at Brigalow wide eyed, "It might just work," Pinet mumbled. "But the Western Front? It's as good as a suicide mission."

"Yes, but Hitler served there. We know where he will be some of the time. With good people and a bit of luck we can stay a step ahead of anyone who might try to stop us. The war should make it hard for them to easily intercept us too," Brigalow added.

"You make a good point," agreed Jie. "And I also think multiple insertions would give us a higher chance of success. If we can find out where Hitler served at various times, we can send people back to multiple locations at different times and, well, hope that one of them succeeds."

"That might work but if we have a few failed attempts, I fear Hitler will go to ground and then what," asked Gonzales.

"It's so strange talking about him as if he's a living breathing reality, even though we know he's been dead for 270 years," Galal said, his head shaking in confusion.

"Yes, it does make your mind spin, doesn't it," agreed Pinet. "But the ball is already rolling on this mission, so we must follow through. Do we all agree on the plan, assuming our technicians can corrupt the data so that whoever is intercepting us can be hoodwinked? Do we go in?"

"Yes," all said in unison.

Chapter 8 – War plans

The first thing the committee needed to do was research where and when they might be able to find Hitler in World War One.

The fact that their operatives had been intercepted twice was a deep concern and no-one could think who might be responsible. It was agreed that they needed to hide their tracks and hope that, once successful, any future group that supported Hitler would never manifest itself.

"You know what else we need to do," Brigalow announced, "We need to be sure that when we die, all of us are cremated and our ashes are scattered so that no-one in the future can send back our bodies and delete us from existence! I'm surprised they haven't done it already."

"Oh my God," blurted Fawcett, "I never thought of that...but you're right, we all have to agree to remove the risk."

"I'm OK with that, what about the rest of you," Pinet asked.

"Yes," "of course", "Indeed," came the responses.

"Then again," added Brigalow, "They might have deleted some of us already and we'd be none the wiser."

No-one had anything to say about that but the looks on their faces were enough. Then Pinet said,

"Let's get to it, dig up everything you can find out about Hitler's service in World War One. The more we can learn the more opportunities we can use. AND if possible, don't record anything digitally. We don't want to leave any records that could be found in the future. Might be best to use encyclopaedias, perhaps download volumes to a computer and disconnect it from the web and destroy it when we're done."

"That's good thinking Jean Claude," Jie said. "And perhaps we can visit some libraries and look at actual paper volumes. They still exist, don't they?"

"Probably in museums, not libraries," said Patel.

"Anything that gets us the information we need is good enough, but we keep it well and truly off the grid," reiterated Pinet.

The research was exhausting and took the committee much longer than they had hoped. It seemed that much had been deleted, but ultimately, they were able to piece together some useful information.

The committee met again and tabled all their findings.

"Who would like to start," Pinet asked the group.

"I will," said Jie. "All right, when the war started, he asked to join the Bavarian Army, and it seems this was granted. It appears that this was a mistake because he should have been deported to Austria, but it was overlooked."

"Do we know where he served," Patel asked.

"Yes. Belgium and France with the Bavarian Reserve Regiment 16," Jie added.

"Anything else," enquired Kuznetsov.

"Not much. Most of what I downloaded was redacted."

"Well, I tried a library and found out what Jie has discovered and more," Kanumbra said, "The Bavarian Reserve Regiment 16 served at the First Battle of Ypres. Hitler served as an Infantry man there. They suffered heavy losses. Hitler's regiment went from 3600 men to 611."

"That must have been awful," Gonzales suggested then added, "Pity they didn't get him then."

"Sadly, they didn't," Kanumbra continued, "But it messed with him by the look of it. The information I found said that he became quite aloof after that and was reassigned as a regimental message runner.

"The Battle of Ypres is not helpful. We can't pinpoint him specifically and it sounds like it was a bloodbath. Anyone we send there would have little chance of surviving let alone getting to Hitler," Pinet thought out loud, "What else have we found out?"

"I found the Battle Honours of the 16th Bavarians," announced Brigalow, "The First Battle of Ypres we know about already, but they were in some heavy stuff more than once...the Somme, Arras, Passchendaele and Fromelles. They were all heavy engagements and disasters for one side or the other, or both."

"So which one do we choose? Or are we taking too high a risk with this approach," asked Pinet.

"Well, we've already put lives at risk and been intercepted at every turn. Hiding behind the veil of war might be risky too, but at least they'll have a sporting chance," Brigalow replied, "and as far as which battle is concerned, I suggest Fromelles."

"Why?"

"Because it was a victory for the Germans. A big one. They repelled a strong attack there and it was one of the Bavarians greatest triumphs," Brigalow explained.

"So, we send someone back to the war, enlist with the 16th Bavarian Regiment and hope he can do the job," Pinet reiterated.

"Yes and no," Brigalow said with a half-smile, "We send someone back as a German, but we have them join the Allies. Whoever is against us won't be expecting that. We throw them a dummy!"

"A what," Gonzales asked clearly confused.

"A dummy, a fake, it's a football term. Essentially, we make it look like we sent someone in as a German operative, but they switch on arrival, change identity and join the British."

"I see," said Pinet. "And they would have to take part in a losing battle and hopefully survive to get to Hitler."

"Indeed, but I know many Australians were captured in that battle, so if they could be part of the first wave they could get into the German trenches. Once captured they could claim to be a German spy," Brigalow explained. "I'm just thinking out loud here. I don't know if it will work but we must confuse those that would stop us. This might be the way to go."

"I suspect anyone turning up in the heat of battle claiming to be a spy would be a red flag to our enemies, whoever they are," Fawcett pointed out, "It all sounds too messy."

"OK, maybe we send in an Australian," Brigalow pointed out. "He'll need to be a member of the," he hesitated as he scanned his notes, "53rd Battalion and he will have to be in the first wave. From what I understand, they got into the German line while the second wave was decimated. Maybe he can then get to Hitler."

"I think this plan is foolhardy," announced Patel, "It does not guarantee success. We will be sending someone to their death. Why can't we send someone back to 1907 again, well before December and have them change identity, removing the risk of war."

"We've tried twice already and, I suspect whoever is intercepting us will now have Hitler under guard. I doubt we'll get close to him regardless," Kanumbra explained, "Do you want to try for a third time?"

Pinet nodded in agreement, "The confusion of war may be our only real option Mr. Patel. It's high risk but so is everything else as we have very much come to realise."

"In that case I propose a two-pronged approach," suggested Jie, "We send two supposed Germans back, switch one to the

Allied side and have the other stay on the German side. Between them we have both options covered. If the people behind the two previous intercepts do the same against our German, so be it, we still have the Allied angle as a backup."

"Could we send them back together and make it look like we only sent one person," Kuznetsov wondered.

"We haven't tried a dual transfer before, but it should work, theoretically," Pinet added, "We should certainly consider it."

"Well then, it appears we have the basis of a plan," Brigalow said, "Let's work up the details and see if we can execute it."

"Yes, but I remind you to keep it all off the record," Pinet told everyone. "We cannot leave any kind of digital trail, or a paper trail for that matter." All nodded in agreement.

The committee members continued to work through the issues. Brigalow had an off the books meeting with the Australian UN Delegate travelling under a fake name and passport. Nothing of the meeting was recorded.

The delegate understood the problem and agreed to quietly source an operative for the task. Pinet negotiated once again with the German Government, he too doing so with stealth, and while they were frustrated by the first two failures, they realised what the committee was up against and agreed to find someone for the job.

The remaining members researched the Battle of Fromelles as much as they could from the data that was available. Again, they discovered that much had been removed but not everything and they found enough data, including why the attack failed.

The frontline at Fromelles was a relatively quiet sector for most of the First World War. The British did try to take the position in 1915 and were decimated but that was soon forgotten after the earlier failings on the Somme in 1916 and so a new attempt was made to take the position and to redirect German resources to intercept the advance and keep them away from the Somme.

The plan wasn't complicated; after a seven-hour artillery barrage, infantry crossed no-man's-land to take the German trenches and at the same time take out a bulge in the line at a place known as the Sugar Loaf.

On the right, the British 61st Division covered around four kilometres of the front and were responsible for taking the Sugar Loaf while the Australian 5th Division was supposed take the rest, around one thousand meters of front line to the left of the British.

Some within the Australian ranks were critical of the plan, because of the distance between the respective trench lines, some four hundred meters of ground to reach the Germans, a horrific distance in an era of lethal machine gun fire, barbed wire, and artillery.

Another quirk of Fromelles was that this area of French Flanders had a high-water table, so trenches couldn't be dug more than a couple of feet before they filled with water, so the Australian and British troops were protected by walls instead of trenches along some parts of the line.

The committee discovered that there was some dispute about how best to start the attack. The Australians opted to climb their walls with ladders, but the British decided to punch holes through theirs to avoid being taken out by snipers going over the top.

At 1800 hours on July 19th, 1916, the advance began. Initially the advance on the left flank went well, with the Australian first wave making the German line. They took approximately 100 meters of the front and even got into the secondary German trenches.

Unfortunately, on the right, the British failed to take the Sugar Loaf where the Germans had a machine gun. They also had a machine gun on the left flank and when the alarm sounded the German gunners, using a textbook crossfire technique, obliterated the Australian second wave.

The British advance was further complicated because of the decision to punch holes through their defensive wall with men machine gunned as they emerged. The piles of bodies stifled their advance, leaving the Australians on the left completely exposed. A detachment of Australians was sent to take out the Sugar Loaf but they too failed.

Those that made the German line could not be supported and after some frantic fighting they were eventually thrown out or captured.

The entire attack was a catastrophe, not only in terms of taking the German trenches and straightening out the bulge at the Sugar Loaf, but it also failed to dupe the Germans and stop them from moving resources to the Somme.

Overall, the casualty count was horrific. In the twenty-four hours after zero hour, the Australians suffered 5533 casualties, the most of any one attack in the war for their army. They also had 400 of their men taken prisoner, a point that the committee noted.

The British lost over 1500 men while the German losses were around 1000.

Many of the Australians trying to return to safety were shot down by snipers in no-man's land and others were killed while trying to scale their own wall. It was indeed a disaster and totally fruitless.

Somewhere though, at the back of this carnage was a 27-year-old German messenger named Adolf Hitler. If a plan could be created to get someone to him, this would be a perfect place to execute their objective. He was still a nobody, and his death would be meaningless.

The committee members agreed they needed to find out who some of those 400 Australian prisoners were and somehow infiltrate them with an operative. From there they might be able to get to Hitler as they passed through the back of the German lines.

At the same time their German operative, would attempt to hunt down Hitler from the German side.

It was high risk, yes, but the war was indeed a good way of covering up their plans and it may well succeed.

If it didn't, everyone knew that things would become much more complicated.

Between the early 21st Century and into the 24th Century the World had seen much turmoil. While there wasn't specifically a Third World War, many historians equated the Cold War of the 20th Century and the Terror Campaigns of the next several decades as the catalyst for a great deal of fragmentation between the West, the East, and several growing extremist factions, driven by an ideology that didn't fit the Western agenda.

With pressure from extremists, the West was forced to fight on several fronts as well as from within their own borders to stem the flow of terror.

Several European nations, France, Belgium, England, Spain, and Germany, were confronted with turmoil from within when factional groups of Neo Nazis unexpectedly grew into an organised and formidable foe.

In 2333, exactly 400 years after Hitler gained power, they sacked Berlin and overthrew the sitting Government and quickly spread their fear into France and Belgium while their supporters in other countries revolted against their respective governments. Some succeeded, others did not but having control of one nation was the foothold they needed.

They blockaded the major ports and brought many European nations to their economic knees. Attempts to unseat them was met with much bloodshed and it was quickly realised that no-one had the military power to deal with them over such a wide area, except perhaps England but they too were fighting against white supremacists on home soil which made mounting a counterattack on the European mainland an unlikely task.

The Nazi conquest was ruthless and unrelenting and not even traditionally neutral countries were spared. Without significant defence, they too were overwhelmed.

As the Nazi successes grew, so did their support. It was like a cancer that spread over Europe, consuming all that was held dear, returning the continent to an era of tyranny and hatred.

Soon the ethnic cleansing that had been a bloody stain on the twentieth century now became a beacon for neo-Nazis around the World, but they were so much more ruthless about it. They didn't bother with concentration camps or gas chambers, they just killed and terrorised indiscriminately to the tune of tens of thousands at first, then hundreds of thousands.

The United Nations was at a loss to explain how they'd grown so powerful under the noses of so many peaceful nations, but it was too late to speculate as most were fighting to maintain their traditional rights and freedoms.

The Nazi approach worked better than any of the antagonists could have hoped. They were able to concentrate their aggression so strategically that none of the defenders were in any position to assist each other, except for perhaps Russia but they opted to secure their borders and make it impossible for the Nazis to enter.

The Russian President, Valeri Oblonsky, a Communist, knew it was only a matter of time before the Nazis once again tried to quell their natural foe, so he ordered that all men aged 16 and over be drafted to defend the Motherland. He knew they had time, given the nature of the fighting in the rest of Europe.

The Nazis would need to make a full commitment to take Russia but to do so meant they had to overwhelm several other nations first, which might take years, allowing Russia to mobilise, train and ultimately defend their soil.

Smaller nations though, like Poland, Austria, and the Balkans, all fell quickly, increasing the Nazi powerbase. Soon after Belgium and the Netherlands collapsed, and while they tried hard to fight on, France too was soon in Nazi control. That once again left England very much alone.

The Neo-Nazis didn't make the same mistake as their founding father though; they immediately crossed the channel by sea and air and invaded England with ruthless abandon.

The British fought hard and held the Nazis for several months, but the weight of numbers and lack of supplies eventually took its toll and England fell along with Scotland, Wales and ultimately Unified Ireland.

After three years of fighting, Western and Southern Europe belonged to the Nazis.

The east though would prove much more difficult to crack. The once famous Iron Curtain that Winston Churchill described after WWII, was again raised in defiance.

The Nazis also stopped at the Turkish border. In this case voluntarily, their control of Europe now ensured that they could take time to consolidate, grow and draw up plans to take Russia, China, Korea, Japan and eventually the Pacific, then America.

The Neo Nazis had negotiated an agreement with extremist groups in the Middle East not to invade and to give them ultimate control of their own piece of the World. They could decide internally how that might be done. It ultimately led to turmoil as extremist groups seized opportunities when the US and other Allied forces left to secure their own borders.

Like Europe, the Middle East was overrun by terror groups, driven by a Caliphate which saw them impose their own form of cleansing. They stole more territory from Turkey, taking all of Africa to the sub-continent.

When the dust settled, it was 2337 and extremists-controlled Europe, Africa, and the Middle East while the US, Canada, South America and Australia remained independent, but for how long? No-one could tell.

The Supreme Leader of the Neo Nazis, Ernst Pfeiffer declared that the Fourth Reich would reign for a thousand years. Their reign was defined by the systematic destruction of democracy and the incarceration, enslavement, or extermination of anyone who didn't adhere to their extremist doctrines. Millions were put to death while those that survived suffered in silence, hoping against hope that they would be saved. It wasn't to be.

But Pfeiffer realised his greatest prize was in Switzerland at Cern where the United Nations facility that housed the Infinity Generator was based.

With this device, he could control the past and maintain the future. He would begin by infiltrating Russia and the United States and start to undermine their respective histories, win the First World War, dispensing with the need for the Second and see Hitler rise to supreme leader of a Nazi World.

He soon realised it wasn't going to be that easy. As his people, with the unwitting assistance of the scientists at the facility, started formulating plans, someone in history had been dabbling with the past according to the IG logs, firstly with an experiment involving a woman sent back to Paris and similar experiments that had no impact on the World's timeline.

Pfeiffer wasn't an astute man by any means, but he had enough intelligence to consider what the United Nations might try to do with their new toy. Given the very reasons for the UN coming into existence, he came to believe they might try to right the wrongs of the past, so he ordered that Nazi operatives be sent back to the early twentieth century with one objective. Protect Adolf Hitler at all costs!

His foresight paid off with several attempts on Hitler's life thwarted during Hitler's teenage years, but Pfeiffer then realised that the people of the past were somehow anticipating his plans.

They might not have a clue who Pfeiffer was, but they were clever enough to cover their tracks and expunge their identities from history so they couldn't be themselves targeted. Pfeiffer also realised that they could probably now get to Hitler without his people being aware. He wasn't sure how but if they could hide themselves from history, they could hide their operatives. That didn't sit well with him. The only thing to do was to take over the IG facility itself back in 2214.

And unlike the people of 2214, the Nazis of 2337 didn't have any hesitation using future tech when they travelled back in time. Why waste such an advantage?

A small task force of five was sent back to deal with the problem at Cern. They were armed with weapons that were highly evolved compared to 2214. It would be like a WW1 soldier facing someone from the early 2000s. They were supremely confident that they would breeze in and exterminate the troublesome IG committee and disappear into the past without breaking a sweat.

The people of 2214 had done well to redact significant amounts of data from the Internet and destroy hard copy records about the facility, but the layout was essentially the same despite several renovations and upgrades over the years.

The Nazi fighters knew where the committee met and would wait for an opportune time to make their move. They studied whatever intelligence they could gather and prepared for the attack.

The five were veterans and skilful killers, unlikely to hesitate in the heat of the fight, not that they expected any such resistance from the UN guard posts. They wouldn't be engaging in close quarter combat.

With their plans made they were sent off by their Commander, Ernst Pfeiffer.

"Your success will guarantee the future of the Reich. You know what to do. God speed!"

The five responded in the customary way, a Sieg Heil salute. They probably weren't aware that the salute was created by Francis Bellamy in the United States in 1892 as part of the Pledge of Allegiance. Bellamy had created it based on a salute that was developed by Roman soldiers. The controversy surrounding the salute after it was adopted by the Nazis and fascists in Italy saw the United States switch to a hand on the heart gesture after an amendment of the flag code in 1942.

The Nazi insurgents were deposited on the outskirts of Geneva in the middle of the night in early 2214, before the first IG experiment took place and thus, before anyone involved could be aware of the existence of the tug o' war that was taking place over the life of Hitler in 1907.

Given the liberal approach to hunting that existed in Switzerland in 2214, a group of five hunters emerging from the forest wouldn't seem out of place at night and so they simply walked into the open unchallenged.

The weapons were slung over their shoulders in gun bags, and they all carried the necessary documentation to prove their legality if ever approached, but these weapons were unlike any hunting rifles that existed in the 2200s. These were high powered automatic weapons with laser guided scopes.

Like cruise missiles of the past, these rifles could guide bullets thousands of yards to multiple targets once painted by the invisible laser sight. The bullets were also self-thrusting, so they didn't lose velocity through the air. Tiny fins that deployed in flight guaranteed they didn't lose trajectory and with their explosive heads, they could penetrate thick steel, concrete and armour plating with ease. In the case of the Cern facility, the projectiles would easily slice through the facade and into a target before they even heard the crack of any penetration through the wall.

Their plan didn't require them to storm the facility. They needed only to find a good firing position and eradicate the committee members in one fell swoop. Once the task was complete, they would steal away, destroy their weapons beyond salvage and commit suicide in a place where they might never be found. It was a good plan!

The Cern Research and Nuclear facility that housed the Infinity Generator was just outside of Geneva, so the insurgents didn't have to enter the city. They simply had to locate high ground, which was oddly difficult, as it turned out. While mountains surrounded the facility, these were too far away to affect an attack, even with these future weapons.

Larger weapons were unable to be transferred back in time because they simply didn't fit and, even though they could have been sent through in parts, they would have been impossible to hide and difficult to move. Otherwise, they could have easily detonated the entire building in one shot but that would destroy the IG machine, so that idea was never on.

The group became frustrated at the lack of vantage points and were starting to worry about attracting unwanted attention as they wandered around searching for an advantageous position.

They knew the roads were probably regularly patrolled and they needed to find cover quickly. For all their efforts it seemed their homework was incomplete regarding the best place to find a shot, which for a sniper was a primary goal. Their arrogance during the planning was now causing problems.

Eventually though they found a building tall enough to give them line of sight to the IG offices. The angle wasn't good, but a stealth drone could be deployed to overcome the impairment.

They could just as easily use the drone to paint the targets as they could with their rifles. Through the drone's camera, they could simply identify each target, log them into the rifle's matrix and fire. It wouldn't even matter if the target moved, the bullet would find them. As expected, the building they found was very secure and they used a device to hack the security codes and spring the door. No alarm sounded. They opted to use a stairwell to get to the roof, significantly reducing them happening across a local resident.

The apartment was on the rise of a small hill and ten stories high, meaning they would be able to look down on the IG office building from an excellent viewpoint. The IG offices were five stories tall with the committee chambers taking up the entire top floor, according to known records.

The architects had made the job easier for the insurgents with floor to ceiling glass across the front of the building, and while security was tight around the facility, no-one would have anticipated a series of sniper rounds from two miles away at an impossible angle.

It was very early in the morning and most people were asleep, with very few windows illuminated. Still, they had to step quietly to avoid the echo of their boots in the stairwell penetrating the neighbouring apartments.

After what seemed like an eternity, they reached the door to the roof. There wasn't any need to decrypt the lock as they were already inside the building, so they nudged the door, while one of the men propped it open, the other four slipped past him onto the roof. The man holding the door wedged it open for an easy escape once the job was done.

The roof was a typical apartment roof with air conditioning units, utility rooms and storage which would help them stay out of sight, but given their vantage point, it was doubtful that anyone could have seen them. They walked to the edge of the roof and looked down on the office of the Infinity Generator complex, noting the top floor windows angled sharply away from them on the street side of the complex. They would need to deploy a stealth drone to make the shots.

They smiled in anticipation as they set up for the operation. They just needed to wait for their targets to turn up.

What they failed to notice was the door of a storage room slide open ever so slightly from it came the muzzle of a rifle. From another door, the same thing and two more rifles emerged from the slatted covers of an air conditioning unit and one more pistol like weapon emerged from a dark corner held by a figure in a matt black suit.

In an instant, four silenced rounds hissed four bullets into four Nazi brains, splitting their skulls apart, grey matter exploding all over the cement of the roof.

Before the fifth member of the party could react, he felt a sting in his neck and blacked out before falling into the pooling blood and gore of his comrades.

"Targets down," someone said into their radio.

"Well done. Bring them in and clean up the mess," came the reply.

"Roger that!"

Chapter 10 – Plots

The nine members of the IG Committee sat at their meeting table, confused by a series of memories that had manifested themselves in an instant. It was now early 2215 and these new memories were mixed up with a reality they had clearly lived through. The new memories revealed an attempt on their lives almost a year ago.

They noted a sudden increase in security and had been moved to a safer location, away from their top floor amenities. It was indeed a strange feeling to have thoughts of something that they all knew to be a very real part of their lives, despite not having experienced it. They couldn't help but discuss what they now knew was a Nazi plot to assassinate each one of them even though it was already well in the past.

They also recalled the aftermath with the sole surviving insurgent clearly not drilled on keeping silent. He made it abundantly clear that the failure was just a delay to the inevitable. His superiority was palpable; despite being vanquished by people of inferior technical ability. He didn't even consider asking how they knew the assailants would be arriving.

Jean Claude Pinet was first to speak on the issue, "It gives you pause; they clearly want us gone and they have a huge advantage. They are in the future looking back while we cannot look forward."

"That's true," added Luciana Gonzales as she rubbed her temples trying to fight off a headache, "but it's pretty clear they don't know a lot about us, so our effort to expunge ourselves from history must have worked."

"Indeed," agreed Pinet, "And it appears we have an ally in the future, his or her warning was well timed and enabled us to post teams across the high points of the ground in anticipation of the attack last year. They were never going to succeed."

"But they may be successful next time," suggested Davis Brigalow. "How do we know this ally will be able to warn us again? These Nazis appear very determined."

"That's true but we are now more aware and have significantly increased security," Pinet explained.

"But what if they go back to an earlier time once again. We will be clueless unless we get a warning like we did on this occasion," said Hamid Kanumbra as sweat beaded on his forehead.

"If that happens then perhaps, we will cease to exist at this point but here we are and I think it would be fair to say that any failed attempt would manifest itself in our memories mixed with the other memories we already have, just like this event did," Pinet pointed out. "We know that a change in history that occurs because of our actions can add those memories to what we already know. Has anyone here experienced anything other than this one event?"

"No," they all said.

"But" Davis Brigalow added, "what if the timelines split and we are carrying on despite our assassination in the past? We could be living in multiple timelines because of the actions we take, and the actions taken by those ahead of us."

"Oh please," blurted Sunil Patel. "Just waking up this morning to a totally different set of protocols and toughened security was the strangest thing I have ever experienced. No need to add more weirdness to the mix."

"I think we must consider everything is possible at this point and things could change again at the drop of a hat, but we also need not dwell on it. Our focus is on our own timeline regardless of cause and effect. We are here, that's all that matters and we have a mission to complete. We should also have faith in the security that has been put in place, as sudden and surprising as it has been. No point getting all bent out of shape over something we cannot control," Pinet suggested and everyone agreed that it was probably a wise approach.

Anastasia Kuznetsov didn't wish to move on just yet, "I think we must consider the bravery of whoever warned us. They took a great risk using the machine under the noses of the Nazis by sending back a warning letter, right to our doorstep. They may not be able to do so as easily again."

"A valid point," Gabrielle Fawcett added. "If these future Nazis can figure out why their mission failed, I fear for whoever it is."

"I agree," said Pinet. "But what can we do? Nothing. We can only carry on with our mission. We opened this Pandora's box, now we must finish the job!" Without giving anyone a chance to continue speculating, which Pinet thought was pointless, he changed the subject immediately. "How are we going with plans for Fromelles?"

Everyone had been working hard on the complexities of the battle, how it panned out and how to best take advantage of it. The research was slow and arduous, but it ultimately paid off. The committee discovered that Hitler's Regiment spent a great deal of time in that region based at the French village of Vlaanderen. They even discovered that Hitler was assigned to the 1st Battalion at the Battle of Fromelles.

They also found that he arrived at the front at 1 O'clock on the morning of July 20, so they had a time and a place. Hitler's regiment didn't leave Fromelles until September 1916. The research also uncovered Hitler's movements during WWII.

He revisited the Fromelles area and specifically inspected a farm and a German bunker D141 at Aubers. It was strongly believed he felt a significant connection to these places after the First War, otherwise why go back there? Everyone agreed it was better than a hunch and could prove vital in finding Hitler in 1916.

Another site that came up in the research was Rote Banke at Rue Delval, which Hitler had sketched, and Befehlstelle Bayern, which seemed much less significant. But at least they had several leads.

The committee created a hard copy schematic of the Fromelles battlefield, hand drawn, so that no data could be stored on computer drives or servers. Hard copies would be destroyed when the operation was complete. They noted dates, times and locations, deployment of forces on both sides, and movements in the lead up to the battle.

"We have a lot of facts and place names, but we need to do more to nail down the battle minute by minute if we can," Brigalow explained.

"And how do we do that," Zhang Jie asked.

"Battalion diaries. They kept handwritten or typed records of the battle as it happened. If we can source that information we can get a clearer picture of events," Brigalow said.

"And where do we get these diaries," Muhammad Galal asked.

"Well, they're online but if we start searching for them, that data is recorded and we risk showing our hand in the future, so we will have to visit and retrieve the data in person," Brigalow added.

"Visit where," came a few voices in unison.

"Canberra; the Australian War Memorial to be exact. It's public record and should be easy to collate."

"Very good," said Pinet, "You will go with Gabrielle. Take separate airlines over different routes. Use false identities. We need to hide our travel as much as we do our online history and no comms while you're away," Pinet ordered.

"Very good Jean Claude," Brigalow answered.

"And we must speed things up. Given what has happened, I don't want to wait longer than we have to before sending operatives back to 1916."

It was essentially a crap shoot now. The committee had to be careful to cover their tracks so that the future wasn't aware of their plan, but they also realised that taking time meant the chances of another insurgent attack increased. It was weird science but a very real threat as they all now knew.

Brigalow took a flight from Geneva to London, then took the Qantas Supersonic Boeing X999 direct to Perth. On the way, while he was dozing, a new set of memories manifested in his mind, another attempt on the lives of the committee members in 2213, before they were even considering the Hitler assassination.

This time the Nazis tried a single assassin but again, their future ally was able to send back a warning just in time and the insurgent was intercepted as soon as he appeared outside Geneva; exactly where they expected him.

Brigalow felt more unnerved by the new mix of information. One attempt could be written off as the Nazis being hopeful, a second attempt made it too real. He knew there would be more attempts and perhaps, eventually they would succeed.

His memory also told him that nothing of the encounter with the Nazi infiltrator was put on record, giving the people in the future no clue as to what happened to their man. They hoped it would protect their informant, whoever it was.

The flight to Perth took six hours, crossing half the planet, then a domestic flight to Canberra. Each time he changed planes, he changed identities, just to keep the records from revealing any travel patterns in the future. Fawcett went via New York and, having headed west was in Canberra before Brigalow.

When they met at the Australian War Memorial, Fawcett too revealed that her memories had altered in transit which suggested all the committee members would be aware of the attempt. Brigalow noticed that she too seemed a little more shaken by the inflight development.

They were ordered not to contact Cern in any way while they were abroad, again to keep from leaving breadcrumbs so they could only assume that everyone else had a similar experience. They'd find out once they returned to Geneva.

At the War Memorial, they entered as a married couple under yet another fake identity, again to throw off the records. They found their way to the research department, spoke with one of the staff about what they were looking for and were directed to the library which was full of volumes about all wars involving Australians as far back as 1899 when Australia fought in Africa against the Boers. There were also computer records, which they were hoping to avoid, knowing that all searches were logged.

"Where do we start," asked Fawcett.

"The Battalion diaries I think," answered Brigalow and they both started searching for volumes.

After a brief look around Brigalow called, "Found it!" They both settled at a table in a quiet corner and started reading through the pages.

"Jesus! It's handwritten," cried Fawcett.

"In pencil," Brigalow added, "It's hard to decipher, a lot of the writing was faded when they created these copies."

"We'll just have to make do," Fawcett suggested.

"Well, here's the battle, in the first few pages. This was their first action. Poor bastards," Brigalow said, shaking his head.

"Why do you say that?"

"It was a disaster, particularly for the Allies. A no win scenario. Bloody reckless and ill planned," Brigalow reiterated.

"So, what's the sense in us sending an operative into that situation," Fawcett asked, even though they'd already discussed it in committee.

"The fog of war. The future Nazis won't be able to easily get to our men in that situation."

"But our men could be easily killed regardless," Fawcett reminded him.

"Very true, but we know which units were captured so we install our man with them."

"That guarantees nothing," Fawcett added.

"I agree but have you got any other ideas? Everything we've done has been intercepted. I would hazard a guess that these future Nazis have Hitler under constant guard from his birth and maybe earlier. We can't get to him in peace time, so it must be war," Brigalow explained. "And, before you say it, yes, I expect they have him covered at Fromelles too, but the war will make it very difficult for them to intercept someone in his vicinity if they're in uniform or a prisoner."

"I see your point. It's high risk either way."

"Exactly," Brigalow said.

With that they set to work, noting the times and specifics of the battle as recorded by the Adjutant of the 53rd Battalion, First Australian Imperial Force. The more they read, the more horrific it became but they were able to note some successes with the first wave making it across no-man's land and into the German lines. Unfortunately, that was as good as it got with the second, third and fourth waves decimated and the soldiers that were in the German line unable to hold on. Those that tried to return to their line were shot down and those that fought on either died or were captured.

Then Fawcett paused for a moment, "What if we win the battle?"

"What," Brigalow blurted in surprise.

"What if we make it so the battle is a success. That will almost guarantee we can get to Hitler or at least increase the odds."

"I don't know," Brigalow said seemingly interested in the concept. "I actually like the idea to be honest but how?"

"I'm sure we can figure something out," Fawcett said with a smile and Brigalow returned the smirk.

Chapter 11 – Battle Plans

Brigalow and Fawcett, upon returning to Geneva, presented their findings to the committee, "This battle was a terrible disaster," explained Brigalow. "It was designed to trick the Germans into moving resources away from the main battlefield on the Somme, which it failed to do. The Germans were also well entrenched and prepared for an attack at Fromelles. In fact, they were expecting it."

"How did they know," Pinet asked.

"The simple answer is that it seemed logical to them that any attack on their line would happen there. They were right," Fawcett said. "And they doubled down on their defences; had secondary trenches made ready, reserves in place which they kept out of range of Allied artillery. There was little hope of success."

"And the attacking battalions went in daylight, which was suicidal and in the case of the Australian battalions, not very experienced in trench warfare like this. They were lambs to the slaughter, that was a certainty," Brigalow added.

"Which prompts me to ask, again, why send our operatives into a failure like this. Surely there are other options," Jie urged.

"I'm starting to agree," added Pinet, "No sense putting good people into a no-win situation."

"Unless we turn it into a win-win," Brigalow announced.

"What? What do you mean," Pinet asked, dismayed.

"We win the battle. We have all the data; we know how and why it went wrong and where the Germans expected the attack to be. So, we change the plan and we win the battle," Brigalow announced, "It's not like we'll be changing history any more than we will with the killing of Hitler. So why not change the game, win the fight, kill Hitler, and be done with it?"

"And what would it take to do that," Patel wondered.

"An elite force, most certainly, and modern weapons," Brigalow said, "And before you say no, I would suggest that doing so would ensure victory and lessen the risk of these weapons falling into the wrong hands, not that they could use them or replicate them in the early 20th Century in any case."

Gonzales backed him up, "Davis makes a good point and it's not like our future antagonists are playing by the rules. They brought back their own weaponry which we are now trying to unravel, without much success I might add, so, why not?"

Pinet sat with a slight frown creasing his glabella, "OK, convince me and I'll take it to the UN Security Council. If they agree, then we will do it."

Brigalow and Fawcett smiled; their plan was taking shape. They briefed the committee on the way the original Battle of Fromelles was developed, how it was executed and why it failed. They pointed out that the failings were extensive, by both the British on the right and the Australians on the left, "But if we can take out their machine guns, silence the artillery and ensure the barbed wire is cut, the situation would be very different," Brigalow explained.

"Those are a lot of ifs," Kanumbra pointed out.

"Yes, but we have hindsight on our side. We also know what the Germans were doing behind their line so we will go in with the advantage," Fawcett explained.

"What about weaponry? And how many operatives will we need," Galal asked and he wasn't alone in that regard.

"I think a task force of perhaps 100, with automatic weapons, side arms and laser guided RPGs, maybe even a drone," suggested Brigalow.

A few of the committee members laughed and Kuznetsov asked, "Firstly, where will we find 100 men willing to take a one-way trip back in time? They will have to be men given the era, not to mention hiding that kind of weaponry?"

"We don't hide it. It's war! New stuff was surfacing all the time. There were no tanks before WW1. The soldiers will simply accept it as some great advance in technology," Brigalow suggested.

"OK, but where do we get the men," Kuznetsov repeated.

"Russia," Brigalow answered cheekily but Kuznetsov didn't see the joke and Brigalow was forced to be serious once again. "I don't know Anastasia, but we will find them."

"I seriously doubt that" Jie added.

"What about battle bots," Pinet announced, which dumbfounded everyone and they looked at him wide eyed and speechless. "The UN has been working on automated warfare. We've had pilotless, self-aware aerial drone technology for years, but I've just learned we also have automated soldiers now. Granted, they're still being tested but they work. No need to send in more than a handful of people to support them."

The rest of the committee members remained in silent shock, they had no idea such a thing existed and didn't know what to say, which made Pinet chuckle a little.

"When were you planning to tell us about that," asked Kuznetsov.

"This has only just come to light," Pinet said, "I agree, we won't find 100 men to send back, but five or ten to control some bots? that should be doable I think."

"What are these bots like," Brigalow asked.

"I haven't seen them but from the reports I've read, they look every bit as human as all of us with a few notable exceptions," Pinet said.

"Such as," asked a few people in unison.

"Well, they don't hold weapons, the weaponry is built in, so that'll look strange and they're hairless of course, but dress them up in WW1 uniforms and send them over in the dark, the Germans will be clueless until it's too late."

"Jesus," exclaimed Brigalow. "Maybe we should have sent one back to do the job in 1907?"

"Two reasons why not; the Security Council didn't want that kind of tech in the field before the war began, particularly inside Austria and they can't identify any individual. They recognise targets," Pinet pointed out.

"Good points," Brigalow added, "So they will have to be programmed to identify all the German uniforms, so they don't kill our guys?"

"That's right," said Pinet.

"What about logistics, how do we keep then armed," asked Galal.

"We have a time machine, don't we," Pinet said smiling even more broadly, "We send back supplies as required."

"Can they handle the onslaught of machine guns and artillery? And what about the terrain," Jie added.

"Of course, they're virtually indestructible, unless they take a direct hit from a shell I suppose, and they have the individual strength of ten men. Just a few of them in 1916 will easily overwhelm a German trench line," Pinet said, "Oh and they can swim, or more accurately, walk under water if need be."

"Holy cow, we could win the whole war with a force like that," Brigalow announced.

"We could," Pinet agreed, "But if you remember, the Allies did win the war in the end, no disrespect to our current allies in Germany and the Middle East," to which Galal nodded his understanding, "so let's not think outside our mission parameters. We are to kill Hitler; that's our prime objective."

"Why not just drop them into the German lines," asked Kuznetsov.

"Again, to reduce the risk of one being somehow overwhelmed and taken by the Germans. They would eventually unravel the tech to suit themselves I'm sure," Pinet pointed out, "And our people will need to be watching so, if necessary, they can use self-destruct, so insertion on the Allied side is the only option."

"Can we inspect these machine men," asked Kuznetsov, "I'm intrigued of course but I also want to be certain that they can handle an assault."

"I will arrange it," answered Pinet.

"You little, ripper" exclaimed Brigalow which resulted in some confused glances.

A few days later the committee visited a UN test facility in the Swiss Alps. It was isolated and top secret, intentionally kept off the grid and off the books, which turned out to be a good thing given the activities of the future Nazis. Five of the bots were brought to the committee for inspection. The lead science technician was, ironically, German, Professor Franz Dietrich, "Welcome. Well, here they are. What do you think?"

The committee members stood gobsmacked, including Pinet, "They look as human as we do!"

"Ja, they have been made to look as real as possible but that's as close as they get to human. The rest is A.I. at its best and the materials are a long way from flesh and blood."

"What *are* they made of," Fawcett asked.

"It's a combination of materials, titanium alloys fused with other light weight elements using nano particles, so the materials are extremely dense but still lightweight. It makes their shells impossible to penetrate," Dietrich explained, "Here, let me show you." He had one of the bots move into a large room, which was glassed on all sides. "This is one of our explosive test labs. We can watch the tests up close without risk. Now watch."

A human soldier arrived, entered the room, and uncovered a standard automatic field gun, capable of 12000 rounds of light weight armour piercing .50 calibre projectiles per minute.

It could tear a tank apart in seconds from 500 yards. He levelled the gun at the bot and squeezed off a few thousand rounds. The staccato buzz of the machine gun sounded like a swarm of angry wasps, and everyone watched as each bullet streaked into the bot and bounced off without any effect, except for a stumble as the unit was knocked slightly off balance, which it was quickly able to recover from. When the noise stopped and the smoke cleared, the bot stood motionless and unscathed.

"Wow," Brigalow blurted, "That's amazing!"

Dietrich was smiling broadly, "Ja, quite incredible. An army of these could defeat any human army on Earth and sustain almost zero casualties. I cannot say the same for the enemy."

"How much would one of these cost," asked Jie.

"We don't like to talk about money, but the first prototype was somewhere around a trillion dollars but they're much cheaper now that we have the production processes and materials in place."

Everyone gulped at the price tag, "What about weapons, what do they carry," Kuznetsov wondered.

"We have equipped them with multiple options which can be used as they assess the situation. Standard are the twin automatic machine guns, built into the arms, 2000 rounds per second. They also carry small arms in their wrists. They can fire rockets from their shoulders; there is a grenade launcher in the chest and in their back a small cannon. They simply crouch and paint the target with a laser and boom," and Dietrich laughed.

"Can we see them in the field," Pinet asked.

"Of course. This way."

Dietrich led the party outside, onto a transport truck which was soon at the field test site. It was a broad area of hills, valleys, and makeshift buildings. They took their seats at an observation post overlooking a battlefield as Dietrich explained what was about to happen.

"The HIT Men will attack from the right."

"Sorry, the what," Patel wondered.

"HIT Men, Humanoid Infantry Technology but, we call them HIT Men for short. I think it suits them," he said with a smile.

"They will enter the field on the right. Their objective is the flagged building on the hill to the extreme left. Between them and the target are many natural obstacles, booby traps, mines, drones, artillery and of course 100 enemy soldiers."

"How many HIT Men are you sending in," Pinet asked.

Dietrich smirked when he answered, "Five."

"Oh, this should be good," Brigalow said excitedly.

"Please put on your noise suppressors, this is going to be loud," suggested Dietrich.

When everyone was settled, Dietrich fired a green flare to signal for the test to begin. Almost immediately the five HIT Men entered the field on the right and took fire from 100 enemy soldiers. Even though they were being regularly hit, they moved like it was a clear day and did so very quickly. Drones fired rockets at the attackers but again there was no effect.

They worked as a unit to over-run the first line of defence, subduing the soldiers with incredibly accurate gunfire from the built-in weaponry, firing blanks in this case.

Artillery was laser guided into the robotic group but after one salvo from the defensive positions the HIT Men were able to calculate the exact positions of each cannon and reply with their own fusillade, wiping them out.

They avoided the booby traps and mines with ease, brought down the drones with rockets and overran the remaining defenders, reaching their goal in a little over 10 minutes. A red flare marked the end of the exercise.

"WOW," cried Brigalow, "They are amazing!"

"Yes, and they did it without hurting a single human soldier in this case. That would not be so in an actual battle I can assure you."

"How many are ready to be made operational," Jie asked, expecting the number would be small.

"We have 2000 battle ready," Dietrich replied which came as a shock to everyone.

Then Pinet asked, "How might they perform in a WW1 scenario?"

Dietrich looked delightfully bemused, "Like shelling peas I imagine. Five of them could wipe out an entire battalion with ease. They would be immune to the effects of WW1 weaponry."

"Even artillery," Kuznetsov wondered.

"I believe so," Dietrich reiterated.

"Impressive Professor. Thank you," Pinet said as he shook Dietrich's hand.

"My great pleasure. I'm sure you will not be disappointed."

The group left, all excited by the possibilities. The Battle of Fromelles was about to be rewritten.

Chapter 12 – The Resistance

Ultimately the UN Security Council signed off on the plan and allocated 10 HIT Men to the task with 30 operatives to support them.

They would be correctly credentialed as members of an elite Allied Corps, answerable to the British Prime Minister, Lloyd George, which would make it impossible for anyone to double check. It was risky but given the era, the poor communications, and the desperate situation on the Somme, it was hoped that no-one would question a new tactic.

The committee members were on tenterhooks, given there had been two attempts by the Nazis to have them eradicated, and so another attempt was expected any time.

The problem with security was they simply didn't know exactly when or where such an attempt might occur. The Nazis had the advantage of being able to pick a time and place that suited them and would no doubt be successful at some point.

Noone really knew what kind of effect that might have and whether the elimination of a committee member in the past would even be noticed by the surviving committee members should the murder happen before the individual was known to everyone else. It was the stuff of nightmares, and it was easier to just not think about it.

The belief was that changing the past would reset the timeline thereafter and now it was hoped that it would correct the future by not enabling the Nazis to ever exist.

There was, however, much conjecture to suggest that a "Quantum Butterfly Effect" as it was called, wasn't an absolute and that changing history might simply do nothing to the present at all or perhaps, because history was something that had already happened nothing would be different now.

This was quickly dismissed given that the committee members were witness to mixed memories from past events they'd never actually experienced but felt that they had been party to. It suggested to them that the Butterfly effect was very real.

As preparations began for the mission to Fromelles and the transfer to Cern of the HIT Men and their operatives for transport back to 1916, a visitor arrived at the Infinity Generator facility, someone that nobody could have expected.

Her name was Janina Zielinski. Security stopped her at the main gate, listened to her story and called through to Jean Claude Pinet and informed him of her arrival. She was searched but held no identification, nor did she carry weapons. Pinet felt that, given her extraordinary story, she was worth the risk, and it was arranged, per her request, that she meet with him and the other committee members under heavy guard.

The committee members gathered in their 'bunker' as Zielinski was brought in. Only Pinet had a clue as to who she was and greeted her warmly despite the four heavily armed UN guards, "Welcome," he said, "I apologise for the scrutiny but I'm sure you understand."

"Of course," she answered in heavily accented English.

"Please, take a seat and let me introduce you to everyone." Pinet gestured to a vacant chair where Zielinski sat.

Everyone stared at her, not because they knew who she was but because of how she was dressed. If it was something new in the fashion world, none of them had come across it before.

Her blouse was sheer to the point where it left nothing to the imagination, like the fabric was simply another layer of skin and a very shiny red, almost like the coating had been spray painted on. Her slacks were not dissimilar although it did appear that certain reservations were catered for. Her hair was short, blonde, and swept back in a slick glistening finish and she looked not to be a day over 30. She settled into her chair and looked around at the other committee members before Pinet spoke,

"Everyone, I'd like you to meet Janina Zielinski." He continued by introducing everyone one by one, "And Janina, perhaps you would like to explain how and why you have come to us."

"Certainly," she answered and everyone noted the strange English dialect. "I am here from the year 2337!" They all sat stunned. It was the last thing they expected, and no-one knew quite what to say so Janina continued, "I have come back to this time to offer you, my assistance."

"That is great news to us," Pinet suggested, "We could use all the help we can get."

But before Pinet could continue, Anastasia Kuznetsov interjected, "Are you, our mole?"

"Yes, I am one of them. I am part of the IGSU, Infinity Generator Science Unit. While we are forced to work for the Nazis, we are secretly working against them. We have been trying to protect you and assist you from our time, but it is risky," she explained.

"So, they really are Nazis," Brigalow said, "It's not just our imaginations."

"Yes, they have taken over Europe in my time. The world is in turmoil. They are trying to stop you from killing Hitler," Janina explained.

Everyone sat completely shocked by the news. No-one really expected the Nazis to be their future foe despite recent events. It was, to say the least, the worst possible irony. It also answered the questions as to their persistent attempts to kill the committee members. It was personal! It took a while for composure to return.

"Have any of your people been caught," asked Zhang Jie.

"Not yet, however, the Nazis realised after the second unsuccessful attempt to erase you that something wasn't right and have been more vigilant. They don't understand the technology and don't know what to look for, which helps us. We have also confused them with a lot of technical mumbo jumbo."

"I see. So, you have made a one-way trip into what must seem a backward world; that's quite a decision for someone so young," suggested Davis Brigalow. "May I ask if you were at risk, was that part of the reason you came back?"

"You are very astute Mister Brigalow and yes, we are all at risk when we deceive the Nazis. Was I about to be discovered? I believe so. I didn't want to take the risk and so it was thought that I should make the journey, not only to survive but to continue the resistance work from this time and help you to eradicate the Nazis from history and, of course the future," Janina explained, "But on the other point you are wrong."

"What point was that" Brigalow asked, clearly confused and forgetting the second part of his statement.

"My age. I am 64 years old!"

The group gasped. She looked every bit a young woman. The texture of her skin was nothing like someone of 64, blemish free and white, more like someone in their twenties and far superior to anyone in the current time.

"How do you look this way," Luciana Gonzales asked.

"Between now and 2337 many things galloped ahead technologically, and that included the slowing of the ageing process. We live much longer than you, by decades."

"And your clothing? It isn't like ours either," suggested Muhammad Galal, who appeared a little embarrassed by her ampleness.

"Clothing too is much more functional and climate controlled. I can wear one layer in any weather and remain comfortable. Oh, and no washing, ironing, or fading," and she smiled.

"Astonishing," exclaimed Sunil Patel.

"But we digress. I'm sure there'll be time for small talk once you are settled in Janina," Pinet interrupted, "May we know of the situation in 2337? How bad is it with the Nazis?"

Janina sat there for a moment looking at everyone's faces, which she noted were full of fear and anticipation. "You must realise that the only difference between my time and now is purely technological. We are more advanced and have overcome some scientific and environmental issues, which I'm sure you can appreciate, but, as far as humanity is concerned, not much is different."

"What does that mean exactly," Pinet urged.

"It means that people still kill each other over differences of opinion; wars are still being fought and now the World has been turned upside down by a new Nazi reign of terror that no-one saw coming," she explained.

"How," wondered Anastasia Kuznetsov, "Surely the crimes of the past were not forgotten. Or were they?"

"We got distracted I suppose. Noone was thinking about a Fourth Reich. They were too focussed on domestic issues and political problems, trade embargoes, tensions over territory. Like I said, nothing much has changed when you look at the way people deal with each other. The distractions of political volatility gave the Nazis an opportunity and they took it," Janina explained but it was clear that she hadn't really answered the questions.

"That doesn't tell us *how* exactly the Nazis came to achieve something they failed to do, twice, in the first half of the 20th Century," Sunil Patel suggested, scowling.

Janina realised she would need to be much more forthcoming and took a deep breath.

"No, it doesn't. Truth is the entire world was caught napping. The Nazis had been building up in secret for years, weapons, manpower, infiltrating governments and corporations at all levels. Noone knew and if they did, they clearly didn't live to warn anyone. Then, in a coordinated attack they got a foothold and spread out across Europe. The fact that they had infiltrated so many countries was to their advantage and they coordinated attacks across several regions. They didn't sweep to a total victory globally, but they did enough to gain control of Europe while they allowed the Middle East to collapse to radicals. They, in turn, somehow managed to overpower Israel and, well here we are. Most believe it's only a matter of time before they sack Australasia before launching campaigns against Russia and the United States. Russia is reinforcing and building defences across its entire border while the US ponders its position. They are in no place to launch a counterattack. They have very few allies left."

"I can't imagine," said Pinet, "It must be horrible there."

"It is for many. They are systematically cleansing the population per the doctrines of Hitler's 'final solution' and many are joining them because they realise it's the only way they will survive."

"What hopes for the Asia Pacific region and the Americas," Gabrielle Fawcett asked.

"The Pacific regions are strong, but they are also a series of islands which means all the Nazis have to do is take over in a series of leaps."

"That didn't work for the Japanese in WWII," added Zhang Jie.

"No, it didn't," Janina conceded, "But the US isn't going to jump to the rescue this time. They must secure their own soil so it's likely they'll sit this one out and secure an alliance with Canada and the South American nations, none of which wants the become a Nazi state, except perhaps Mexico. The US is negotiating with them."

"But won't that simply give the Nazis more time and more resources to work with," Muhammad Galal asked.

"Yes, of course but the Americans are not ready to fight on such a massive front. They wouldn't even know where to start," Janina added. "South America is a failed state which leaves the US, China, Australia, Canada, and Russia to fight them off. Australia will surely fall without the support of its allies and while China is strong and is also securing its borders, they won't lift a finger to help anyone else, so that basically leaves North America alone."

"How do you see it ending up," Hamid Kanumbra asked then added, "Will the World be split into new superpowers?"

Janina looked at him with a half-smile, "Yes, I believe that's how it will go. China, Russia, and North America will stand alone; the rest of the world, barring South America, will be held by the Nazis. I don't believe they will hold to their deal with the Middle East and will ultimately wipe them out. I then expect the fight will be over South America, although I think that will be a difficult campaign for the Nazis. The terrain alone will make it a long, hard battle but the opposition there is weak and there's already a lot of unrest, so who knows?" She paused. "That's another reason I came back. The Nazis are going to be quite pre-occupied with a Pacific and then South American campaign which I believe will give you time to complete your mission."

"How do you know," Pinet asked, "They've tried to kill us twice."

"True, but they haven't considered a third attempt yet. I'm sure they will but they're starting to realise that controlling vast amounts of territory is difficult and they're struggling to create the infrastructure to run their empire. While their victory in Europe was essentially flawless, they are being troubled by resistance groups. Believe me, they are stretched to the limit in some respects and," she smiled broadly, "we aren't giving them a free pass either. The Infinity Generator keeps breaking down for some strange reason." Her smiled revealed her perfect, bright white teeth.

Without even a second to absorb the information Kuznetsov said, "So your disappearance is likely to set off alarm bells, yes? They will know now that something is wrong and probably tear the place apart to find out what and who betrayed them."

"Perhaps, but we play on the former neutral status of Switzerland and have convinced them that we do not see them as an enemy," suggested Janina. "And my disappearance won't be too suspicious. My mother is quite ill, and I told them I wanted to be with her when she dies."

"And they believe that," Kuznetsov asked, wondering the age of Janina's mother in 2337.

"Well, it's true but also, when it comes from the Swiss Government, yes, they accept it and we took full advantage of that. Believe me, they have enough problems without worrying about my honesty. Having a country simply yield is a breath of fresh air to them."

"Clever," Pinet said, "a simple act of submission and the heat turns down."

"Precisely."

"So, what happens now Janina," Pinet asked, "What do we do?"

"You can start by telling me what you have in mind. We know you are trying to kill Hitler and were aware of the first real attempt and the follow up mission but from there you went dark, and a good thing too," Janina revealed.

"Well, we had to. And thank you for the warnings. If you hadn't risked your lives then we would be dead, that is certain," Pinet suggested.

"That is true, but I believe you now have a window, and my people are watching for anything that might reveal your plans. I think between your attempts to keep your activities off the record and my people screening any data that might be logged, we can smite the Nazis at their dawn!"

"Well Janina," said Pinet, "we appreciate you coming here and if I may, I must say it's an incredible sacrifice to leave your ailing mother, knowing you will never see her again."

"Thank you."

Pinet and the other committee members set about explaining their plans for Fromelles, the HIT Men, and the data they had about Hitler's whereabouts at the time. Janina listened intently, not saying a word until they were finished. She pondered for a few moments then said, "It's a good plan, except for one thing you couldn't have even considered."

"And what's that," Pinet asked.

"The Nazis are sending back weapons to Germany before the war and will be training soldiers so they will win WW1."

"How much time have we got," Pinet asked.

Janina frowned., "If you go now, you might catch them off guard, but I cannot guarantee it."

"What about our HIT Men, will they be effective against Nazi tech," Brigalow asked her.

"HIT Men," Janina asked, clearly confused.

"You don't know about them?" he added.

"Not at all," she replied.

"Interesting. So, no Nazi robot fighters in 2337," Pinet asked.

"None that I'm aware of," she answered.

Pinet smiled, "Well something has finally worked in our favour. Keeping our robots off the grid could have been a master stroke.

He did wonder though, how such tech could have been kept quiet so far into the future.

Chapter 13 – A New Plan

The committee members realised that their plans for Fromelles were going to be useless if the Nazis managed to send back high-tech weaponry to Germany in the years before World War 1. It would give them an advantage that would make them unstoppable.

Not only that, but they would also be able to roll over the defenders quickly and the war of attrition that became the Western Front trench line from 1914 to 1918 would never happen, thus ending the conflict much sooner.

No-one could really envisage what the World might become with a German victory in that era. History books were clear about the fact that Adolf Hitler started down his tyrannical rise to power because of the German failings in WW1 and the economic kneecapping of Germany through the Treaty of Versailles, so what would a victory do to him?

Janina Zielinski was quick to counter that. From her understanding of the Nazis in 2337, they would make sure he rose to power regardless and there would be a continued effort to take control of Russia and ultimately the rest of the World. They would simply use their technology to smite their foe with ease and put Hitler up as the Supreme leader of the World. It made sense.

They all agreed that their plans for Fromelles would be impossible if the Nazis equipped the German Army with future weapons before 1914, so an idea was presented to intercept them, but Janina was quick to point out a major issue with that plan.

"You could stop one or two delivery attempts but how long before they were wise to it and sent back a task force to intercept you?"

"Yes, I agree," Pinet conceded, "It would be a tit for tat exchange, bouncing around through time and I don't know how that might end up."

"My people will, of course, try to slow the Nazis down," Janina revealed, "They will indeed try to warn us about delivery dates and times. What we do with that information is critical."

Luciana Gonzales volunteered a thought, "If we know exactly when and where they are emerging and we opened a wormhole at the same time, what will happen then?

"I really don't know," Pinet answered. "Any ideas Janina?"

"Well, it's an interesting thought. How long can you keep the link open," she asked.

"A few minutes at best with our current technology," Pinet suggested.

"Hmm, in 2337 we have achieved portals of 30 minutes, I don't see how we can stop them given their time advantage and we would have to be very exact to block them, assuming only one window can open from the same source regardless of when it happens," she mulled it over for a moment when another idea was tabled.

"We don't have to block them," Jie added, "We only need to open the vortex for a short time just before they do, deposit an incendiary device and, boom," He made an explosion gesture with his hands.

"A pre-emptive strike," Pinet said in surprise, "That could work and no risk to personnel. We could do it as many times as necessary!"

"Of course, there's no guarantee that you will get them every time and we're assuming that we will be notified of every Nazi transfer; that's doubtful. They only must be successful once or twice. If my people fail to warn us before any such delivery, they win," Janina pointed out.

"Of course. I understand," Pinet said, "Your connections may well be aware of a transfer of weapons but not be able to warn us. They could of course try after the fact but that wouldn't matter because the weapons would have been used 423 years earlier so even if they warned us minutes after the fact it would be irrelevant. We might not exist to receive the information. It makes the mind spin."

"In which case we pre-empt their arrival by sending back a detachment of HIT Men to wait for the Nazis and destroy them each and every time they emerge," Jie explained.

"Do we want to risk HIT Men head on with 2337 Tech," Sunil Patel said, "This is all becoming pointless. There must be another way, or we simply let history be history and let the future be the future." The last remark drew a scowl from Janina Zielinski.

"Perhaps," said Kuznetsov who had been listening intently to the many dilemmas that had been raised, "But they will know what we know soon enough and understand that no-one wins if we keep countering each other's moves. They may have the advantage of being in the future but that doesn't mean they will keep trying repeatedly. I suspect after a few attempts they won't want to waste resources, even if they can anticipate our counter moves."

Janina smiled, "You are right, they are very impatient and are likely to change plans if thwarted. They might even give up on that approach entirely."

Pinet looked worried, "So we are playing cat and mouse; hoping your people give us good intel and then hoping after a few strikes against the Nazis they give up and try something else?"

"Exactly," Janina confirmed, "They have issues in 2337 and can't afford to waste too much effort in the past, not in terms of firepower anyway."

"Ok, so we're agreed, we try to intercept them at every opportunity and hope they waver," Pinet asked the group.

All indicated their approval.

Zang Jie then looked at Janina, catching her eye and asked, "Why haven't your people destroyed the Infinity Generator to stop the Nazis sending back people to intercept us and the transfer of weapons? That to me would be the easy solution."

"You would think so from this perspective, but security is tight. No weapons let alone explosives are allowed anywhere near the facility and the fail-safes make it near impossible to overload the system and damage the machine," she advised.

"OK, so tell me how you manage to send us warnings without them realising, let alone the obvious power spikes such activities create," he added.

"All very good points. We must use the machine quickly and quietly. We have honed the process to use lower power thresholds depending on what is being sent, so a letter for example doesn't need the kind of power that human delivery or equipment does, but you are right, there is still a spike," she explained. "We offset that through a series of dampeners. They were retrofitted before the war, and the Nazis don't know what they are. They've never asked and we never said anything. A stroke of luck, I'm sure you'll agree."

"Another course of action would be to send someone back to make sure the IG is never created," Patel said but before he drew Janina's scorn again, he added, "But that doesn't solve the issue of the Nazis in 2337," and he gave her a knowing smile and nod.

"Very true. And if we're going to all this trouble to extinguish Hitler, then we must now consider that the future Nazis are part of the same issue," Pinet suggested.

"Thank you," said Janina.

"Tell us," asked Kuznetsov, "what are their weapons like, what are they sending back?"

"Well, it's likely they will send back guided bullet tech with high power laser rifle delivery systems, similar to what they have tried to use against you."

"Tech we haven't yet started to understand," Kuznetsov added.

"Very true but they also have aerial drone tech that can think for itself, paint targets, carry thousands of micro cluster bombs as small as a, what would you call it? Nail? Yes, a small nail. With one drone they could simply paint an entire battalion and kill each soldier instantly. Wouldn't even matter if they were walking, running, or even under cover. They are AI assisted, like mini smart bombs," she explained.

"Good God! How can we stop that," Kanumbra exclaimed.

"If I may, I have an idea," Kuznetsov declared, "What if we made it impossible for the future Nazis to have their advanced weapons?" She turned to Janina once again. "Would I be right in saying that these weapons use resources that aren't available now? Some kind of technicality, metal, compound or component that is yet to be invented?"

"Yes. Many of the advanced systems in my time use newly developed synthetic components," she answered then said, "One in particular that is crucial."

"And what might that be?"

She laughed, "It's what gives the weapons the capacity to paint targets. It's like an infrared/x-ray laser which lights the target and keeps them lit for a time, like warming them with a magnifying glass just enough to enable the projectiles to hone in."

"And?"

"They are useless without the lens. It's hard to describe but it's an AI flexi lens that changes the light frequency aimed at each target individually so that tens of thousands of smart projectiles can fire at once and always be on target without confusing one painted target from another."

"Bloody Hell," boomed Brigalow, "What's it made of?"

"That's the interesting part. Something very rare called Lunicite and, as luck would have it, it's only found in one place."

"The Moon," Kuznetsov declared.

"Correct," replied Janina.

"But what is it exactly," Patel asked.

Janina tried to explain, "Twenty percent of the Moon's surface is silica, but when they started mining on the Moon in 2276, or will start I should say, they discover a variation of Silica that has much greater potential. It's flexible, can be made into the clearest material ever known and able to be manipulated electronically. It will also adapt to almost any visual situation. Extremely expensive and thus only the military can afford it. So far, no such element has been found on Earth."

Pinet considered the revelation, "Then we must convince the UN to ban mining on the Moon! They will see sense in that, I'm sure." He looked at Janina. "Will that be enough?"

"It will set back weapons development about fifty years, yes, but they will still have a sixty-year head start on you," she explained.

"But the odds will improve for us, yes," Pinet asked.

"Oh yes, you will have a sporting chance, albeit a slim one," Janina confirmed.

"That's better than nothing," Pinet added. "OK, we draft a report to the UN using an offline computer. I will deliver it myself. Let's hope that it will do the trick."

Once again everyone agreed. They would arrange ballistic intercepts preventing the Nazis from delivering future weapons to the early 1900s if needed and convince the UN to ban mining on the Moon and hope that would be enough to kill off the smart weapons of 2337.

Jean Claude Pinet was soon on his way to New York under a series of fake identities to meet the UN Secretary General, Blair Odette.

Once in New York, Pinet travelled by Taxi to the United Nations building where he handed a security guard a handwritten note and asked that it be delivered personally to Blair Odette. The man looked at him with great suspicion, "It's a piece of paper," Pinet exclaimed, "What harm can it do?"

"The guard looked at the envelope again and shrugged. "Wait here!"

Pinet stood on the street looking out over the East River, which was bustling with activity, water taxis, people fishing, ferries, leisure craft, all oblivious to the possibility that their world might change at any second. He smiled at the thought that they wouldn't know the difference if it happened at this exact moment.

After about fifteen minutes he heard a whistle and looked around. It was Blair Odette. She motioned him to join her and they started walking. "What's all this about Jean Claude?" They'd known each other for many years, and she had no doubt that the note was genuine when she saw the handwriting.

"I have a report you need to read. It's critical to our mission. It also shows how we can deal with the future Nazi threat," he explained.

"Yes, I have read your reports to date. How quaint to produce them offline and have them physically couriered here. No-one has done that in decades," She smiled.

"I know, but we cannot risk any traceable data being left for the Nazis to harvest."

"That makes sense. So, what's the latest?"

Pinet explained to Odette the plans of the Nazis and the counter activities they planned to slow them down, but when he reached the part about banning mining on the Moon, she stopped walking.

"You do realise that won't be easy," she exclaimed.

"Why not? The Outer Space Treaty still applies does it not? No one can lay claim to anything beyond Earth. Use that argument," he urged.

"Yes, but that applies to planets and moons, not what's harvested from them. No nation can claim to own Mars for example but if they go there and bring back rocks. They own the rocks. The same applies to mining," Odette explained.

"Then we just change the rules," Pinet added.

"But the agreements already exist; to allow harvesting of rare minerals in the future, they cannot be simply torn up."

"And yet that is exactly what is required. Urgently!"

"China won't be happy. They have a controlling interest in electronics. They may just ignore us," Odette said.

"And it will be to their detriment if they do. The Nazis will overrun China in the future, that is certain," Pinet said, "If China takes a stand now, they will most certainly topple in the future. That we already know!"

"They wouldn't believe us even if we could tell them. They would just laugh," she said, shaking her head, "And we have other countries that are keen to mine off planet too. Japan, India even Australia. They won't be easy to sway."

Just then Pinet saw pictures in his head that he'd never seen before, a memory of something that had changed and he stopped walking.

"What is it, Jean Claude," Odette asked.

"The Nazis have made another attempt to kill one of us. Thankfully they failed again. We killed two of their operatives. They tried to use one of their attacks drones this time but didn't get a fix on anyone before we intercepted them," he explained, clearly shaken by the new memories.

"When did this happen?"

"Five years ago! They are trying anything to get to us. We must stop them, Blair. They won't stop until we are eradicated. We are their greatest threat."

As she listened, Odette too felt ripples of weird memories relating to the attempt by the Nazis, "It's good that you are all off the grid now. Makes it so much harder for them."

"Yes, but not impossible." He looked at her intently, "You must get the ban passed as soon as possible. You must!"

"I'll try but it may well mean having to go public with some of our discoveries, at least to a government level. I don't know how that might be received or if it might reveal your hand to 2337," she explained.

"I understand but at this stage we don't have much of a choice," Then he looked hard at her. "If we can eradicate Hitler, we eliminate the Nazis past, present and future. That shouldn't be hard to sell.

"I'll do my best," she answered, "but it's complicated."

"Read the report, it makes everything clear," he said as he handed her a sealed envelope.

Blair Odette nodded but the look on her face gave Pinet no confidence of success.

Chapter 14 – Pfeiffer

The leader of the Nazis (2337) sat in the chambers of the Reichstag in Berlin, his ten generals standing before him. This was the first time there had been a lull in the Nazi advances across Europe.

"Gentlemen, congratulations, we have done very well to this point. You should be proud." That was as much praise as he would offer them. He thought too many accolades made men soft, "We hold Europe to the borders at Turkey and Russia and we have taken England," his steel blue eyes focussed on General Felix Voight who gulped when they locked eyes, "What is happening on the Eastern Front General?"

"The Russians have secured their borders. They are building a strong defensive perimeter and drafting all men over 16 years of age to hold us back, but they have done nothing aggressive yet Sir," Voight explained.

"It is of no consequence. We can wait, even if the rest of the World is dealt with first, our natural enemy, Russia, will ultimately yield," Pfeiffer said, then he turned to General Emil Lutz, "What of the situation in England General?"

"We have control militarily, but the English are stubborn and there is resistance politically and on the streets. Small attacks really, nuisance value only," Lutz wasn't easily scared and Pfeiffer respected him for that.

"But you are taking casualties, yes?"

"We are but we are killing many more of them. We will break them sir," Lutz said confidently.

"Good. That's what I like to hear. Now, what is happening on the Turkish border?"

General Oskar Sauer stood to attention snapping his heels together with a loud clack, "Sir I can report that all is quiet, no issues at all sir!"

"Very good and they continue to think we are all friends," Pfeiffer asked.

"Indeed, they do sir."

"Let's keep it that way for the time being. Now Ziegler, how are we going with weapons production? We need to build up supplies before our next advance."

General Noah Ziegler was a quiet man, task driven, not into small talk and always kept his answers brief, much to Pfeiffer's frustration, "It goes well."

"That's all?"

"Yes sir."

"When will we have enough attack drones to advance in South America?"

"Soon sir," Ziegler replied.

"Aggghh," Pfeiffer yelled, "I want specifics, a week? A month, a year?"

"Hard to say sir, a few months perhaps."

"I do not want to wait that long. We need to keep moving, take ground while they are unprepared. We cannot stall or we will find ourselves..." but he didn't continue, a tendency of his when he was frustrated. "What of our governance in Europe, are we making any progress there General Graf?"

"Sir, yes and no. Some authorities are cooperating. They seem to understand that a business-as-usual approach is their best option, others not so." Pfeiffer was about to ask for clarification which General Engel Graf anticipated, "Sir, French provinces are fighting change more so than those of any other country. They have not accepted that they are now part of the Reich."

"And they will not; not for a long time," Pfeiffer paused, "No matter. Keep working with the authorities as best you can. If anyone resists too much you know what to do. You will eventually have people in place that will be more obliging."

"Yes Sir!"

"Now General Wolff, what is the status of our efforts to quell the antagonists in the past," Pfeiffer asked.

General Maximillian Wolff noted the venom in Pfeiffer's tone. "Sir, as you know, we have made three attempts to overcome the aggressors from the past and we can only assume they have failed on each occasion."

"Can you be more specific?"

"Unfortunately, Sir that is proving difficult. They appear to have deleted themselves from their historical matrix. We don't know who they are, only that they must be in Cern. There are no records, they have made certain of that and no clues as to what happened to our people, sir."

"Do we not have our own records, after the first attempt," Pfeiffer asked.

"Well sir, we have a record of the delivery of our taskforce but there is no mission log, so no, we have no electronic record."

Pfeiffer growled with frustration, "How could you be so stupid? These people are a real threat to us and now we don't know who they are. We must stop them Wolff, do you understand that?"

"Yes sir, I do, but we are fighting an invisible foe, however I don't think we need to know who they are; we can intercept events or change history ourselves. If I may sir, I suggest that we change tactics. Fight them on our terms."

"And how do you propose we do that," Pfeiffer asked with an unhidden sarcastic twang.

"We have posted guards in the Fuhrers pre-birth and post-birth years to protect him after the two attempts on his life."

Pfeiffer couldn't take it anymore, "Get to the point Wolff!"

"Sir, they are always a step behind us, but they are crafty. I suggest we send back someone they might trust, one of our own to infiltrate the IG facility in Cern in 2214 to seek out the people who would stop us and eradicate them. Stealth rather than aggression sir!"

"At last, some lateral thinking. Very good Wolff, see to it." Then Pfeiffer gave Wolff a cold stare, "Do we have such an individual?"

"Not yet sir. We are looking for someone."

Pfeiffer rolled his eyes, "What about the facility itself, all is well there I hope?"

"Yes sir, we have the full cooperation of the scientists and technicians. They are doing everything we ask without question."

"Does that not appear strange to you?"

"No sir, they are absorbed in their work, they don't care who runs the Government as long as they are funded and working on their precious toy," Wolff explained.

"And what of the missing scientist? Um, Zielinski. Does that not concern you?"

"No sir. Her mother is quite ill. She is returning when that is dealt with, "Wolff said.

"You are certain of this?"

"As certain as I can be sir," Wolff replied, shifting slightly in his stance.

Pfeiffer stood and leaned with both hands on his desk, head down, "And how go our deliveries, the weapons destined for the German Army pre-WW1. Have we sent the shipments?"

"I beg your pardon Sir," Wolff asked appearing confused.

"The weapons Wolff! Have we delivered the weapons?"

General Wolff shifted unsteadily again and appeared to be quaking a little, "Well sir, the first attempt failed for some reason. We created a vortex and sent the shipment, but we don't know what happened. The equipment left the facility, but there are no indications of a successful transfer."

Pfeiffer's face reddened in a rage and he exploded, "Your incompetence in this matter has frustrated me one too many times Wolff. I have lost patience. I'm relieving you of duty!"

"Sir? But…"

Before Wolff could protest, Pfeiffer raised his fully restored World War II vintage Luger and squeezed the trigger, shooting Wolff in the head. "Does anyone know what happened to the shipment," he demanded but the generals remained silent. "Then someone bring me the lead scientist. Surely, he can explain the problem." No one moved, "DISMISSED," Pfeiffer yelled.

The next day the lead scientist for the Infinity Generator was ushered into Pfeiffer's office after being *invited* to Berlin from the Cern facility. As Professor Jonas Kupper stepped through the door, Pfeiffer welcomed him with a handshake, "Welcome Professor. Refreshments? You must be hungry, yes?"

"Thank you, I'm fine," replied the Professor.

"Very good." Pfeiffer didn't stand on ceremony as he invited Kupper to take a seat. "Tell me Professor, what happened to the first arms shipment to the Germans in 1910?"

If Kupper was scared, it didn't show; he crossed his legs and leaned back in the chair. He even smiled, "It is unknown. We opened the vortex and sent the materials and the men back to the designated time and place. It looked to have been nominal."

"But?"

"As you know, we can only discern the eventualities through the documented history of that era and there is no indication of any change in events; Germany still lost the war. In fact, nothing changed at all, not even to a minor degree," Kupper said.

"What do you think happened," Pfeiffer asked, again.

"I can only offer theory of course, but it could have been a disruption in the field, which may have erased the shipment," Kupper stated.

"Erased, as in deleted from existence?"

"Yes."

"What would cause that," Pfeiffer wondered.

"A power issue, an unstable wormhole or even a solar flare," Kupper explained and he sounded convincing, but Pfeiffer wasn't yet sold.

"What about human error?"

Kupper paused as if considering the possibility, "I suppose that could have come into it. It takes only a minor augmentation to skew the vortex."

"Which means what?"

"They may have ended up sometime else," Kupper concluded, "Where and when we may never know BUT I don't believe it was human error. We have checked the figures again. Everything looks flawless at this end."

"I have another theory Professor Kupper," Pfeiffer announced which Kupper reacted to with interest, "It was deliberate. Someone made sure the delivery failed. What say you to that Kupper?"

The professor noted the sudden dropping of his title as the tension in the room increased somewhat, "If that is what happened, then I know nothing of it."

"But you are in charge and you oversee the deliveries, yes?'

"That is true," Kupper gulped.

"So, is it possible for someone to jeopardise a delivery under your watch," Pfeiffer asked as he glared at Kupper.

"I..." Kupper was nonplussed at the idea, "Um...it would have to be someone who, not only had intent but was able to hide the data so that everything seemed normal."

"So, you agree that it could have happened that way?"

"I don't know. Perhaps," Kupper said dubiously.

"In which case Professor I suggest you do some investigation. In fact, I will send someone to assist. There needs to be a complete audit of the IG logs and a reconstruction of the data. If someone has manipulated the records, you will report them and they will be dealt with," Pfeiffer demanded.

Kupper realised he was in no position to argue as two Schultstaffen officers came into the room, summoned by Pfeiffer's silent hail. Kupper looked at them and felt a twinge as he recognised the jet-black uniforms from the 1940s. It made him shrink inside.

"Are we in agreeance Professor," Pfeiffer asked, ripping Kupper's gaze away from the SS Officers.

"Yes of course. An audit. Good idea. It will be done," Kupper answered, his initial confidence now well and truly scuttled.

"Very good. I look forward to your report."

The SS officers escorted Kupper from the room and hustled him to the airport where he was shuttled back to Cern with an SS Investigator. If anyone at the IG facility was manipulating the Nazi's work, it would soon be known, and they would be executed in front of the entire staff of the facility to send a message. In the meantime, all deliveries were suspended, which very much grated on Pfeiffer.

It didn't take long for Kupper to make contact. He reported that there was indeed an anomaly in the data. It appeared that the calculations were correct except for a glitch, as Kupper called it, which resulted in the shipment being lost. He told Pfeiffer that it was an oversight and one that was not of intent. "Mistakes happen," was what he said to Pfeiffer in conclusion.

Ernst Pfeiffer was not a patient man. The idea that it was a simple error didn't wash and the excuse made him angrier and, truth be told, he just didn't believe Kupper, who he assessed as being someone who would hide the truth to cover his own back.

Pfeiffer spoke to the SS Investigator who also conveyed his opinion that this wasn't as simple as a glitch. Whoever was manipulating the data was indeed very good at covering their track, or something else was happening that Kupper couldn't or wouldn't explain but both agreed that Kupper was hiding something and that couldn't be allowed to stand.

"You know what to do," he told the SS Investigator.

The Officer called a gathering of all the staff at the IG facility and announced that there had been an error which caused the loss of the shipment. He announced that these kinds of *mistakes* would not be tolerated.

"The Reich rewards hard work and obedience," the officer told the gathering. "BUT the consequences for inaction, deliberate manipulation, subversion and sabotage are significant!"

With that he pointed a gun at Professor Kupper and shot him through the forehead. He was dead before he hit the floor resulting in shrieks, screams, cries of anguish and hysteria with some of the assembled faculty. The officer sneered at the group and further announced, "Let this serve as a warning to whoever would jeopardise future shipments." Nothing more needed to be said.

A few days later a new delivery was arranged, a series of high-powered rifles with guided projectiles and cluster bombing drones. They would be sent back to 1910 with expert personnel to school the Germans on how to operate them.

Ernst Pfeiffer was about to receive a call telling him how the transfer went when he felt weird, like something was going to happen but he didn't know what. He shook his head, confused by a mixture of thoughts which suddenly became different thoughts, although he couldn't comprehend what his mind was telling him or what he'd just been thinking about. Just then the communicator beeped.

"Yes," he answered.

"Sir, the soldiers have been despatched to 1916 with the weapons as planned!"

"1916," Pfeiffer was confused but didn't know why. He shook off the feeling. "OK, very good," he replied, then asked, "and they arrived safely?"

The voice replied, "Yes sir we believe so, the men are in full World War One attire and are carrying the weapons of the era. They will blend in perfectly sir. The Fuhrer will be well guarded."

"Very good," Pfeiffer said as he clicked off the communicator, but he couldn't help thinking that something was off. He just couldn't understand what or why.

Chapter 15 – Back to Fromelles

Jean Claude Pinet closed the communication interface on his personal tablet and smiled, "Great news everyone," he announced to the IG Committee members, "the UN has successfully gazetted a total ban on Lunar mineral exploration and extraction. Noone can mine the Moon. Ever!"

The group cheered and applauded at the news.

"Oh, I'd love to see their faces in 2337," Sunil Patel gloated.

"I agree," added Janina Zielinski, "But the truth is they would be totally unaware of what we did. They will briefly realise something is off but not know what, because it would have been erased since historically, mining never happened."

"But we have had multiple memories of things we know happened and that were changed or stopped. Mixed memories, why is this different?" Davis Brigalow asked.

"Because of the timing. You experienced things within your lifetime, we erased something long before the Nazis existed in 2337, so they could never have experienced the alternative," Janina explained.

"I see. So, we experience a paradox while their state is altered by the historical change. Cool," Brigalow said with a beaming smile.

The group didn't have much time to celebrate the victory; they knew only too well that the future Nazis would still have a technical advantage as well as a better position in time to counter any direct attempts to kill Hitler or disrupt Nazi activities. Those complexities aside, the plan to install operatives on the WW1 front line at Fromelles was back on track. If all went well, they would turn a disaster into an Allied victory and kill Hitler in the process.

"We know the Nazis used an elite squad to protect Hitler in 1916. There is evidence of that in the German archives. They were probably sent back from 2337. For now, they appear to have had no influence on the war. I suspect the Nazis are simply watching over Hitler," Pinet explained, "and I hope with our HIT Men we are able to exact a savage beating on the Germans at Fromelles."

"I do see one issue Jean Claude," Gabrielle Fawcett announced, "When David and I did the research in Australia, we discovered that Hitler didn't reach the battle front until the early hours of the morning, which means the battle was raging for many hours before he got there."

"What's your point," Pinet wondered.

"If the HIT Men are as lethal as we've seen in tests, they will overcome the Germans much sooner than that and Hitler won't even have arrived when the battle is over."

"Hmm, you make a very good point. So, we must hold back, let the battle unfold and, once we have reached a point where Hitler is in the field, we strike," suggested Pinet but he could see that not everyone agreed, "What is it, Davis?"

"My people, the Australians were slaughtered. We have a chance to erase that but if we wait, they will die anyway. Surely, we can do both. Slow the attack until Hitler arrives," Brigalow suggested.

"I see a risk in doing that," Zhang Jie said, "Two issues in fact. One, the commanders on the ground won't want to hold back if they have superior weapons available and two, a slow approach increases the risk of failure or perhaps successful interception by the future Nazis." He looked at Brigalow, "I'm sorry about your countrymen Davis, but their initial sacrifice is necessary to give us the advantage we need."

Davis Brigalow looked glum but nodded in agreement as Janina Zielinski added her thoughts, "I propose that we delay the transfer until midnight, six hours after the launch of the battle; that way we can use the darkness and the confusion of the battle itself as cover to slip into the fight. Once there we can turn the tide, overrun the Germans and kill Hitler. We know where he'll be and when he'll be there and thus terminated him."

Pinet agreed, "It's a good plan Janina. Does everyone agree?" They all did, including Brigalow, which Pinet appreciated. "Thank you everyone, especially you Davis. I know it was a difficult decision, but we will save some of them, I'm sure."

"Yes, Jean Claude. I know."

The plan to win the Battle of Fromelles was set. The opening stages of the fight would go as they had in history, when Australians crossed no-man's land and entered German trenches under lethal machine gun crossfire.

Hitler's regiment would be called up, and it would be then that the vortex would open and send the HIT Men into the fight. That also ensured that no-one on the Allied side would have time to realise who or what they were as they went about their business. They would then carry out the plan as it was drawn up, hitting the German machine guns and artillery up and down the line, quelling the defence and opening the way for the advance to succeed.

The HIT Men and support crews were moved to the IG Facility at Cern and briefed on the mission. The men realised they would never be coming back and would have to live out their lives in a time that would be very much inferior to their understanding of normal. It would be hard, but when they signed up for combat, they all knew there would be risks. Probably nothing like this, though. Still, they accepted their fate in whatever form it might take.

As the taskforce was made ready the human soldiers were given inoculations, "What's this for," one of them asked.

"Spanish Flu, for after the war. It has lifetime protection," the doctor said. The soldier simply nodded.

All was ready. It would take five jumps to get the squad back to 1916 with the IG machine only capable of holding eight people at a time or in this case humans and robots. The whole operation would take around an hour due to the recharge required to power each jump, so the first groups would have to wait near the battlefront until everyone arrived.

They didn't know what might welcome them at the back of the lines where they were going to emerge, but it was likely they would see a lot of activity as the battle raged and a lot of confusion as the reality of the situation unfolded.

The first transfer was set to arrive on the battlefront at 2300hrs on July 19, 1916, and the transfer completed by Midnight. It would then be a case of moving forward and beginning their assault at 0100 on July 20th, the same time Hitler was due to arrive behind the German line.

The group leader, Captain John Williams, an Australian spoke briefly with Brigalow before he was sent in, "I'll do what I can to save our mates sir. Rest assured."

"I know you will Captain, but the mission is your priority. Don't get caught up in the emotion, this will be nothing like you have ever experienced. It was a bloody, horrible war with millions of needless deaths. Oh, and expect the English to try and take charge of you and your men, they ran the whole show, very poorly a lot of the time," Brigalow explained.

"Understood sir!"

With that, Williams accompanied by five humans and two HIT Men entered the machine. The control room wound up the power and the interior of the room glowed and brightened to the point that it was impossible to watch.

Then quite suddenly the light extinguished and the machine wound down, the room empty. A voice emanated from a speaker, *All clear, successful transition.*

The committee members watched nervously as the remaining jumps were executed without incident.

When Captain Williams emerged from the vortex, he was met with a sight he could never have imagined. Even though they were well back of the front line, he could see the battle ahead with flashes of artillery and flares accompanied by the clashing sound of machine guns, rifles and shell fire and the smell of cordite mixed with other unfamiliar scents. He could see the beautiful horror that was unfolding before his eyes.

Williams took cover with his comrades and HIT Men and waited for the rest of the assault group to arrive. The spot they chose was perfect for the insertion with no-one noticing their arrival which was something of a bonus. He looked at the HIT Men as they took up defensive positions. In the dark they looked every bit the WW1 soldier but up close there was no hiding their lack of humanity. No matter, they were here to do a job, and an explanation would come later, if necessary.

The second group, the third and fourth came through quickly and Williams felt nervous pangs as he waited for the last group to arrive. The arrival point glowed with the last vortex opening when a voice called from the inky darkness behind them, "Oi, you fellows. What are you doing?"

Williams turned around as did the rest of the group, his night vision and smart goggles identifying a British sergeant approaching their position. Williams called back, "This is our rally point sergeant. We're waiting for the last of our men to arrive before we go forward."

"You should have been in there hours ago," called the Tommy.

"Sorry Sargent, we were delayed. Won't be long now," Williams added.

Just as the Tommy arrived at the scene the vortex opened and from seemingly nowhere eight soldiers emerged right in front of him. Before he could react a Hit-Man strode forward and brushed passed the sergeant to join the others, "What in blazes is going on," he blurted.

Williams didn't have time to explain as the last of his troops emerged. He decided it best to ignore the Tommy and move out, "Right, let's go," he ordered.

The Sergeant stood with his mouth gaping, "Wait just a minute. Who are you? What is that...thing," but he got no reply as the mysterious combatants moved towards the shimmering lights and cacophonous noise of battle, "Double time. Move," Williams demanded.

Despite the pockmarked terrain and the roads crammed with every manner of vehicle, they made good time. The night vision gear helped immensely. As they got close, they all switched on their mapping telemetry which would guide each group to their jump point. Williams didn't mince words, "Good luck. See you when it's over."

"OoRah" said the other men while the HIT Men remained silent. They would be able to find each other via their Wi-Fi transponders once the job was done.

Williams, his four fighters, and two HIT Men moved through the calamity of the forward medical stations, ignoring the screams and cries of the wounded.

Most people took little notice of them, their attention elsewhere but a few caught a quick scope of the weird future soldiers before they vanished at speed towards the front line. Williams wasn't concerned about how the Allies might react to their presence, he just wanted to get to the jump point and be ready for zero hour, 0100, now only 30 minutes away. They'd made excellent time and even better, no sign of any future Nazi interception.

Williams and his unit were moving up to the frontline wall that defined the Australian part of the line. As written in the history books, the Aussies used ladders to make the jump into no-man's land. He noticed several men lying around, wounded, some severely and he knew there would be a great many more out there, but he was to carry on regardless of the pleas for help that would most likely come.

Working his way through the crush of men, medics, and equipment, they reached the wall and secured a ladder. Williams checked the time on his heads-up display, 0045. The scene was nothing short of calamitous. The cries of the wounded were not something anyone was ready for and the screams coming from over the wall were somehow louder. The only people who were silent were the dead, of which there were clearly a great many.

An Australian private sat with his head in his hands sobbing and rocking back and forth, blood soaking his uniform. Williams analysed the man with Meditech software via his helmet cam. The boy, probably 18 years old, wasn't wounded but he was psychologically damaged. The readings of heart rate, brain wave function and the adrenaline and cortisol levels in his system were all red lining. He had witnessed something that his mind couldn't take, probably his best mate being blown to bits or something equally horrible.

Williams shifted uneasily at the smell of blood mixed with cordite while the noise around them remained horrifically loud. Even though he was a combat veteran, he'd never experienced anything like this. Wars in the 2200s were much more distantly fought and clinical. This was a meat grinder of epic proportions. One of his comrades vomited.

Despite the confusion, they were attracting attention, mainly because of the full-face helmets the soldiers wore. The combatants of 1916 wore tin hats which did little to protect them from anything but a clod of dirt. The combat helmets Williams and his party wore were so advanced they could warn you of incoming danger and the smart suits they wore under their uniforms were linked to compact personal computers which could quite literally move the soldiers to safety with a lurch if the helmet sensors detected an oncoming projectile. Advancing on a front such as this should be easy despite the incessant spatter of shrapnel and bullets.

Williams checked the time, 0059, "One minute," he announced on the comm link. He received four short and affirmative responses. They were ready.

The seconds dragged as they waited for 0100 and Williams began to understand how these men felt in the cauldron of what he had studied at military college. They didn't just teach soldiers about tactics and weapons in 2215; they studied all the great battles and wars in history. They spent time deconstructing the tactics of great and not so great generals on the battlefield and tried to find out where they went wrong during some of those infamous losses. Williams enjoyed that very much and was able, many a time, to reconstruct a battle and turn the tide.

Their computer technology enabled students to demonstrate their solutions to all their classmates and commanders on holographic displays. Williams was a supreme tactician and even managed to give Napoleon Bonaparte a victory over Wellington at the Battle of Waterloo by concentrating his attack on the right flank, cutting off Wellington's capacity to escape.

As he crouched by the ladder waiting to cross over, he realised that computer classes and theoretical recreations were of absolutely no use when you were just one man in a meat mincer like this. His tactical training and superior weapons would, however, make a huge difference here.

At 0100, no whistles were necessary, all knew their tasks and they climbed over the ramparts onto the soil of no-man's land. The HIT Men immediately targeted German machine gunners on the Sugarloaf and elsewhere along the line and fired a synchronised fusillade at each target. All evaporated in flashes of white light that turned the battlefield into daylight for a few seconds. The sudden change in sound was evident, and the task force moved forward, heading for the German wire.

Chapter 16 – Fallout

Jean Claude Pinet sat with the rest of the committee members dumbfounded by what was now apparent. Gabrielle Fawcett, the committee's North American delegate had vanished. Even more shocking was that they had a new committee member sitting before them. Their memories were incredibly messed up. They all remembered Fawcett even though she hadn't technically been a committee member in this new timeline.

Even more staggering was the stranger who now sat amongst them, a young woman who seemed to be very much at home amongst the group. They all had memories of working with her, but they didn't know her from a bar of soap. It was a truly weird situation, and they all stared at her like she was an alien, which she clearly noticed, "What? You're looking at me like I stole your lunch!"

No-one responded at first, then Pinet piped up, "Well, um, Miss….er" He realised he couldn't recall her name.

"What's going on," the woman asked.

"We don't know who you are," Zhang Jie announced, "You weren't here yesterday. Gabrielle Fawcett was and now she's gone.

"Oh," said the woman, "and does everyone have the same recollection?" They all nodded to which she simply said, "Jesus!"

"Yep. We know of you but until today none of us had ever spoken to you," Davis Brigalow explained.

"And yet I know you all so well. I looked after your cat when you went on your trip Davis," she said.

"You did?" Then he asked, "What trip?"

"To Australia to study up on Fromelles," the woman explained, "You're the reason this whole thing went ahead."

"I went with Gabrielle; I mean we both met there," Brigalow added.

"Well, I don't know who she is and you went alone," came the response.

"This is truly bizarre," Muhammad Galal said, "What happened to Gabrielle, where is she?"

While everyone was talking, Pinet tapped away on his personal tablet, "She works for NASA!" They all looked at him in astonishment as he continued, "Gabrielle is Deputy Administrator, one of their most senior people it seems. Somehow her timeline changed and she never joined the UN."

The nameless woman chimed in with a thought, "Clearly, we caused something to change after Fromelles. Something big. Her life was changed by those events long before her birth, events it seems she was ironically a part of. But we all knew this could happen, didn't we?"

"Well yes, but we never really expected it," Pinet replied, "We thought it would be more like one of us just not existing for some reason," then he turned to the woman, "and you are Kelly Antoniadis, right?"

"Ah, so you do remember me or does this mean you all have to get to know me again," Kelly wondered.

"I'm afraid so," Pinet said seeing the look of disappointment on Kelly's face.

"But this could be a good thing because you're in the unique position of knowing firsthand what we all did up to this point. We have mixed up foggy memories of things that clearly happened, but we didn't directly experience," Jie explained, "So you need to brief us, get us back to reality, so to speak."

"That's becoming obvious, but shouldn't we look at the data from Fromelles first, see what happened," Antoniadis suggested. She was clearly the only one with a lucid mind now.

"You're right of course; we can reintroduce ourselves later," Pinet added, "What do we know?"

No-one spoke for a while as they pawed over articles and history books reading how the battle unfolded; none of them had anticipated the outcome. The battle was won and the HIT Men were, no doubt, responsible for that.

What they didn't anticipate was how widely effective they would be in the overall theatre of World War 1; they expedited the end of the war, saving hundreds of thousands of lives. The Treaty of Versailles was still imposed on Germany, the Nazis still gained power in March of 1933, stole allied weapons technology which meant the Second World War and the Holocaust still happened.

On the plus side, Japan never figured in the Second World War because they were utterly unable to compete technologically which saved the Pacific. Interestingly that kept the United States neutral, but the European Allies were able to defeat Germany on their own terms and again, Hitler died a martyr in his bunker in Berlin and the future of white supremacy and thus, the Nazi takeover in 2337 wasn't erased.

Russia however didn't divide Germany after the war because the USA wasn't pressing them and the borders changed little after the conflict.

Pinet was distracted by many thoughts and shook his head to try and clear up his memories. What he knew as real was no longer the case and was now augmented by what was actual but alien to him, "What do we know?"

Davis Brigalow was first to speak, very keen to learn the consequences of their actions for his countrymen at Fromelles. While he had the memory of what he read at the Australian War Memorial Archive, it was mixed with memories of a new reality at Fromelles and the handwritten data they kept before the insertion helped fill in the blanks. Again, everything was kept off the digital spectrum to avoid the future Nazis getting hold of it, "The casualties were low it seems, around 1500 men and according to the notes we wrote and my memory, that's several thousand fewer than the original battle. It's a good result."

"A good result," Pinet blurted in frustration, "We failed completely! We didn't kill Hitler! Why not?"

Just then Luciana Gonzales sat up straight, "Here it is! Hitler wasn't there!"

There was a collective response, "What?"

"He wasn't there according to this report from, um," she paused to check the document, "Bundesarchiv; the Bavarian Guard didn't turn up that night. They were deployed elsewhere," Gonzales added.

"That can only mean that someone is guarding him or protecting him," suggested Sunil Patel.

"We already knew that," added Pinet.

Then Janina Zielinski said, "That might explain the killing of your people in 1907. I agree the Nazis from my era have been watching over him but how could they have known about Fromelles?"

"They didn't," Zhang Jie suggested, "I think they're protecting him by keeping him away from all conflicts. That's why he wasn't there. They're hiding him."

"That will just make our task all the more difficult," Muhammad Galal said and no-one disagreed.

Pinet rubbed his face with both hands in pure frustration, "We need a new plan."

Kelly Antoniadis looked grim, "What if we kill his parents, erase his birth?"

Many of the committee members looked at her in horror, "We can't do that," Hamid Kanumbra said which resulted in several nods of agreement.

"We can't do it because the Nazis would be expecting it," Pinet added, "No, we need to come up with something that they couldn't possibly anticipate."

"Surely, they can't watch all his ancestors. Could we go back a few generations," Antoniadis asked.

"Maybe, but I doubt that any such data exists. I don't know how good the Austrian records were back then. You're talking the 1800s," Pinet explained, "And besides, it means sending an operative into what would be a prehistoric existence for them."

"We should at least consider it, shouldn't we," Antoniadis urged.

"I will only consider it if we cannot think of something more feasible and don't think for one moment that the Nazis haven't considered your idea. I very much suspect they are watching over him as far back as they can trace his bloodline," Pinet noted and many nodded their belief in his theory.

Anastasia Kuznetsov had been very quiet until now, but when she spoke, she made her thoughts very clear, "I'm sick of this. We try something and they intercept. We try something else and they hide Hitler and our world changes. We are losing this fight and are doing it to ourselves. We need a totally different approach, a new plan that doesn't mess with our minds! There must be a better way."

No-one replied immediately but it did prompt a thought in Pinet's mind, "Kelly? From where you sit, is the World now better or worse because of us shortening the Great War and subsequently reducing the impact of WW2?"

"That's not easy to answer because the World as I knew it may not be the same as the one you experienced. Clearly, I wasn't a member of this committee at all in your reality, not until today."

Pinet understood her point but then challenged her, "You were with us in your timeline, before Fromelles, so you would have the same understanding of what the World was before it changed wouldn't you?"

"I guess so. OK, let's see," she checked her tablet briefly, "OK, the United States is the supreme power in the World, dwarfing even Russia and China. That's certainly a big change in my mind. Economically I'm guessing it's much the same, boom and bust all the time. The climate still suffers and there's still widespread poverty in the third world," she explained, "How does that compare to what you know?"

"The data seems to correlate with what I knew before; China, the US and Russia were all superpowers, so that's changed dramatically," Pinet answered. He looked over at Jie and Kuznetsov as they shifted uneasily at the news of their nations, "Should we consider going back to Fromelles and reversing what we have done?"

Some of the committee members were a little astonished that he would even bring up the possibility, most saying no except for the two communists when Gonzales said, "It's not our decision to make. That would have to go to the UN Security Council or a full sitting of the United Nations."

Pinet corrected himself, "That's true, I'm just throwing up ideas for debate at this stage. I will take it up with the UN and see how they feel about the state of play globally; they might decide to leave things be."

"That remains to be seen," Kuznetsov announced as Jie nodded in favour of her remark.

Pinet let it slide, "I think I know the answer to my next question but is the US a positive power globally today," he asked Antoniadis.

"Yes, for the most part. Being a superpower draws a lot of criticism but they're not threatening everyone with all-out war or sanctions if they disagree with something. I think the best word to describe how things as they are now is stable."

"And no blowback from China or Russia," asked Jie which was clearly on Kuznetsov's mind too.

"Honestly, I don't know what the relationships between the three were like in your old timeline but, after the two world wars, both were happy to sit back and watch the World take shape and keep to themselves. They never grew into anything to rival the US," Antoniadis told him.

"Interesting," added Kuznetsov, "And yet we still appear to have seats at the UN and here."

"Probably because you both represent very large geographic and populous parts of the World," Antoniadis suggested.

The discussion went back and forth for some time all the while the changes in the timeline becoming clearer in everyone's memories. They still weren't accustomed to having memories of events that they never experienced. The best way they could describe it was the same as recalling the plot of a TV show or a movie.

As they talked Pinet's personal tablet vibrated on the table. He saw the caller ID and tapped the answer icon putting the caller on speaker, "Hello Gabrielle."

"What the hell happened? Why on Earth am I sitting in an office in Houston," Fawcett screamed.

"It's a long story Gabrielle and we will get you up to speed. Truth be told, we weren't sure if you would recall anything," Pinet explained.

"Well, I sure as hell do. I was at the facility one second and here the next! And I remember everything and a lot more that I didn't know before."

"We know," Pinet reassured her.

"So when can I come back," Fawcett asked.

"Well, it's a little more complicated than that Gabrielle."

"What do you mean? I was there yesterday."

"True but the event has caused substantial change and, well, technically speaking, you never worked here. There's another person in your seat."

"What?"

"It's true Gabrielle," added Brigalow. "She's been with the committee for years while you went down a different path it seems."

Fawcett was breathing heavily, clearly at her wits end, "Who is he or she?"

"My name is Kelly Antoniadis. Pleased to meet you, Gabrielle."

"Um. Hi," Fawcett said, "This is so weird."

"I know this is all very strange. I'm sitting at table with friends and colleagues that I've known for years who have never met me before. It doesn't get much weirder," Antoniadis replied.

Fawcett laughed, breaking the tension. "Well, you sound lovely. I'm sure you're a good fit." She turned her attention back to Pinet. "What am I supposed to do now, Jean Claude? I have a stack of mission briefs on my desk, and I don't have a clue what to do."

"I'll see what I can do Gabby. It'll take some explaining but I'm sure we can get you back." Then he looked at Kelly, "Of course your position remains in place, rest assured."

"Thank you," Kelly said.

Then Gabrielle, feeling a little better having talked to her colleagues, asked sarcastically, "So, is Hitler dead yet?"

Chapter 17 – Breakthrough

Ernst Pfeiffer sat in his office at the Reichstag in Berlin, where the Nazis had restored Germany's traditional seat of power. He looked from his window over the River Spree, which was busy with river traffic, mainly barges transporting goods. Despite the harsh approach to their foe, the Nazis also knew that the economy had to be maintained to enable a prosperous future.

Pfeiffer was distracted momentarily from the issues the Nazis faced, of which there were a great many. There was rebellion is some areas, particularly England and French resistance had begun to frustrate him as they attacked Nazi supply systems, administration centres and their own government officials who had relented to the Nazi takeover.

Occasionally a resistance member was captured but they never talked, not even under the extremes of torture. They were more than willing to die for their cause. Pfeiffer respected that, but it made his plans more difficult. These rebels had to be subdued before they could concentrate on their next offensive.

Then there were the people that were threatening his very existence with continued attempts on the Fuhrer, Adolf Hitler in the past. If they were to succeed, the Nazi Party would be erased and thus the Nazis of 2337 and he couldn't allow that. These people were able to hide themselves from the historic records, but he knew where they were.

Nevertheless, several attempts to send people back to eradicate them had failed. He considered delivering a bomb to their facility in Cern but that would have eliminated the Infinity Generator, and he wasn't keen to lose such a valuable device. Who knows how crucial it might be in the future when dealing with the past.

Pfeiffer was suddenly snapped out of his moment of respite by a knock on the door, "Enter!" It was his personal assistant who announced the arrival of their newest lead scientist on the IG Project. He was an outsider, handpicked by the Nazis and a party man through and through. As valuable as all the scientists and technicians were on the project, he didn't quite trust them. Pfeiffer smiled as he entered, "Welcome Klaus, it is good to see you my old friend."

The man was rather tall, almost awkwardly so, in his mid-forties with a pasty white completion, vivid blue eyes and short slicked back black hair, almost Hitler like without the moustache.

"Thank you, Ernst," answered Klaus Haas, "It is good to see you too. Congratulations on your success so far. You must be pleased."

Pfeiffer waved off the compliment then snapped his fingers towards his assistant, a signal to arrange refreshments. The assistant stood to attention and clicked the heels of his jackboots before turning, closing the door and setting off on the task.

"How have you settled in at Cern," Pfeiffer enquired.

"Very well thank you, it's a nice town and I have a good team it would appear."

"Are you certain you can trust them Ernst? I have my doubts."

"Yes, I received your mission brief and I'm aware of your concerns, but they do not know that I am a party man, and my credentials do not reveal anything. If they go snooping, they will find out about my educational history and my past achievements in science, but there is no connection to us," Haas explained.

"Very good," replied Pfeiffer, "Let's keep it that way," to which Haas nodded. Pfeiffer changed the subject, "So tell me what you're working on?"

Haas smiled broadly, "You will be pleased to know that I am developing something that will give you a significant advantage over the future and the past with the IG machine."

Pfeiffer raised his eyebrows, clearly interested in anything that might help the cause, "Well, what is it Klaus, you know I'm not a patient man."

"Only too well," Hass said and the pair laughed. "I think I know how to augment the Infinity Generator so that it can be controlled using time dilation."

Pfeiffer's eyes glazed over, "What the hell are you talking about Klaus?"

"I think I can make it go forward!"

Pfeiffer looked at him, unable to hide his delight, "Forward in time?"

"Yes. We would do it by...." But Pfeiffer cut him off.

"I don't care how you do it. Just tell me how soon."

"Well, once I've done my calculations, a bit of retrofitting and written the new programs...maybe a few months, six at the most," Haas suggested.

Pfeiffer's face was beaming, "You know what this means? We can go back, deal with those imbeciles in the 2200s and then come home. We can literally clean up that mess."

"Well, not quite Ernst."

"Why not? If we can go forward, we can get back here, right?"

"We can adjust the machine in the here and now, but if we go back, the machine will still be like it is now, only able to go back," Haas explained.

Pfeiffer paused and his face reddened when he realised his stupidity, "So could we adjust the machine back then?"

"It's not really that simple Ernst but there may be two options. One, we connect with their machine and maintain a wormhole for the duration of our arrival and departure into 2215. This creates a dual portal so we can slip into their facility via the machine's vortex and return. The downside is we cannot stay long. Two, we go back one way and arrive externally, which means attacking the facility to get to the machine and make the changes to get home. Both are equally risky," Haas said.

"That sounds perfectly feasible. Make it happen," Pfeiffer ordered.

Haas didn't look too pleased and didn't wait for his long-time friend to ask what the problem was, "You realise you would be walking into hostile territory and would have to take over the facility and hold it until we finish the retro fit no matter how long it took. One mistake and we're stranded."

"Yes, yes, I know all that," Pfeiffer said impatiently, "We have the advantage of surprise and firepower. That won't be a problem."

"That's not what I've heard given your previous attempts to infiltrate their time," Haas reminded his friend. Normally that would result in a tirade or worse, but Pfeiffer made allowances for his friend.

"That is true Klaus but if we get directly inside with your two-way portal, then half the problem is resolved."

"True," but again Haas revealed doubt on his face.

"What else Klaus," Pfeiffer demanded feeling his frustration welling up.

"We won't be working with the kinds of computers that operate now. By our standards, their equipment will be ancient. It might be a tougher job than you think."

"Then figure it out before we go Klaus. Surely you have access to the archives?"

"I do. I'll see what I can learn. Perhaps we can create a way of interfacing with their computers before we go or perhaps building compatible machines to take with us."

"Good. Very good!" Pfeiffer cried excitedly, "This is the opportunity we've been hoping for. I knew it was the right thing to bring you in."

"Perhaps you should have done so from the beginning Ernst," Haas pointed out.

"Probably," was all the Pfeiffer said.

"One other thing Ernst if you will permit me. Might I suggest you make no further attempts on the facility in 2215 in the meantime. Let them think you've given up. If we wait a while, they will ultimately think we have changed tac. We will lull them into a false sense of security," Haas suggested and the idea was greeted with a nod of approval.

Just then the refreshments arrived and the two men spent some time chatting about their past adventures. Intellectually they were poles apart and probably should never have become friends, but they connected when they were both much younger and the friendship had endured. Pfeiffer left his assistant to deal with the next few hours' worth of appointments so he could enjoy the company of his friend but eventually something came up that he had to deal with, "I'm sorry Klaus, duty calls it seems."

"I understand. I should be getting back to Cern. Seeing you was the last thing on my "to do" list, however the most joyful of tasks," Haas said with a wide smile.

"It's been a delight to see you again. Let us not wait so long next time Klaus."

The pair shook hands which was followed by a Nazi salute, "Heil Hitler!"

As Haas walked out Pfeiffer called to him, "Keep me up to date with your progress with the retrofitting of the IG machine, it is your number one priority now Klaus."

"I will," he said before he disappeared through the antique mahogany floor to ceiling double doors which abruptly closed.

Weeks went by with little to report, Pfeiffer decided that he should visit Cern himself and *inspire* the scientists.

The arrangements were made and Pfeiffer, along with his entourage of security officers took off from Berlin Tegel International Spaceport in the Nazi's private jet, one they seized from the deposed German Government.

The high-speed aircraft, adorned now with a red swastika on its tail, and painted matt black, would make the journey in a little over thirty minutes accompanied by a squadron of modern Scram interceptors.

The flight went smoothly and Pfeiffer was ushered to a waiting armoured vehicle for the short drive to the Infinity Generator where he once again met his old friend, Klaus Haas who gave him a formal tour of the facility.

At the end of the tour the IG staff and science faculty were assembled where Pfeiffer briefed them. As always, he chose a place where he could look down upon his audience. He didn't read from an autocue display, he preferred to speak off the cuff.

"Heil Hitler!" he cried, following it with the Nazi salute.

The gesture caught some of the faculty off guard. Scientists had a reputation for being somewhat removed from reality and Pfeiffer did it to see how they reacted. Interestingly, most returned the gesture immediately, but some looked a little dumbfounded.

Pfeiffer was amused, "Thank you, thank you. It is so good to be here to see the vital work you are doing for the Reich. I want you to know how important you are to me and my party. We value your work significantly and feel you are a critical cog in the Nazi Party machine. With the Infinity Generator we can right the wrongs of the past, and now, according to your team leader, Klaus Haas, we will soon be able to ensure our future."

Pfeiffer was careful not to draw any attention to the friendship he had with Haas. He didn't trust these people, but he had nothing concrete to implicate any of them to anti-Nazi groups. He just had a feeling.

"I am supremely confident that you will succeed in cracking the puzzle that will enable us to move forward in time. I believe with your talent and the limitless resources the Nazi Party offers you, this can be done and done very soon!" He held a gaze at the group to help them understand that he wasn't going to wait long and then threw in the carrot, "I'm a generous man, you may not know this, but to the individual or group here that solves the riddle of forward time travel, I promise you a valuable prize. It will be up to you to make a choice, perhaps a home or a work assignment. Whatever you wish, within reason, I will deliver!"

Pfeiffer knew that money talked in most levels of society and offering a blank cheque was going to reveal those who were loyal and perhaps weed out anyone that might not be so willing to help the Party.

The reaction from the group again was variable, from elation to subdued surprise. Pfeiffer was recording the audience members through his security detail's body cams, and they would later analyse the data and see if there were any anomalies in the mood changes and body language of the individuals.

Unlike Adolf Hitler, Pfeiffer didn't build his speeches to a rousing crescendo, in fact he preferred to be brief and get to the point.

"May I conclude by saying how proud I am to have you all working for the Reich. Your contribution to our cause and more importantly our continuity as a Party and a Nation is the most important things you can do and the reason why I feel so very close to this project," he said, wanting to make them understand that he was watching them intently, "I look forward to your success! Now back to work!"

Haas shook Pfeiffer's hand being careful to keep it brief and as impartial as possible to avoid undue suspicion from any of the

IG's scientific staff. The meeting broke as Pfeiffer was ushered back to Haas's office where he asked, "Do you think it worked? Will they now be more focussed?"

"Perhaps," answered Haas, "But we are dealing with complexities that are very challenging."

"Are you saying you won't solve the problem?"

"I must be honest; we can solve it, but it may take longer than I had hoped. Of course, there's always a chance that we will achieve a breakthrough sooner. I am hopeful we will Ernst."

"I'm counting on it Klaus. With the capacity to go back and forth through time, we can guarantee our future. We can go forward, see what the World is like and if, for some reason, we are not happy with how things are, we can make the corrections at whatever point in time is required," Pfeiffer explained, "You have to succeed."

"I will Ernst. I promise you."

"Very good. I do not doubt you my friend," and he smiled, "Well, I must go, I need to be back in Berlin for a party briefing tonight."

"Of course, thank you for making the journey. It was good to see you again," Haas said with a smile.

With that Pfeiffer returned to the airport in Cern and boarded his Nazi jet. Four of the Scram interceptors circled the airport in anticipation of his take-off while others taxied to the end of the runway for a multiple take off. The interceptors would provide a protective cordon around the jet.

Pfeiffer's advisors had warned him that he was most vulnerable during landing and take-off because of the slower speeds in those situations. At altitude and at high speed, the jet was almost impossible to attack unless you had a scram interceptor. The pilot pushed the engines to full throttle and the plane quickly built-up ground speed before rotating into a climb, gaining altitude quickly. As it rose the radio squawked, "Smoke trails coming in from four directions!"

At that moment one scram interceptor evaporated, follow by another.

The remaining two peeled off as the other rockets screamed after them, leaving the Nazi leader exposed.

As the Nazi jet climbed, two more rockets were launched and found the jet's heat trail, zigging hard towards their target, now only seconds away.

"Deploy counter measures," cried the pilot just as the plane was shuddered by a huge detonation.

Chapter 18 – A Whole New Plan

It had been several months since the attack on Fromelles and now, a United Nations report was released into the actions of the IG Committee which concluded that they had indeed managed to save millions of lives and improved the lives of a great many other people in the years that followed the Great War, notwithstanding the tyranny of the Nazis in World War two Europe. The fact that they had failed in their goal of eliminating Hitler was unfortunate.

The UN Security Council agreed that the Nazi's of 2337 must be protecting Hitler and getting to him would be much more difficult. They also agreed that the committee needed to think of a very different approach, one that could be executed quickly, effectively and most importantly, could not be intercepted or reversed.

It sounded simple enough, but it was far from that. What could they possibly do? One thing the UN did decide on was to bring in a new team to try and foster some fresh ideas Think tanks that spit balled all sorts of concepts. Nothing was left off the table no matter how ludicrous.

One idea was to send an incendiary device directly into Hitler's house in 1907 and burn it down, but when it was pointed out that the portal must merge into open air outside of any kind of structure, the idea was scotched.

Another idea was to train attack dogs to hunt him down and kill him but for that they would need his scent and in 2215, that was hardly available to them. They could try teaching the dogs to attack on sight, but it was felt this would be to haphazard and again the idea was shelved. Besides, Hitler's protectors would no doubt be close by and shoot the animals before they could get to him.

Many ideas were debated and each one rejected for one reason or another. The UN wanted certainty and so far, the chances of success for even the best idea to date was estimated to be 5%.

But then an idea was tabled that seemed to have merit. The more it was investigated, the better it got, so much so that the UN Secretary General was brought into the discussion. That was quickly followed by her travelling to Cern.

Jean Claude Pinet greeted the UN Secretary General, Blair Odette as she arrived, "It's good to see you again Blair."

"You too Jean Claude, I have news which I could not share with you through normal channels," Odette explained.

"Of course," Pinet replied.

They drove back to the IG facility and made their way quickly to Pinet's office. Odette was briefly introduced to the other committee members and was astonished to meet Janina Zielinski whom she previously learned had travelled back from 2337 to help their cause. She was also thrilled to see that Gabrielle Fawcett was again on the committee after the machinations of the Fromelles adventure.

She sat down and looked at Pinet, "Have there been any more attempts on you or the other committee members," she asked.

"No, thankfully, not for a long time. I hope they have decided it's all too difficult," Pinet said with a half-smile.

Odette smiled back, both knowing, that the Nazis would never stop trying to get to him and his team, "What do you think they'll try next?"

"God only knows. I just hope we're ready for it. It's not a good feeling waiting for an assassin to appear every minute of every day, and night. I don't sleep much."

"I can't imagine," Odette added then she said, "Some very strange things have happened since we started toying with time Jean Claude."

"I know, but we can't stop now, particularly when we know what the future holds for humanity," Pinet said frowning.

"I'm not here to shut you down, I'm here to give you a solution," Odette told him.

Pinet's eyes widened in surprise, "A solution?"

"Yes, well THE solution. I couldn't email this through or call your tablet. Too much risk of the data being discovered in the future and if they learn this, they will act and that will remove perhaps our very best chance of killing Hitler," Odette explained.

"So, what have you discovered," Pinet asked, clearly excited.

"We have been consulting with historians, to see what more we can learn about Hitler's life, the places he lived and worked, and an interesting piece of information came to our attention. I think it is the key to our goal," she said.

Pinet couldn't stand the cloak and dagger, "Blair, you're toying with me. Get to the point!"

She smiled knowing she could play this game a while longer but decided it was time to explain what she'd learned, "OK, here it is."

For the next fifteen minutes she spoke and Pinet listened, not uttering a word. The more she said, the more excited he became. The idea was brilliant and would be 100% successful should they be able to deliver the package but then Odette revealed the one stumbling block.

"For this to work we will need the Russians, and they won't agree without putting a heavy price on it, probably a more hands on approach to the IG for starters. We might all be getting along these days, but business is business with the Russians."

"Hmm, I can understand that. Nothing gets done without a price, not even if the prize is freedom for all but we can negotiate, surely," Pinet asked.

"I believe so. If they can deliver on this then I think the price will be worth it, whatever they ask."

"So how do we go about this? We can't just call the Kremlin and say, 'hand it over' that would leave a trail," Pinet suggested.

"Very true. You and I will have to go to Russia and talk to them off the record. The whole thing must be off the books and on a handshake agreement. We can do everything formally after the job is done."

"They won't go for that. They'll want guarantees up front, signed sealed and delivered," Pinet said, "And before you say it, I know, that would leave evidence on record for the Nazis to exploit. Someone must go there in person." Then Pinet saw Odette smiling, "What."

"Well, you will be going there alone as a tourist under an assumed identity. We must keep you hidden. As for the carrot, I will sell it in the guise of a deal for a bigger Eastern Block representation on the UN Security Council. I'm anticipating they'll ask for that regardless, so why not use it to our advantage?"

"That's a good idea but without formality, they'll just think it's all talk," Pinet pointed out.

"That's why I want you there. You have firsthand knowledge and experience that they need to know, to sell the concept."

"That's true but if I may, we should also take Anastasia Kuznetsov. She's Russian for starters but she will be more believable than I might be at the Kremlin," Pinet added.

"Of course, I was getting to that. She is very much a part of the plan. I would also like you to take Janina Zielinski if you're agreeable. She is Eastern Block, yes?" Pinet nodded, "More importantly, she is from the future and will back us up. What do you think," Odette asked.

"I have come to know her and I trust her. She has been most helpful. She has certainly improved some of the operational aspects of the IG and improved our power consumption efficiency. Yes, she should go."

"Good, it's settled." Odette said smiling, "I sure hope this works!"

"Me too," Pinet said nervously.

Arranging travel for Janina Zielinski proved somewhat difficult given she had no form of identification in this era. She couldn't travel under her real name for the same reasons that the rest of the IG committee couldn't, so an alias was organised and papers drawn up.

It wasn't something the United Nations was comfortable doing but there was much more at stake than their reputation. Finding time to sit down with the Russian President also slowed the process and Blair Odette wondered if he was just playing games when he rejected every date they put forward. Eventually though he agreed and a date was set.

The quartet set off as individuals on four different travel schedules, leaving on different days and arriving in Moscow separately with several days of separation, just to be safe.

It was also suggested that Zielinski wear a disguise so that cameras couldn't record her real image, just in case that data was somehow dug up in the future. They took no chances.

The group converged on the Kremlin and found each other in the President's lavish waiting room at the appointed time. As was Dimitri Chadov's custom, he kept them waiting just long enough to be annoying.

When they were shown into his palatial office he smiled broadly and greeted Blair Odette with a hug, "Blair, so good to see you. It has been far too long."

Odette was equally disingenuous when she answered, "Thank you Dimitri, you are too kind."

"And you too Jean Claude, welcome. It is surprising to see you here. I can only wonder what this is all about. So much mystery. It must be important, hmmm?"

Pinet didn't want to play Chadov's silly game of one-upmanship, but what choice did he have. "You will be pleased you saw us Dimitri."

"Perhaps," he replied then turned his attention to Kuznetsov and Zielinski, recognising the features of his kinsfolk, "And who are these radiant creatures and why have you kept them hidden from me?"

Odette smiled, realising that Chadov had made a diplomatic faux pas. "Dimitri, this is Anastasia Kuznetsov, the Russian Federation's representative on the IG Committee, although I'm sure you have met previously."

Chadov's face reddened, "Of course. Forgive me Anastasia, I forget myself sometimes."

"It is as honour to see you again sir," she replied, giving her leader the dutiful respect he deserved and expected.

"And this is Helena Mazur, one of our most esteemed scientists," Odette told Chadov, knowing it was untrue. She would correct that when the room was cleared of the President's entourage.

"You are Polish?" Chadov asked.

"Yes," Mazur (Zielinski) replied.

"Ah excellent. I love Poland, beautiful women and a country that has long suffered the tug of war between east and west. Tough people the Poles," Chadov said clumsily, clearly taken back by Janina's beauty.

"Thank you," was all she said in response.

He blushed again then stepped behind his desk and invited everyone to be seated, "So what can a humble Russian President do for the United Nations?"

Blair Odette waited for the room to clear before she spoke which only piqued Chadov's interest, "Firstly Dimitri I wonder if we can keep this discussion off the books and I mean, no digital record at all. The security of the World hinges on you agreeing to that."

Chadov's demeanour changed immediately. He may have been a playboy, but he knew when something needed to be taken seriously. He clapped his hands then said, "OK, the room is dark, I assure you Blair, this meeting is completely off the record," he paused then added, "For the moment."

Blair Odette knew he could have been faking her, but she didn't think so and simply said, "Well if there is any digital record of this discussion, the future is doomed and I'm not playing around Dimitri. We have first-hand knowledge. Now you understand the way the IG machine works and what we're trying to do?" He nodded, "OK, so you should realise that the machine exists in the future still, and the wrong kind of people have control of it there." she didn't elaborate and turned to Janina Zielinski.

"Mr. President, I am not Helena Mazur. I have come here from the year 2337. I am a technician at Cern, and I worked on the IG machine."

He didn't realise it, but his mouth dropped open and eyes widened in total shock, and it took him a moment to speak, "What is your real name?"

"That is something I will not divulge, it's simply too dangerous to leave any traces of my presence for the Nazis to use against us," she explained.

"The Nazis?"

"Yes. In 2337 they rise up against the nations of the World and take control of Europe including England. They stop at the

Russian border and have a truce with the Middle East, which I'm sure they intend to break. They are biding their time but will ultimately take them out followed by the Pacific, Russia, China, South America and when they have overcome all of them, they will turn on North America. And before you ask, yes, they will succeed!"

Chadov was speechless this time and looked at the other three delegates, then asked a question of Anastasia Kuznetsov, "Is this true comrade?"

"Yes sir. Helena learned these things in her time from the resistance networks she worked with." Kuznetsov then changed tac, "Our attempts to kill Hitler have been thwarted by the Nazis on several occasions and they have made attempts on our lives too. They realise we can wipe them from existence if we succeed and they are protecting Hitler through their IG machine," and she continued to give him detailed facts about several events that had led to this meeting.

The explanations, coming from a fellow Russian, were enough to convince him that a dire future awaited the Russian Federation and the World as a whole. "And if the UN had not sanctioned the elimination of Hitler, we would never know what the future holds," she concluded.

"My God," he exclaimed.

"Well Dimitri," Janina said, "I think I would have come back to warn you regardless, so you would ultimately have been made aware, and we would be sitting here anyway."

"Yes, of course. I'm sorry but this time travel nonsense is very confusing," he said then snapped back to reality, "So how can Russia help? What do you need from us," he asked.

Jean Claude Pinet cleared his throat before he spoke, grabbing Chadov's focus. "You have something that we need, something that will guarantee our success. It is really our only remaining option. Until now we have been intercepted or, as was the case with our Fromelles offensive, they simply kept

Hitler away, so we couldn't get to him. We needed a new plan and, according to our research, you have the weapon we require."

"We do?"

"Yes. You do."

"What is it," Chadov asked.

"It's a war trophy, one that your army collected in World War 2, and we need it to kill Hitler," Odette said.

Dimitri Chadov looked completely perplexed, "What kind of war trophy?"

Jean Claude Pinet smiled. "A very special one."

Chapter 19 – Retribution

Inside a dank cell in Berlin, a near naked man lay panting, his hands and feet brutally tied together, the wire cutting into his skin, his body covered in welts and bruises.

An SS officer stood over him with a modified riding crop, festooned with metal barbs. He raised it and whipped the man across the back, causing another series of rips in the man's now pasty looking skin. The man flinched but was so weak he could no longer scream, he just squeaked.

The officer asked him the same question for the fiftieth or perhaps the hundredth time, the man had long ago lost count, "Who organised to attack your Fuhrer?" Use of the word *your* was deliberately antagonistic.

The man didn't answer seemingly resigned to his fate which he expected would be slow and painful. The SS officer had already realised this man was well trained and disciplined and probably wouldn't break but at least he could enjoy the process of inflicting pain on an enemy of the Reich.

The man had been subjected to several forms of coercion to no effect. He was now without fingernails, toenails and the burns on his torso were hideously blistered and weeping, some already showing signs of infection after several days of sleepless and relentless interrogation.

"We know there were at least four of you surrounding the airport with laser guided anti-aircraft weaponry," the officer told the man yet again, "And two of your comrades are dead, the third, like you, is being questioned."

The man scoffed sarcastically then coughed, his weakened state turning his moment of mirth against him.

"You think it's funny? Well, here's something you don't know, The Fuhrer, Ernst Pfeiffer is alive and well!"

The man reacted to that with a hacking laugh and managed to squeeze out a single word, "Bullshit!"

"Oh, it's true I assure you. You see, the Scram interceptors guarding the Fuhrer's plane blocked your rockets and the Fuhrer escaped with a few bruises. You failed," the torturer advised.

The man, lying face down on the disgusting floor, covered in the blood and refuse of his isolation looked up at his antagonist, "I saw the plane explode. Pfeiffer is dead and good riddance," and he spat at the SS man's boot.

The officer laughed, "You are mistaken. You saw a scram interceptor explode as a hero of the Reich sacrificed himself to save our great leader. That's what you saw."

"I don't believe you," the man mumbled as he coughed up a wad of bloody phlegm.

The officer sneered at the man with seething hate but resisted the temptation to lay another blow on his victim, "Hmm, I wonder how I might prove my claim. Perhaps Ernst Pfeiffer himself can convince you?"

"Oh, you'd like that wouldn't you?" asked the man. "He's just going to walk on through the door and introduce himself."

"What if he did? You would know you failed. What then?"

"I would kill him here and now," the man said.

The officer laughed loudly, "Oh I would certainly like to see that. And how would you execute your attack? A bite to the ankle perhaps," and the officer laughed again.

The more the officer toyed with the prisoner the more the man believed that their attack at Cern Airport was successful.

The prisoner smiled in defiance which resulted in another swat from the riding crop, this time across the face, a barb piercing the ocular surface of his left eye, tearing a jagged line across it.

The man winced as the eye watered profusely, "I don't care if you kill me, fast, slow. It doesn't matter. I go to my grave knowing that Pfeiffer is dead and gone and your precious Reich will crumble without him."

"WHERE ARE YOUR COMRADES? WHO ARE THEY," demanded the officer one final time.

"Go to hell!"

The officer wanted so much to kill the man lying on the blood and shit stained floor, but he was under strict orders and took his hand off the pistol strapped to his hip which made the prisoner smile once more. The sting of the barbs didn't feel so bad this time, the man knowing his death would not be in vain. Pfeiffer was indeed gone.

"Is that all you've got? Just kill me. I go to my death a happy man. You can't change that."

The officer didn't respond this time except to tap a communicator on the collar of his jet-black uniform, "He's ready."

The man heard the words but didn't understand the meaning then thought, *at last they're going to end this. Time to die* and he relaxed, smiling just as the cell door opened. He was blinded briefly by the burst of light from the corridor which hurt his injured eye but then the light was blocked as someone entered the room. He saw the large frame of a man and the silhouette of his bald cranium. The man limped across the floor and stood over the prisoner but didn't immediately speak. The SS officer stood to attention and snapped his heel, "Heil Hitler!"

The man saluted back but said nothing for the next few moments as he returned his gaze to the near dead man on the floor who was now looking up at the face of the new arrival and he shuddered in shock and fear.

"You have been very brave my friend. I admire your strength but, as you can see, you have wasted your life and now you can die knowing you did indeed completely fail!"

Ernst Pfeiffer didn't kick the man or whip him he just let the knowledge of his being very much alive sink into the prisoner's brain and when it did. The man screamed and lunged at Pfeiffer, to no avail.

"Shhhhhhh," Pfeiffer hissed. "It will all be over soon."

Pfeiffer snapped his fingers and another SS officer came into the room dragging another prisoner, a woman and Pfeiffer looked at her saying, "I believe this is your wife, am I right Herr Polson, Frederik Polson? freedom fighter?"

The man squinted and when his one good eye adjusted, he could see the woman clearly. She was gagged and dishevelled from rough treatment and didn't look to have been tortured but he could easily read the terror on his wife's face.

"Spare her. She's done nothing."

He realised his mistake immediately. He would have been better off denying her completely. At least then she would have had a vague chance.

Pfeiffer grinned slightly. "At this point I would normally threaten to harm your wife unless you speak, blah, blah, blah, but I don't need to."

Polson frowned, not understanding what that meant. Then he saw Pfeiffer pull a large hunting knife from its scabbard and plunge it into the woman's torso, once, twice, three times. She dropped to the floor, unable to squeal because of the gag, convulsing as her body oozed life right next to her husband who was screaming in a rage. Pfeiffer waited.

The Man ranted and raved for several minutes while Pfeiffer cleaned his knife and returned it to the scabbard, not saying anything. Finally, Polson was out of breath and lay there sobbing as he watched his wife die, helpless to do anything.

Her last memory of him would be his broken body on a filthy cell floor, knowing he too would be dead soon.

Pfeiffer, satisfied that the man was now broken spoke, "I do not need to hear your confession Herr Polson," and then he showed Polson something, "Do you know what this is? It's a tiny camera. Looks like an ant doesn't it. We have hundreds of them, and, after your attack, we sent these back through our time machine to see who tried to kill me. When we collected them from their lead depository the facial recognition software did the rest."

Polson's expression weakened even further, if that was possible, realising what that meant, which Pfeiffer noticed, "Yes, Herr Polson, we have traced your movements and those of your dead colleagues. We found your base and obliterated it. They are all dead I assure you. You are defeated. No survivors."

Polson grunted in utter frustration, again lunging at Pfeiffer who didn't even bother to flinch at the pitiful attempt.

"Herr Polson," Pfeiffer tisked, "I really do admire your tenacity. If only you were on our side, what an asset you would have been."

Polson spat one last time, realising his torture had been nothing more than retribution. They never needed him to crack. They just wanted to punish him.

"Of course, the cruellest thing I could do is not kill you Herr Polson and leave you to live out your days with the image of your dying wife knowing that you are the reason she lies there. Such a pretty thing too. Pity." Pfeiffer fumbled at his right hip and there was a click as a holster popped open. "But I am a generous man and have decided to do you a favour Herr Polson, because you are so brave." Pfeiffer lifted his antique luger and aimed it at Polson's head. "Goodbye!"

BANG!

Ernst Pfeiffer returned to his office at the Reichstag, satisfied that another resistance group had been nullified. Even so, they were able to mobilise in quick time and almost executed the perfect ambush.

It was clear that the resistance operated in cells so one group knew nothing of any other. Finding one group didn't open doors to others. During the investigation that uncovered Polson's resistance group, the SS identified one of the Reichstag's staff, a clerk, who had leaked Pfeiffer's movements to the Cern cell.

The young man confessed and gave up his contacts hoping it would save him. He was shot in front of all the staff, just in case there were others who were thinking of doing something stupid.

Pfeiffer was fed up and ordered ruthless vengeance from now on. People would be shot on suspicion. If terror was the only way to quell an uprising, then it would be so.

He was also becoming incredibly frustrated with the lack of progress at the facility in Cern. Many more weeks had passed and, yet, they hadn't made any progress on the IG machine's capacity to go forward in time, despite assurances from his good friend Klaus Haas. He was about to call his friend when Pfeiffer's Personal Assistant knocked and entered.

 "What is it," Pfeiffer demanded.

"Sir, Klaus Haas is here to see you!"

"Really? Why was I not advised," Pfeiffer demanded.

"He did not announce he was coming sir."

"Well show him in!"

The assistant snapped his heels and gestured for Haas to enter Pfeiffer's office, "Hello old friend, it's good to see you are well," Haas said as he strode up and hugged his friend.

"Ah, just a couple of bruises Klaus, nothing more."

"That limp tells me otherwise," Haas added.

"Yes well, the Scram took a hit close to us and shook us up pretty good. It's just a cork. Nothing more."

"It could be a compound fracture, and I think you would still be walking without a compression skin," Haas said and the two men laughed.

"Please sit Klaus," Pfeiffer said then ordered refreshments which his assistant immediately arranged, "I was about to call you. Do you have good news?"

Haas beamed a broad smile, "Better Ernst. We have cracked it. In fact, we have conducted an experiment which I hope will confirm our success."

"What kind of experiment Klaus," Pfeiffer asked.

Haas looked at his wrist and tapped the smart screen, "Any second now."

As he spoke the surface of Pfeiffer's desk shimmered and both men watched as something materialised on the surface. In a few seconds an antique Nazi clock manifested itself on the tabletop.

"What is this Klaus," Pfeiffer asked in surprise.

"That is the clock from my office, one from this very building dating back to 1942. I wanted to give it to you to show that we have succeeded."

"But I don't understand Klaus, what are you showing me?"

"I sent this three days ago!"

Pfeiffer's features almost cracked as he smiled. He didn't smile very much but now he was filled with joy, "You did it! Oh, my friend, this is amazing. Thank you!!"

"There's more. We can also portal freely into a building, even a submarine if we have the coordinates, so there are no limits to what can be achieved now."

Pfeiffer stood and walked around to his friend and hugged him, a very unlikely gesture from a Fuhrer but he was ecstatic, "You have done me a great service Klaus. You will be rewarded. This is extraordinary," and he gestured towards the still working clock.

"What will you do now Ernst," Haas asked.

"Ah, first thing is to infiltrate the IG facility in 2215 and eradicate that threat, retrofit your technology and come home. Then, who knows; take a peek at the next hundred years and make sure we are still operating."

"Ah ok, so then, I must warn you of the paradoxical issues. You cannot emerge at a time when you are living or have already been but going forward should be ok if you return at a time later than you left."

"I am aware. I will add one hundred years to my age, for the journey forward, just to be safe."

"Hmm make it 150 years, Ernst, you will outlive us all I think." The two men laughed then Haas added, "I would very much like for you to be there when the mission to 2215 is sent back. I would be honoured if you could witness it, perhaps even 'push the button' so to speak."

"Well, given that the most recent threat has been eliminated, I doubt that another attempt will be made. And my security is being ramped up as we speak, so yes, I would be thrilled to do so!"

"Very good. Next week then? If you have a team ready, no sense waiting," Haas suggested.

"I like the way you think Klaus. Yes, indeed, next week," Pfeiffer agreed.

"Excellent," Haas said as the pair smiled.

A week later Ernst Pfeiffer stood in the control room at Cern watching as a small Nazi Commando Unit made ready to transit back to 2215 and take control of the IG facility.

"Once they have secured the machine, I will send back our technicians to retrofit the necessary equipment for a safe return to 2337," Haas explained as Pfeiffer nodded.

Haas ordered the machine to be spooled up, and the commandos stepped into the portal. They knew what they had to do, kill any combatants but spare the rest for the time being, at least until their worth could be assessed, perhaps bringing some forward for interrogation. IG Committee members were to be captured also, if possible, otherwise eliminated.

The computer program took over, and the energy build up could be felt vibrating through the floor as the quantum reactors reached their peak.

"Would you like a closer look Ernst," Haas asked.

Pfeiffer was very excited and nodded like a child in a candy store. Haas led him into the transfer room where Pfeiffer met the commandoes and wished them well.

"Better stand back Ernst, they're about to jump," said Haas as the portal glowed and the men were absorbed into a bright white light before vanishing before Pfeiffer's eyes, "Amazing," he said.

"Yes, indeed it is," Haas answered proudly. "You will soon have control of the IG unit in 2215."

"Not only that my friend," Pfeiffer gloated, "We are on the cusp of controlling all of time. The history and the future!"

Chapter 20 – The Final option

Several transports had left Russia from different airports on different days travelling to different destinations but only one contained the cargo that the United Nations needed to eliminate Adolf Hitler from history and thus expunge the Holocaust and by default, the new Nazis from the future.

Initially it was thought that heavy security would be required but that idea was scrapped as it may have attracted the wrong kind of attention. Civilian transports were used to make things look routine.

The IG committee members understood the Nazis were, likely, protecting Hitler throughout history and probably his parents and previous bloodlines. Their last attempt to initiate a military strike against him came to nothing, although it did shorten the First World War significantly, but the aftermath was the same with Hitler installed as Nazi leader and all that followed across Europe.

IG Committee Chairman, Jean Claude Pinet sat in his office, nervously biting his fingernails waiting for news of the delivery from Russia. The Russian President, Dimitri Chadov, upon learning of the future threat to Russia was more than happy to hand over the prize, won by the Russian Army in World War Two, the one thing the UN believed could do the job.

They'd already tried assassins before the Great War and robot soldiers carrying future tech into WW1 but none of it worked and they expended some very good people along the way. Now they would try something different, something that they hoped the Nazis couldn't even imagine let alone intercept.

Still, Pinet was concerned. He believed that if the Nazis were protecting Hitler, they were most likely watching the facility in Cern too, so getting something like this delivered undetected needed to seem as ordinary as possible. As he nibbled at the edge of his thumb, his private tablet bleeped and vibrated on the desk and an encrypted message appeared on the screen, "Rosemary has landed." The message didn't say where, but he knew it was London.

As with everything the IG committee had done since the early attempts on their lives, the entire operation was kept off the grid. An encrypted message about someone named Rosemary wouldn't seem odd, he hoped. He smiled at the news but that wasn't the end of it.

The delivery now had to get from London to Cern. Again, with concerns that the Cern Airport was under surveillance, the final journey would be by Ferry, across the English Channel then by road, a trip of approximately ten hours depending on the traffic.

One thing that hadn't changed in hundreds of years was traffic. Infrastructure was never quite up to date with vehicle numbers it seemed. The item would be carried by agents posing as tourists and finally handed over to a contact who would get it on a food delivery truck which regularly visited the facility. Anyone watching wouldn't be suspicious of a truck they'd seen several times over a long period. Just to be safe, the item would be dropped at the loading dock with the rest of that weeks' supplies. Once inside it would be collected and delivered to Pinet's office.

Pinet didn't sleep well that night. He knew the truck would arrive at the facility around 8am but he ordered everyone to stick to routine. A crowd milling around a loading dock would appear strange, so only a handful of people knew it was coming. He rose, feeling exhausted from tossing and turning most of the night, remembering nightmares about the ferry being torpedoed or the truck blowing a tyre and going over a cliff. The images repeatedly played in his unconscious mind. He was relieved to get out of bed.

As he tried to enjoy his breakfast, croissants and coffee, the tablet bleeped again, "Rosemary is home. She can't wait to see you."

Pinet scoffed down his food and gulped the last of his coffee before driving to the office, arriving at the normal time. He drove an old, weather-beaten car that wouldn't attract attention and always parked in the worker's section of the facility.

He generally dressed in overalls, so he looked like just another worker. He entered the building through the tradesman's workshop, again to avoid unwanted attention. The other IG committee members had similar disguises.

After getting inside, he took the overalls off, changed from boots into shiny leather shoes and walked into his underground office. There he was met by a staff member from the loading dock holding a large black case, which he took from them. It had been hidden in a crate full of vegetables. He unlocked the door to his office and placed the case on top of his desk and waited.

The rest of the committee members arrived at various times from different departments and congregated in the meeting room. As soon as they were assembled, Pinet took the case and placed it on the conference table, "We have it," he told them and they all sighed with relief.

The case looked like any other, aside from the encrypted electronic locks. It was about the size of a standard suitcase and quite heavy. Pinet correctly surmised that the weight was caused by the protective interior of the case more so than the contents itself, designed to make electronic scans impossible, "So who wants to take a look?"

Everyone nodded although he could tell they also felt somewhat apprehensive. Pinet plugged a digital keyboard into a socket on the lid of the case and four sets of tally lights strobed and then blacked out. He typed in his code as the first set of lights illuminated one at a time. The first latch clicked,

Hamid Kanumbra did the same then Luciana Gonzales and finally Zhang Jie. It was felt that one person having all the codes would be a risk. When Jie tapped the last character, the lid popped open slightly.

Pinet took a deep breath. "OK, here we go."

He eased the led lined case open whereupon everyone saw that something box like was wrapped in a black silken bag. He took the cover off a box which was made of Perspex, no doubt designed to display and protect the contents, which had been sealed like this for a great many years. They all gasped as they looked at the 270-year-old relic.

No-one said anything for a moment, then finally Davis Brigalow piped up, "So you think this will do the trick huh? It's low tech," and he laughed nervously.

"I believe so, it's not something the Nazis could ever imagine being used against them," answered Pinet.

"Unless it's a fake," Muhammad Galal said.

"That's a risk we'll have to take," Pinet said.

"So, how do we, um, use it," Sunil Patel asked.

Pinet shrugged, "To be honest, I don't really understand the science, but it should be simple enough. We have evidence to suggest this is the one thing that will work!"

Again, they all nodded, somewhat hypnotised by what they saw. Pinet put the bag back around the box and sealed the case, "This goes into the safe with 24-hour security until we need it."

"The question now is where and when do we deliver it," Anastasia Kuznetsov suggested.

"That's what we need to decide," Pinet said then added, "We have complicated matters with our previous attempts so getting to him may be much more difficult."

"Do we need to get close," Kelly Antoniadis asked.

"Probably not but I think the closer, the better. I want to be certain," Pinet replied, "What do you think Janina?"

Janina Zielinski had worked with more advanced knowledge of the IG machine given she was from 2337 and was more technically aware of its limitations.

"It's more a question of when rather than where but I would be concerned about just dropping something into some timeline without assurances. I would want to get very close, if possible, perhaps have it personally delivered."

"I agree," said Pinet, "We will only get one shot at this."

"Perhaps we can use someone who is already there? One of our operatives from Fromelles perhaps," Brigalow suggested.

"You assume that's when we do the delivery and yet we know he wasn't there, or at least where we expected him to be," Pinet pointed out.

The location and timing of the drop was now the most crucial part of the exercise as well as the complexity of finding yet another operative to go back to whenever was deemed most appropriate.

Even then, walking up to Hitler would be impossible without drawing unwanted attention from his protectorate. It would likely be a suicide mission.

"Any ideas? Anything at all," Pinet pleaded.

"We've been over this a thousand times," Sunil Patel replied, "And we still don't have an answer. Our clumsiness has resulted in him being almost untouchable."

Pinet shot him a steely glare, but he also knew that Patel was right.

Gabrielle Fawcett then lit up like she'd had some kind of revelation, "What if..." then she paused as her mind ticked over, "We know where he lived in the early 1900s, yes? What if we deposit the package at the home of his birth? Put it somewhere that no-one could find it?"

Pinet looked up at her, "Yes! They are probably anticipating a frontal attack but if we deposit the weapon in waiting, they're not likely to be as attentive. It could work!"

Fawcett continued, "The operative would only need to monitor the situation and wait for things to unfold. They would have a front row seat."

"Indeed, they would," added Kuznetsov, "so where was he when he was born?"

"I have it," Pinet replied as he strode to his office, returning with a reference book, "He was born on April 20, 1889, in the town of Braunau am Inn in Austria."

"We need to know where," added Jie, "Was he born at his home or in a hospital?"

"Given the era it was most likely a home birth, but we should find out for sure," Pinet agreed and continued to thumb through the book before retrieving another and then several more.

Everyone worked through the chapters looking for a clue until Zielinski slapped the table, "I have it!" Everyone stopped and looked up in anticipation, "He was born in a rented apartment, Salzburger Vorstadt 15!"

"Excellent," announced Pinet, "We have a place and a time, now we simply need to deliver the box and make sure it stays put."

"Perhaps we should do it before Hitler's parents moved in. I doubt the Nazis will be watching the apartment before they get there," Kuznetsov suggested.

"That's a very good idea," Pinet beamed, "That way it can be secured and all we need do is wait for the right moment."

"It looks like Alois; Hitler's father moved into the apartment around 1873. Before that he was in the south of the country," Kuznetsov explained. "So, if we go there before 1873, it should be relatively safe. Our operative could secure the device and wait."

"They'll be waiting a long time," Brigalow suggested, "16 years? That's a big ask."

"Have we got any better ideas," Pinet asked but no-one answered, "Then that's the plan!"

The committee began the search for someone to infiltrate the town of Braunau am Inn. They couldn't advertise for candidates for security reasons, instead using a word-of-mouth approach to find potential agents.

There was indeed a risk that the news might get out anyway, but they could only ask that the information remain confidential and hope that it stayed that way. They weren't detailing the mission initially, just interviewing candidates and assessing their potential for insertion into the chosen era. Only when a candidate proved perfect for the task would the mission be revealed.

1870s Austria was a time of change, just after the Austro-Prussian war which led to a dual monarchy with Hungary and the dawning of the Austro-Hungarian Empire, a close partner of Germany. The Austro-Hungarian Empire would last until the end of World War One.

Interestingly, 1873 was the year of Austrian Emperor, Franz Joseph's Jubilee and it was a time of much celebration and progress in the country with significant levels of construction and expansion. The committee agreed it was a very good time to slip someone in.

The person would need to be fluent in the Germanic languages and know the history of the era, or be able to learn it. They would also need to be strong of mind. Going from

2215 to 1873 would be a huge challenge and one that could be psychologically difficult.

The search was proving fruitless with all the volunteers balking at the idea of living out their lives in the lead up to WW1 and who could blame them?

Weeks went by without luck, so the search was expanded. Contacts inside the United Nations Security Council were used to put up potential candidates but again, when it came to the crunch, no-one wanted to be thrust back to a time preceding the automobile.

The committee knew they were asking a lot, and it was looking like it would have to be handed over to the military so a volunteer could be assigned to the task. While that was indeed an option, it didn't sit well with the concept of blending in. The military of 2215 was strict and disciplined and such a demeanour in 1873 would be out of place in the civilian world, even in Austria. It could so easily attract the wrong kind of attention from Hitler's minders when the family moved into the apartment.

The other issue that was raising concern was security. With so many candidates being vetted, the fear of a security breach was becoming a worry. While most candidates that failed to qualify were sifted out before knowing anything about the mission, wagging tongues always gave the committee a headache. All they could do was have them sign a confidentiality agreement and hope for the best. Adding that a breach could see a catastrophic time paradox occur was generally enough to convince most to remain silent. Of course, once the mission succeeded, none of the candidates would ever know what it was all about anyway.

Then luck finally fell in favour of the committee as a married couple presented themselves for assessment. Rudolph Fischer and his wife Nina were university academics with a fascination for the era, and both spoke the native Austrian language but were also fluent in German. The difference between the two was minuscule, just a few words and dialect variations. They were recommended by the Secretary General herself, personal friends who had studied the era extensively and yearned to experience it firsthand, never believing that such an opportunity could ever exist. After passing the initial security screening, health, and psychological tests, the couple sat with the IG committee to learn of the reasons behind the mission.

Jean Claude Pinet, after completing introductions, addressed the couple, "First of all I will remind you again that no digital record of this process is ever to exist. You cannot tell anyone! If you go on this mission, you will for all intents and purposes simply disappear. I'm sorry if that's distressing but it is essential. There will be no goodbyes. Do you understand?" The couple nodded, although Pinet noted Nina's apprehension and homed in on it, "Is that a problem Nina?"

"No sir. I mean, yes, it is somewhat. My mother is ill and may well pass soon," and she shed a tear.

"I see. In that case I doubt we can offer you the task. I'm sorry," Pinet said.

"Wait. we both want this," Rudolph announced, "If we can get Nina's mother the medical help she needs, we will go. I suppose what I'm trying to do here is negotiate." Pinet raised his eyebrows in astonishment as Rudolph continued, "Her needs are beyond us financially but with the right treatment she may be cured or at least have her life extended for many years. That's what we ask for our services."

Pinet was stunned, "Your motivation is to help Nina's mother? You will go back 342 years in time if we help you? What is your mother's name?"

"Miriam. Miriam Reigler," Nina said.

"Right. Miriam," Pinet confirmed as he looked at the candidate profiles on his tablet. "So, your interest in the era, is that real?"

"Oh yes. We may have embellished things a little, but we have studied the time and the history of Austria extensively. It is a fascinating place," Rudolph explained, "And we have always said if we could build a time machine and go there, we would. As it turns out you have one. Correct?"

Pinet smiled. "You know we have. That's public knowledge."

"Of course. So, we qualify. We have the motivation and we want to do this, so what say you," Rudolph asked.

"Well, wait a minute," Pinet stuttered, "It's not as simple as that. There are many things to consider. What about the way you live now, the comforts you enjoy? How will you cope in 1873 without personal tablets, data streaming, high speed travel, modern food and other conveniences? These things all need to be considered."

Rudolph looked at Jean Claude and smiled. "You speak as if we have no idea what we're going to face but the truth is the opposite. We know exactly what it will be like there. We feel a kinship with the era and the folk who lived then. It was a time of great change; the people were finding their voices, and the country was forging ahead. Why would we *not* wish to witness that firsthand?"

"And, from a woman's point of view, I am captivated by Austrian society. The struggle for suffrage for example occurred around this time," Nina explained.

"That's true," Pinet said. "But it was also a time when the husband had legal control over his wife and women's freedoms were heavily restricted, am I right?"

"You are correct. Austria didn't outlaw adultery or rape until 1989 for example, but I have Rudolph, I will not face those kinds of issues," Nina added.

Pinet looked at her and could see she had already anticipated his next question but asked anyway, "What if something happens to Rudolph; an accident or perhaps, after your mission is complete, he is recruited and has to fight in the war and is killed, you will be alone and..." he didn't elaborate further because he could see she got the point.

"I am willing to take the risk. We will accept whatever happens regardless," and Nina squeezed her husband's hand, and he gave her an approving nod, then she added, "And you underestimate my motivation. I want this for my mother yes, but I want it for me too. I love Austria. Its history, its climate, it's people. I want this more than you can know."

Pinet looked at the other committee members and received affirmative nods, "OK, we would be willing to assist Miriam for you; I give you my word on that, but you don't know what the mission is yet. We will be asking a lot of you to be sure. This may be the deal breaker. There is a risk involved."

Nina looked at Pinet squarely in the eye, "I am not scared. I fear more for my mother than I do myself. I want to do whatever it is you need if it means my mother will live out her life comfortably."

"Very well," Pinet answered, "But again I remind you of the secrecy. If you say no, everything we tell you is never to leave this room, or we will have to prosecute. Do I make myself clear?"

"Yes. Of Course," they both said.

Pinet took a deep breath. "We want you to go back to Austria in 1873, we've already established that, but we want you to go to the town of Braunau am Inn and deliver a package."

"Is that all," asked Rudolph.

"Not quite. The package is critical in a United Nations mission that we hope will correct an atrocity in the history of the World," Pinet said as he saw a light spark in Nina's eye.

"Hitler." she said.

"Yes. In short, we are going to stop him from becoming the Fuhrer and prevent the Nazis from ever existing and thus stop the Holocaust. The United Nations has signed off on the mission, and we have, we believe, the tool to do the job."

Nina and Rudolph looked at each other and smiled then turned to the table of IG delegates, "When do we leave?"

The rest of the meeting was spent going over all the details, including the previous attempts at Fromelles and the shortening of the war by a year, which came as a shock to both.

They'd always believed the Great War had ended in 1917. After everything was laid out for them, they never wavered and the deal was agreed to on a handshake.

Chapter 21 – Infiltrators

Rudolph and Nina Fischer were incredibly knowledgeable about the era they were headed back to, that was indeed a bonus for the mission, but the downside was their lack of mission experience. It would be fair to say they were inept when it came to hiding in plain sight and the focus of their training was designed to give them some of the skills that would not only enable them to execute their mission, but to stay alive if faced with potential danger.

Their ages were also a hindrance, both in their mid-forties and as academics, they were not overly fit, particularly Rudolph. While there were certainly advantages in being older, such as the likelihood of avoiding the attention of Nazi observers, the inability to overcome a physical threat from a trained antagonist who would, likely, be much younger, was a concern.

Training also focussed on ways they could access the Hitler home and deposit the package. It was made very clear to Rudolph that the content would need to be removed from the case and deposited in the right place but hidden from view. He accepted that without question. He didn't need to know about the technicalities of triggering the device.

Given the era, it wasn't likely the apartment building would be like Fort Knox, but a few basic skills needed to be developed. Once the package was in place, their role would simply be one of overwatch, to make certain it wasn't disturbed, which could be a very long time.

To the relief of the IG committee, the Fischers proved very astute in their understanding of the various new skills they needed. Whether or not they could execute those skills in the new reality they would soon face was an unknown.

After several weeks the time came to send them back. Arrangements had been made to move Nina's mother to a care facility that could give her the medical aid she needed and, while deeply saddened by the requirement to just disappear, the Fischers accepted the reality of their choice without complaint.

They entered the Infinity Generator chamber dressed for an Austrian winter in the late 1800s. It would be cold indeed, but they were used to it, although the kit they had in 1873 would be nothing like the warming materials available in 2215 so they would feel the cold. That was certain. They carried two matching bags, one with clothes and other personal amenities and the other with the weapon.

They were ordered to keep it hidden until it could be deposited in the home, preferably in a wall or under the floor where it would not likely be stumbled upon. There it would remain until it could be activated.

As they stepped into the chamber, Jean Claude Pinet farewelled them, "God speed, both of you! You are doing something great for humanity and are saving perhaps millions of lives."

"Thank you," replied Rudolph, "We are privileged."

"And Nina, the arrangements for your mother are well in hand, you need not worry."

"Thank you," was all she said as a tear rolled down her cheek.

Pinet took a deep breath and shook hands with both before stepping back, "Good luck," was all he said as the Infinity Generator spooled up and the white light enveloped the Fischers before they vanished from all they'd known, headed back 342 years to kill Hitler.

No sooner had they disappeared when a warning alarm clanged. Rather than spooling down the IG machine vibrated with more intensity and the light of the vortex increased to a blinding level, "What's happening," Pinet shouted but the technicians and scientists were dumbfounded, "Call security, NOW!!"

The glow didn't dissipate as several armed men entered the room, focussing their weapons on the void. All civilians, including the IG committee members left the chamber room, unsure as to what went wrong.

"What has happened to the Fischers," asked Kelly Antoniadis.

"I don't know," Pinet replied, "I hope they got through."

Pinet and the others looked through the glassed wall of the control room which was full of frantic activity, and it soon became clear that the technicians had lost control of the machine.

Pinet couldn't see the IG chamber from where he stood but he could certainly hear the noise of the machine's generators but then he heard gunfire. The technicians in the control room looked into the chamber, horror on their faces. The gunfire subsided and the technicians, responding to some kind of prompt from within the room, raised their hands.

Pinet wanted to run, as did everyone else but they didn't know what had happened and, as it turned out, wouldn't have made it too far in any case.

The access door to the IG chamber flung open and a dark clad figure holding a large weapon burst into the antechamber that separated the IG machine from the control room raising it to Pinet's head, "Hande Hoch!" the man yelled. Pinet didn't need a translation, instinctively putting his hands up, as did the rest of the committee representatives.

The door opened again as another darkly clad soldier walked in. Pinet could see his security team had all been killed. He could also see more soldiers emerging from the vortex and recalled Janina Zielinski saying that the Nazis of 2337 had managed to keep their wormhole open for up to 30 minutes. It was then that the penny dropped.

The apparent leader of the group barked orders and several soldiers started down the various corridors, checking the facility room by room with occasional spurts of gun fire before the civilians and technicians were herded out of the control room and antechamber and taken to the upper-level board room where they were forced to sit on the floor with their hands behind their heads.

Somehow the invading force had managed to supress the facilities HIT Men robotic soldiers too. Pinet didn't know how, given Zielinski's lack of knowledge about them, but he assumed the Nazis gained the knowledge and found a weakness. It didn't really matter now.

After several more minutes a soldier appeared and spoke to the leader who nodded and seemed to relax. He removed his helmet and balaclava and scanned the people his troops had rounded up, "Who is in charge?"

Jean Claude raised his hand, "Me."

"And who are you," the soldier asked pointedly.

"I'm Jean Claude Pinet, Chairman of the Infinity Generator Committee." There didn't seem much point hiding the fact now.

"Gut!" announced the Nazi, then he added, "Please do not try anything stupid, we have the building and your security forces are all dead."

Several people shrieked in horror, but the Nazi didn't respond until their cries died down. "You need not worry; we are not here to kill all of you."

"Why are you here then," Pinet asked.

The soldier smiled, "You have been trying to do things that we do not like so we have come to stop you."

"I see," Pinet said. "And I'm guessing you have managed some breakthrough with the IG machine in 2337 that enabled you to enter through the machine itself, impressive."

"I do not understand any of that but, yes," the Nazi answered.

"Are you not concerned that you are now trapped in 2215 with no hope of going home? You will ultimately be overcome once the authorities realise what has happened," Pinet suggested.

The soldier smiled widely. "I wouldn't be too sure of that Herr Pinet."

Janina Zielinski couldn't contain herself, "What does that mean?"

The soldier looked at her. "And who are you?"

"I am Helena Mazur, a technical officer here," she said, "What is the breakthrough you seem so happy about?"

The soldier wasn't sure whether he could reveal anything about their technology but then came to the realisation that they would be aware soon enough when several of them were taken to Berlin in 2337, "We can go forward in time now, so we can go home."

"WHAT," Janina exclaimed as many of those in the room gasped in surprise at the news. Janina said, "I don't believe it."

"I assure you, it's true. Our technicians will be here soon to retrofit the device so that we can go back, or forward as the case may be," he scanned the prisoners smiling again, "And I'm pleased to say that many of you will be joining us."

Naturally several exclaimed fear at that news but Janina was concerned that technicians she knew personally would be arriving to update the 2215 IG machine. She knew that her cover would be blown and that would most certainly mean her execution was inevitable.

"Do you really think you can hold the facility long enough to fit your device," Pinet asked.

"Yes, I think so," the soldier said flippantly, "We have much better fire power than you and our technicians have the 2215 schematics and have developed the device to fit your system, so it shouldn't take long."

By now several more soldiers had arrived, streaming through the vortex and taking up strategic defensive positions throughout the building. Once the contingent of Nazi soldiers had arrived, several white coated technical personnel appeared, their apparent leader finding the soldier in the board room. Janina recognised him immediately.

He spoke to the soldier briefly and turned to leave as he cast an eye on the prisoners. He saw Janina and clearly recognised her but said nothing. He was one that Janina trusted and she felt relieved. She couldn't be sure that it would be the same with some of the others. Not all were willing to disrupt the Nazis, and a few were happy to go with the flow, perhaps even blow her cover if there was some kind of advantage in doing so.

"So," the soldier said, "please make yourselves comfortable as we complete our work. The technicians will soon have the machine ready for our return journey. In the meantime, we will be deciding who will accompany us."

"What does that mean," Pinet demanded.

"We will vet everyone, take those we think are important and the rest we will let go," he said.

"You'll just let some of us go," Pinet asked.

"Oh, not you Jean Claude, you I think will be taking a little trip with us, as will all the other members of the committee," to which the soldier then said, "So please raise your hand if you are on the IG committee."

No-one moved.

"Oh dear. That is too bad. I was hoping this would be painless but, if you insist," and the soldier raised his gun and fired a single shot through the head of a young woman sitting a few feet away from him. Her head exploded showering those nearby in blood and brain matter.

Once again, the soldier waited for the screams to fade away before speaking, "Raise your hand if you are on the IG committee. I really do not wish to do that again."

This time all of them complied, except for Kelly Antoniadis.

"Ah, sehr gut! Please, would all the committee members gather over there," he pointed to a side wall in the board room, "Technicians and scientists over there and everyone else against the remaining wall. Dunker!"

Everyone did as they were asked.

"You didn't need to kill her," Pinet said to the soldier. He knew he was probably pushing his luck.

"No, I didn't, but it did speed things up I'm sure you'll agree." And the soldier sneered again, "I will leave you for a while. When I come back some of us will be taking a little trip to Berlin."

Hours went by and the prisoners were getting tired, hungry with many needing to use the amenities. They were allowed to do so under guard while others retrieved food and water from the canteen.

Pinet knew that the UN would be concerned that he hadn't reported in after the Fischers were sent though and would be reacting accordingly. Silence would be met by a defensive condition response. Armed forces would be here soon, if they weren't at the facility already trying to assess the situation and plan an incursion.

The fact that the Nazis had chosen to use the upper board room meant that they were clearly visible, but they didn't seem to care.

Then another thought struck Pinet. The Nazis arrival at the moment the Fischers were sent made him realise that the Fischers had probably failed or ended up in the wrong era;

perhaps even been sent to 2337 when the Nazis infiltrated the vortex. He had no idea. He looked at the faces of his fellow committee members and could see they too had come to the same conclusion.

It felt like hours, but it was probably only another ninety minutes before the soldier returned.

"Good news, we have retrofitted the machine and updated the software. It is now capable of going forward," His sneer was evident, "Our people are very good, are they not?"

Pinet shook his head but said nothing.

"But before we take you to our time, I have a little surprise for you," He stood to attention, as did all the other soldiers in the room, snapping their boot heels together,

"HEIL HITLER!!"

Just then the towering figure of a man strode into the room. He had a limp which was obvious and his head was bald. Janina recognised him immediately and shielded her face just in case he knew who she was although they'd never met.

"Guten tag," said the man, "I am Ernst Pfeiffer!"

When Rudolph and Nina Fischer emerged from the transfer vortex, they were faced with something they could never have anticipated. Instead of emerging outside the Austrian town of Braunau am Inn in 1873, they found themselves in a forested area as expected but it wasn't Austria.

The trees for one thing, were not the pines and firs of an Austrian forest. The other thing they immediately noticed was the heat; it was stifling and certainly not an Austrian winter.

Rudolph looked around. There appeared to be no signs of human activity. No roads or villages anywhere. He looked again at the trees. He was no botanist, but he knew enough to recognise them, "These are Eucalyptus trees Nina. We have landed in the wrong hemisphere I think."

"What," she said in astonishment, "Where do you think we are?"

"If these trees are what I think they are and it is indeed 1873, we can only be in one place," he suggested.

"And where is that, Rudolph," Nina asked.

"Australia!"

Rudolph could see the shock on her face then Nina asked, "Do you suppose there was an error? Australia instead of Austria?"

"I don't know. I suppose it's possible, but we will never figure it out. If we are where I think we are, then we are on the opposite side of the World, almost as far from Austria as you can be on Earth," he said.

Nina wept at their plight and Rudolph soothed her. When she settled down, he said, "Well, there's only one thing to do. We find civilisation and get ourselves on a ship back to Europe as soon as possible."

Nina smiled then frowned, "We won't get there in time, will we?"

"No, the journey will take months, but we'll figure something out," he assured her, "For now though, we need to find out exactly where we are."

Chapter 22 – Interrogation

Ernst Pfeiffer stood over Jean Claude Pinet with a sneer on his smug face, "You have been a pain in my side for a long while. How should I deal with you I wonder?"

Pinet didn't answer and continued to stare at the speckled designs in the grey office carpet upon which he sat. He knew that his life was probably going to end and very soon, now that the Nazis had infiltrated their complex.

They had modified the IG machine and could now transport people back to 2337. He writhed inside at the horror of it all. He was equally distressed by the apparent failure of their mission, which had only just been executed when the vortex was interrupted. He wondered what effect it might have had but couldn't concentrate on the puzzle under the current circumstances.

Pfeiffer was angered by Pinet's failure to respond and kicked him in his left side causing Pinet to slump over and cough.

"Now, I wonder if you would perhaps like to see what the world is like in my time, hmm? You might like it." He looked around the room, "I'm sure many of you have the kinds of skills we're looking for in the Reich. We have so many plans with our machine."

"We would not have the advanced knowledge of your own scientists' Herr Pfeiffer," Pinet said, "and I'm sure you are aware of that."

"Oh, but you are all highly intelligent people. I'm sure some retraining would be all that is required," Pfeiffer suggested before adding, "Of course we will not need all of you, that is true. We will take the best of the best back with us. I'm not certain as to what to do with the rest of you."

"What are you hoping to achieve by coming here? You cannot destroy the machine, or you will be stuck. Your trip is rather pointless," Pinet explained pointedly.

Pfeiffer didn't appreciate the jibe, "We will do enough to disrupt you and take your best people with us. That should be more than enough to stop you."

Pinet looked up at Pfeiffer's unsavoury face, "You have a problem Ernst. For a start, I wonder how you intend to hold this facility. You must be expecting a breach and when that happens, you will have to leave and coming back to this time will be more difficult, I'm sure you realise that. You can't return to a time where you have already been. That would be very messy I think."

"Perhaps, but we have the advantage of being able to pop in and out of any time that suits our needs so you will never know where or when we will be, and we can send people to this exact moment repeatedly. Just different people," Pfeiffer snarled.

"That's true I suppose," Pinet said, "But we have stifled everything you have attempted so far. That must really irk you."

"Ah but now I know your names and will soon know where you are from and who your families are. With that knowledge I will be able to dispose of the threat you have become. You will simply cease to exist," Pfeiffer announced which caused a stir amongst the captives.

Pinet didn't hesitate, "Be careful Ernst. Dispose of the wrong person and you may change things enough to eliminate this facility or change the way it is used. You know as well as I that change has ramifications through time."

"I am all too aware of that. You have been trying to erase us by killing the Fuhrer have you not? That I cannot tolerate and that is why I am here. To erase the threat," Pfeiffer declared.

"Then why don't you kill me now?"

"In good time Herr Pinet. You have knowledge I require before that and I intend to extract it from you, and your colleagues."

"What information, Pinet wondered.

"Well for instance, I'm told you have just transferred operatives into the past. You have managed to set up an auto erase on the logs, so we don't know where or when, but I know why. You must tell us who they are and what they will try so we can stop them," Pfeiffer demanded, and if you will not, I'm sure someone will squeal. You can't all stay quiet, hmm?"

"I don't know what you're talking about. We sent no-one," Pinet stated unconvincingly.

"Tut tut Herr Pinet; you cannot hide the energy signatures even if you can erase the logs. My people know this. Where did they go," Pfeiffer demanded.

"So, this is the interrogation," Pinet asked.

Pfeiffer smiled, "I'm trying to give you the opportunity to do this the easy way. It's a onetime offer. Refusal will have consequences and you really don't want to know what happens after that, but I can assure you it will be very painful!"

"Of course it will," Pinet said with an obvious squirm that delighted Pfeiffer, "But that's how you people roll isn't it? Terror, hate, torture and murder The World doesn't seem to have progressed much at all."

"Oh, but we have. The future, our present will ensure the purity of humanity. In time the tyranny you allude to will subside and the planet will see unparalleled peace and prosperity," declared Pfeiffer.

"You delude yourself. While ever there is tyranny, there will be people who will rise. You Nazis never have figured that out and that will be the reason for your demise." Pinet's remarks resulted in another kick to the kidney.

"You seem to forget that we now have the power to travel across time in both directions. From now on we control time and therefore control the World in our own time and beyond!"

"But you can only do so much with the past. Even now you grasp 2215 by your fingernails. Within hours, perhaps only minutes our security forces will breach the facility and kill whoever is still here. You have no time," Pinet reminded him and got a knee to the jaw for his trouble, but he was right.

"Enough of this," and Pfeiffer turned to his men, "Sort these people out. Bring those that have anything we need and kill the rest!"

There were shrieks of horror from the captives as Ernst Pfeiffer strode away but then he stopped and looked back at Jean Claude, "You, Herr Pinet will be the first to try a trip forward in time. We need to know absolutely if it will work. You are our guinea pig!"

Pinet smiled, "So you were stupid enough to come back and fit an untested system. Why am I surprised? You may well be stuck here Ernst." And Pinet laughed.

The remark wiped the smirk off Pfeiffer's face and he stormed off shouting, "Bring him with the others as soon as you have them sorted. We return to 2337 as soon as possible. Vet them quickly," Pfeiffer demanded.

"Sieg Heil," came the collective response.

Soldiers herded the captives into smaller groups and quickly asked their names, titles, and their areas of expertise. Many were sobbing at the prospect of being taken away from life as they knew it. The dilemma was that if you weren't useful, you would probably be killed, so lying about what you could do was as good as suicide. All hoped that a breach and rescue operation was close at hand.

Jean Claude Pinet did his best to calm everyone down and he was assaulted once again for his troubles. He sat with the other committee members watching the process with people, having been interrogated, grouped into two categories, those who would be leaving and those who would soon be dead.

Pinet then looked across at Janina Zielinski as she was confronted by one of the interrogators. Whatever was said resulted in more questions and before long three interrogators were questioning her. One of them left and returned with a scientist who had travelled back with the Nazis. The guard pointed at Zielinski, "Who is this woman?"

"How should I know?" the scientist replied but even Pinet could tell he was lying which the guard also noticed.

"You lie" and the guard buried the stock of his weapon into the man's stomach. The scientist fell and coughed, "We can now replace you with one of these people, so don't think for a second that you are indispensable," the guard added.

When the scientist gained his breath, he looked at Janina and said, "I'm sorry," then turned to the guard, "She is Janina Zielinski. The one who is missing."

The guard immediately pointed his weapon at Janina, "Stand up," he demanded and led her away, presumably to reveal the discovery to Ernst Pfeiffer. She didn't look back at Jean Claude or the others, probably in the vain hope that they wouldn't be implicated in her ruse. Pinet wondered if she revealed herself to save him.

At that very moment there was an explosion downstairs followed by gunfire. The difference between the weapons was clear, the staccato fire of the Nazi weapon was much more apparent in terms of power than the guns of 2215, much more rapid too.

Jean Claude Pinet realised that if their rescuers broke through, the Nazi guards might just kill everyone in the room out of hand. Right now, they looked surprised but not in a panic which Pinet read as a good thing, for the moment. He turned to his colleagues and said, "We don't have much time. Get ready to run. They will kill us if the UN soldiers get close. Does anyone have access to a weapon?" No-one did. "Never mind. Watch the guards and if they start to get skittish, we make a break. Grab anything to defend yourself."

For the moment the vetting process paused, and all the guards and interrogators stood and grouped into a defensive formation as the gun play continued. Then another explosion, louder this time followed by more staccato exchanges. It was clear the UN soldiers were closing in.

Pinet looked again at the Nazis and saw they were now looking apprehensive. The second in command sent one of his men to check on the situation with the IG machine when the building vibrated as the IG power generators ramped up.

The gunfire quelled and everyone waited and wondered what might have happened. The Nazis were wondering the same thing.

Then something bounced into the board room followed by a blaze of light that blinded everyone. It was followed by a series of concussion grenades which bounced and exploded, shaking everyone to their cores.

It was lucky that all the captives were sitting because what happened next, happened so fast that no-one standing could respond. A spray of automatic weapon fire criss-crossed the void hitting the Nazi soldiers multiple times. They didn't even have time to squeeze off any rounds in reply. Their body armour was high tech but at this range the velocity of the hits was enough to penetrate their suits and kill most, leaving the rest with severe wounds.

When the gunfire died and the smoke thinned, all the Nazi guards were down. Thankfully most everyone else in the room were unscathed, except for the ringing in their ears and a few nose bleeds from the concussion blasts.

The UN Commander in charge yelled, "Where are they?"

Pinet pointed to the left, "The IG room! Careful, Pfeiffer is there. The soldier looked confused. "The Nazi leader," Pinet screamed.

The UN soldiers headed up the corridor towards the transfer room just as the building shook violently and the bright light from the transfer chamber cascaded down the access way. Then the generators wound down, the light faded and there was silence.

Pinet stood up and brushed himself off, as did everyone else. They all waited, wondering what happened when the UN commander walked back into the room. He looked at Pinet, "They're gone."

Pinet's gut twisted, "Was there a woman in there, one of ours?"

The soldiers shook his head, "I'm sorry, the room is empty."

Jean Claude and the rest of the committee members and many staff ran into the IG room but all they saw were UN soldiers. The Nazis had managed to fire up the machine and presumably returned to 2337 and they had Janina, "Oh no," Pinet said.

"What will happen to her," Gabrielle Fawcett asked out loud.

"I don't know, I don't even want to think about it," Pinet replied but he was thinking about it, as was everyone else. They would probably execute her, and the others that helped her. Their future allies, who had been feeding them critical information, would probably now die and give the Nazis yet another advantage.

Pinet didn't hesitate, "OK, we need to find out what happened to the Fischers. We need to know where they are and why they have failed in their mission." No-one moved, "Quickly, check everything. There may be a clue the Nazi's missed!"

People scurried in all directions, checking logs, computer data, encrypted files, whatever they could to see where the Fischers landed. Then one of their interns noticed something and called to Pinet who strode over to the main computer terminal of the IG machine. The cadet pointed at something. Jean Claude leaned in to take a look. He examined the thing for a moment and then stood with a huge smile on his face.

"What is it Jean Claude," asked Sunil Patel.

Pinet turned to the committee, "The idiots didn't consider how to take their device home."

"What does that mean," Fawcett asked him as everyone stood there looking confused.

Pinet pointed to a device that had been plugged into the main IG quantum computer, "This device is what they created to make the machine go forward in time. They left it here. They either had no time to retrieve it, or they didn't think about how to get it back while it was being used."

"Or, one of our sympathisers in 2337 made this happen," suggested Anastasia Kuznetsov.

"Indeed, that may well be the case, which is very fortunate, because we now possess the device and the software to make it work for us," Pinet said with a grin.

It was only at that moment that the penny really dropped with everyone on the committee and they all laughed. Being in the future was no longer to the Nazi's advantage. Their stupidity, or whatever it was, had just levelled the playing field.

"Janina was right about them, they are arrogant to a fault," Muhammad Galal said, then added, "Can we save her?"

"Doubtful, but we have to try," Pinet said.

They then returned to the board room and saw the now shrouded body of Kelly Antoniadis. There was silence for a few moments before Pinet announced, "That could have been any one of us."

Everyone nodded in agreement, "What will we tell her family," asked Luciana Gonzales?"

"The usual," Pinet added, "She was killed trying to keep the peace."

"That's essentially true," Sunil Patel agreed.

Pinet looked back at his fellow committee members, "Well, I need to make some calls and get this cleaned up," and he waved his hand around the room full of bodies and bullet holes, "If anyone needs anything like counselling, it can be arranged. I need you all at one hundred percent. We have a lot of work to do. First and foremost, we must find out what happened to the Fischers!"

Chapter 23 – Back to the Future

This time it was Janina Zielinski who sat on the filthy floor of a prison cell. The slime she was soaking in was a mixture of human waste, vomit and blood from previous victims. Her flesh was swollen and bruised. Her half naked body was covered in welts and burns from relentless torture.

Despite the modern techniques available like brain stem spasms, these Nazis preferred the old ways and took great delight in it.

Janina was exhausted and was about to drop off to sleep when speakers in the cell blasted her awake with a shrieking siren. Torture didn't always mean inflicting pain. Sleep deprivation was another tactic the Nazis employed. Janina thought about giving up but snapped out of it; she wasn't going to betray her colleagues. Instead, she tried to convince the Nazis that she was a lone wolf.

If she could hold out until she was dead, they might just believe it too. The cell became silent and, in a few minutes, she drifted off again, managing a few sacred moments of bliss before the horn shocked her awake again.

Janina had lost track of time completely. She had no idea if it was day or night or what day it was. Perhaps she'd only been in there for a week, but to her if seemed much longer. While she was awake, she contemplated death again. When she snatched a few vital minutes of sleep she rejoiced at some happy dreams but always, in the back of her mind, was the knowledge that the door would soon open again and her torturer would return to hand out another hour or two of pain and punishment for defying the Reich.

Almost on cue, the door burst open but this time it wasn't her torturer, it was a soldier, then another and then two more.

They said nothing but grabbed Janina who winced in pain as they dragged her from the cell and into the dark corridor.

She was zigged and zagged through the bowels of the Nazi fortress, no doubt designed to confuse anyone stupid enough to escape.

A few minutes later she exited the labyrinth into the brightness of day, briefly blinding her after spending however long, in pitch darkness. It took her eyes quite a while to adjust after she was dumped on the ground, but when she could look around, she saw several Nazi uniforms, most of them armed soldiers in a line.

The gorilla like figure of Ernst Pfeiffer stood close by and she saw a row of white coated scientists and physicians kneeling with their hands tied behind their backs, seven of them in all. They showed no signs of having been tortured but the terror on their faces spoke volumes.

When Ernst Pfeiffer realised that she was lucid and able to absorb the scene he strode over to her, his heavy boots crunching on the courtyard gravel. "Thank you so very much for joining us, Janina. I'm glad you could spare the time," he said then added, "I hope you're finding your accommodations comfortable."

She didn't answer but managed to smile because she knew it would piss him off, which it did. He grabbed her mottled hair which was matted with dry blood and other gore, "You see these men and women? They are your colleagues, people you love and trust and who no doubt trusted you. I am giving you one final chance to give up your co-conspirators. Tell me now and they go free and you die quickly and painlessly."

"It's only me. No-one else," she squeaked.

"Oh Janina, I haven't told you the good part yet. If you refuse to give them up, then I kill these people one by one. It's a simple transaction really. Your life and the lives of the other traitors to save the lives of the innocent," Pfeiffer explained.

She knew how the process worked and looked over at the seven. She knew them all. Four of them were clueless, that was certain, one was indeed up to his neck in conspiracy, but the Nazis clearly didn't know that and the other two probably knew something was going on but that was all. That's what she hoped anyway.

"I've told you everything. I acted alone. These people are innocent."

"That's what I thought you would say," Pfeiffer noted as he nodded to one of the soldiers which resulted in the sharp crack of a rifle and the head of the first scientist exploded, one of the innocents.

Janina slumped as cries of terror and anguish erupted from the six remaining hostages, "Please Janina, tell him, for pity's sake," said one of the female scientists.

"Yes Janina, for pity's sake, tell us what we know to be true, that there are others in your traitorous group who need to die," added Pfeiffer.

She shook her head, "You are as stupid as you are ugly. There isn't anyone else. How many times do I have to say it?"

Pfeiffer nodded again and another gunshot saw a second scientist hit the ground headless, followed by the expectant shrieks of horror from those remaining.

"You can save these people Janina. All you have to do is point out your co-conspirators. Then it can be all over for you. I know that's what you want," Pfeiffer teased.

"What I want is an end to the Nazis and if I can't have that, then I don't want to be here," and she spat on Pfeiffer's left boot.

He nodded again and the third scientist fell.

"Surely you can see how this is going to end. These people will all be dead because of you. You don't want that," suggested Pfeiffer.

"Of course, not but there's one thing you will never understand Ernst."

"And what might that be," he asked with a dismissive tone.

"They are but a few individuals. If they all have to die for the greater good, so be it!"

Pfeiffer looked at her in surprise, "You don't care if these people die?"

"Of course I do, but what you don't get Ernst," she continued to use his first name as a sign of disrespect for his position, "is that I am not going to break. You can kill all of us and I still won't tell you anything."

"So, you will let them die, for what," Pfeiffer asked.

"To ensure that you never know if it's just me or a huge network trying to undermine you. Seven or eight lives are worth that," Janina said then added, "So go right ahead, finish us off. I'm over it."

Ernst Pfeiffer had never been spoken to like this before. Moreover, he was completely taken back by her defiance. Her strength under incredible duress impressed him. She could have been a great asset to the Reich with her resolve, but alas, she was the enemy, beyond salvation. "Very well."

Pfeiffer was about to give the order to kill them all when his aid burst onto the courtyard looking quite flustered, "Mein Fuhrer," he called.

"What is it," Pfeiffer yelled in frustration.

"Sir, we have a problem."

"What now," Pfeiffer demanded.

"It's a message sir."

"From whom?"

"Jean Claude Pinet sir! He demands that you spare the life of Janina Zielinski or suffer the consequences."

"WHAT?!" Pfeiffer screamed in a rage as he stormed out of the courtyard and back to his office leaving his SS officers and troopers nonplussed. There was no order to kill the remaining scientists, and they dared not do it without his say so. They didn't know what to do so they waited.

Janina Zielinski simply smiled.

When Pfeiffer returned to his office, he read the message from Jean Claude Pinet. It was succinct but there was no doubting the intent. Pfeiffer punched his desk and the antique tabletop cracked, "How did this happen," he screamed, "How did they manage to send us a message?"

His aid was terrified but knew he had to answer, "It would appear sir that you may have left our technology on their device." Pfeiffer shot the aid a look of evil intent having been personally blamed for the error and the aid corrected himself clumsily, "I mean whoever it was that fitted the device, they are to blame of course...sir!"

"So, you are telling me that those idiots in 2215 now have the capacity to move forward in time too?"

"Yes sir, that is correct."

"BRING ME KLAUSS HAAS," bellowed Pfeiffer. The aid was about to move when Pfeiffer changed his mind, "No wait. I will go to him. Make the arrangements."

"Yes sir!"

"And bring that bitch Zielinski and the scientists too. I have an idea," Pfeiffer added.

"SIEG HEIL," cried the aid as he gave the Nazi salute, snapping his heels and making a hasty exit.

A day later Pfeiffer, Janina and the remaining scientists were in Cern at the IG facility. Pfeiffer was in the office of Klaus Haas demanding answers, "Please my friend, explain to me how we managed to leave valuable technology in the past for our enemies to use against us?"

Haas didn't look particularly worried but decided to be cautious, "Ernst, you took scientists into a hostile situation. They were ill equipped. As I understand it there was no time to retrieve the device or delete the software. They cannot be blamed for wanting to escape."

Pfeiffer was furious, "You should have known but you said nothing!"

"Of course," Haas conceded, "But you did not tell me of the potential for conflict. I was led to believe that your insurgency would take over the facility, hold it and bring back the antagonists. That clearly didn't happen."

Pfeiffer didn't like being made a fool of, not even from someone he called friend, "Be careful Klaus. We are friends yes, but this is business. They do not mix well."

"Of course, Ernst, I'm sorry, but there's little can be done about it now."

"On the contrary," Pfeiffer replied, "I believe we have an ace up our sleeve, and I intend to use it."

"Zielinski?!"

"Yes! I want you to send Pinet a message and invite him to parlay; Zielinski's life for the device."

Haas smiled, "That's brilliant. I'll see to it."

Pfeiffer relaxed then looked at Haas, "Do you believe she is acting alone Klaus?"

"I have seen nothing to suggest that my people are trying to undermine the Reich. I am confident they are all with us."

"I don't know. It's hard to believe that she could disrupt us without help, particularly given that several of our actions were intercepted after she disappeared," Pfeiffer suggested giving Haas a look that could only mean he was likely being duped by his own people.

Klaus Haas gulped, "I vetted them all myself when I got here. No-one set off any alarm bells. I don't imagine that they could hide their fear when it came to the crunch."

"Maybe but I'm still convinced we have enemies within the facility," Pfeiffer added.

"Then I will flush them out," Haas announced.

"Yes, you will Klaus and you will do so very soon, and I don't think I need to explain the price of failure," Pfeiffer said pointedly.

"Of course," Haas replied realising he'd painted himself into a corner.

Messages and demands were negotiated back and forth between 2215 and 2337 via a stable, two-way wormhole established by the Nazis.

Pfeiffer made sure that the device was part of the negotiation pointing out that it was the only way to save Janina Zielinski. He knew that Pinet would have no choice but to meet the Nazi demands. His final message was received and the terms agreed to.

The next day the IG transfer room shimmered, and Jean Claude Pinet emerged from the vortex with a security detail, carrying a case. The wormhole, as agreed to in the terms of the parlay would remain open so that Pinet could return home immediately with Janina.

Ernst Pfeiffer was pleased with himself when he saw the case, but still had to force himself to be polite, "Welcome to the Nazi Reich of 2337 Jean Claude."

Jean Claude ignored the Nazi reference and simply said, "Thank you."

"Do you have the device?"

"Of course," Pinet answered." Then asked, "Where is Janina?"

Pfeiffer snapped his fingers and two guards dragged a haggard, bruised and bloodied woman into the IG transfer room. "Here she is. I'm afraid she wasn't very cooperative."

Pinet was shocked at the sight of her but bit his tongue. As much as he wanted to lose his temper and serve Pfeiffer a tirade, he knew better of it. "Are you all right Janina?"

She looked up at Jean Claude. "I'm just peachy," which made him smile.

The remark annoyed Pfeiffer and his patience evaporated. "Show me the device!"

"Of course."

Pinet laid the case on the floor and typed in the security code when Pfeiffer reacted, "Slowly Jean Claude. No tricks."

"I'm hardly in any position to play games," Pinet replied which made Pfeiffer smile this time. Jean Claude Pinet had raised his hand to indicate that nothing untoward would happen then finished entering the code, popping the lid of the case. He opened it slowly and turned it around so Pfeiffer could see the contents.

"Klaus," Pfeiffer ordered

Klaus Haas walked over and looked in the case, spent a few moments investigating the device and turned to Pfeiffer nodding.

"That's everything Jean Claude," Pfeiffer asked.

"Yes. We have completely removed all your equipment. It is all here intact. No tricks I promise you," Pinet reiterated.

Pfeiffer paused as Haas whispered something in his ear which appeared to pique his interest, "And what of the software?"

"Deleted as you requested. It's useless to us without the device in any case," Pinet told them.

Then Klaus Haas had a thought, "And you have not replicated our device," which raised Pfeiffer's eyebrows in surprise.

"No, we have not. Of course we considered it, but there was no time and, frankly, it's beyond our capabilities as you know," Pinet told Haas.

Haas smiled and took the case, "Of course. Just checking. In any case it's useless without access to xillinium."

Pfeiffer was confused momentarily until Haas gave him reassuring nod again. Pfeiffer then nodded to the guards who threw Zielinski at Pinet's feet, "We will see you soon Jean Claude," Pfeiffer sneered.

Pinet gave a gracious nod, helped Janina to her feet and headed for the void.

"I look forward to it Ernst," Pinet said with a smile before disappearing into the light.

Chapter 24 – The Fischers

Rudolph and Nina Fischer struggled through the bush, searching for civilisation. They still carried the bag that contained the World War 2 relic that they had been charged with delivering to the future home of the Hitler family in Austria, but they were certainly in no position to do so.

Rudolph's suspicions about where they were deposited by the IG machine were confirmed when they disturbed a mob of Kangaroos which bolted after being startled by the pair as they stumbled along in search of a settlement.

The heat was stifling and Nina was struggling, having had nothing to eat or drink for the better part of the day. It was now growing dark, and she was beginning to panic.

Being academics, their forest skills were basically nil which meant one or two more days in this wilderness would undoubtedly see them perish. Rudolph noticed Nina's complexion; she was dehydrated and in desperate need of water, "It should be cooler after dark; we can rest then."

"And after that," Nina asked.

"We might get lucky tomorrow," he replied.

"Well, we need something to happen or there won't be a day after that I fear," Nina added.

The pair struggled on, pushing aside shrubs and branches, looking for a place to rest. They'd been walking for endless hours and hadn't found any sign of humanity, nor had they discovered a creek or a pond.

They were hot, sunburnt and overdressed, forcing them to shed their overcoats. Movement proved particularly difficult for Nina who was wearing a bodice and petticoat, which was extremely inconvenient in a wooded setting. It was already filthy and tangled with twigs and grasses. To add to their misery, they were constantly harassed by flies.

They heard a rumbling sound and, when they broke out of some thick vegetation into a clearing and saw storm clouds in the distance. A grey curtain of rain quenched the bushland. They could even smell it, but it was nowhere near and quickly veered away.

The clearing did have one positive though; they were able to see down into a valley and noticed gullies which could lead them to a creek or perhaps a river. They decided to camp where they were for the night, snatch some sleep and hope they had better fortune in the morning.

As darkness descended an exhausted Nina Fischer, drifted off to sleep. Rudolph was about to lay down on the grass and sleep a few hours too when something caught his eye.

At first, he thought it might be lightning from the distant thunder clouds, but when he turned his head in the direction of the glint, he realised it was a campfire. There were people in the valley, and they weren't too far away. He wanted to wake Nina and tell her but thought better of it. They could sleep now and make for the camp in the morning. He felt too excited to sleep but eventually his fatigue got the better of him and he fell into deep unconsciousness.

As dawn broke, they were awakened from their slumber, not by the light on a new day but by voices not far away. Rudolph jumped to his feet and scanned the area looking for the source. It took all but a second for him to see the men, a group of three, all with rifles. Rudolph, being a historian noticed they were not flintlock weapons, but lever action, which was more common in the later 1800s, so he was satisfied they were in the right era.

The trio all wore big round hats, long sleeved shirts with canvas pants held up by braces, and old dirty brown boots. Their skin was darkly tanned from exposure to this environment over many years. One of them spoke and

Rudolph understood the remark. "I see the mob on the rise, about two hundred yards."

The accent was Irish, but the reply wasn't, "I see em Paddy, now shut up before you scare them off!" This time the accent was a peculiar mix of English cockney, Irish and other variations of English mixed up into a twangy drawl Rudolph didn't recognise. The third man said nothing at all.

As they stalked the kangaroo which were oblivious to the danger, the trio spread out to give themselves a better chance of nabbing a roo. Rudolph noticed two of the kangaroos were standing face to face and kicking each other in mock battle. He thought it a curious activity but considered it was natural for these creatures.

When the men got close one signalled and the trio fired. One of the boxing kangaroos fell, instantly dead, another tried to hop away but was mortally wounded. The rest bolted.

The sudden triple blast woke Nina who screamed in shock, which in turn attracted the attention of the hunters, who now looked towards the odd pair. One of the men said something and the fellow known as Paddy ran off to collect the kangaroo that had just been shot. The remaining pair moved towards Rudolph and Nina, their guns pointed to the ground, which Rudolph saw as a good sign.

"Good morning," said the apparent leader of the group. "You look to be quite lost."

Rudolph could see that Nina was afraid, but he had a feeling there wasn't anything to worry about, "Yes, I'm afraid we're a bit out of our depth."

"That's obvious. You're certainly not dressed for this part of the world," the man said.

"Well, again I cannot disagree," Rudolph added. He knew the most difficult question was about to come.

"So, I hear an accent, what is that? Where are you folks from?"

And there it was. Rudolph had to think fast. "Well, it's a long story. We've been travelling for a long time and, yes, we got lost along the way. We were following a road but somehow it turned out to be nothing and by then it was too late." He didn't reveal much with the explanation, but it sounded feasible to him, and it was.

The man smiled, "Well it happens often, believe me. Are you headed to Melbourne then?"

"Yes! That's right, Melbourne," Rudolph said taking the opportunity offered.

"Where have you come from?"

Another question that was difficult to answer but a generic answer was again all Rudolph offered, "Oh up north, you know?"

"Yes, I do, everyone wants to get in on the action," the man suggested.

"Action," Rudolph replied, perplexed by the remark.

"Why, gold of course. the goldfields? I assume that's what you're doing here," the man said as he scratched his forehead, clearly confused by the dumbfounded couple.

"Oh, well, yes and no. We're teachers."

That seemed to have a very positive effect on the pair as Paddy returned with the kill. "Oh, that explains the clothing because you certainly don't look like prospectors." The men laughed.

Rudolph smiled. "No, we're certainly not."

"I'm still trying to work out the accent," the man said, "Where did you come from?"

"Originally?" Rudolph asked and the man nodded, "Well, Nina and I are from Austria, but we lived in other places as well, most recently Switzerland."

"Ah I see, well yes, I can hear that." He then looked at Nina. "Madame, you look like you've been without food or water for a while, may we be of assistance?"

Nina smiled and nodded, "Yes, thank you."

"My name is Bill Williamson. I'm the manager of these parts, this is Paddy but he's, well he's Paddy." The men laughed. "And this bloke is a mad Scotsman named; well, we call him Scotty. It saves us a lot of bother," and they laughed again as they shook hands with Rudolph.

"My name is Rudolph. Rudolph Fischer and this is my wife, Nina. I'm pleased to meet you and so glad you found us," Rudolph said.

"Well, you're only a little way off course but I think we need to get you to the homestead, fed and cleaned up before you continue your journey," Bill suggested.

"That sounds wonderful," Nina said as she stood and brushed herself off.

"And perhaps my wife, Jane, can help you with that dress. It's taken a bit of a beating," Bill added.

"Yes. Thank you for your kindness," Nina said.

"Don't mention it," Bill replied.

Then Rudolph asked, "Was that your campfire we saw last night?" The question drew a swift glance from Bill.

"No, that would have been those no-good cattle thieves. We've been trying to catch them but they're slippery beggars. Good thing you didn't approach them, they may well have shot you both," Bill said with a frown.

"You have cattle," Rudolph asked as he salivated.

"Yes, quite a herd in these parts, one of the biggest properties in the colony of Victoria. Herefords mainly, great meat and there are plenty of mouths to feed these days with the influx of people to the colony," Bill explained.

"Beef. That sounds very nice," said Rudolph. "I could eat anything at the moment."

Bill looked at him and said, "Have you ever tried Kangaroo," and Paddy held up the fresh kill as blood drained from the bullet hole in its head. As he held the animal up by its tail, he was beaming a smile that revealed a few missing teeth.

"Um, no, I haven't,' and he looked at Nina who seemed to have gone white which Bill also noticed.

"Well, you're in for a treat. It's a very fine meat, once you get used to it," The trio laughed. "Come on, this way, we have water, I'm sure you're parched. We'll get home in time for lunch."

"That sounds great, thank you again," Rudolph said.

Bill started his next sentence the usual way, "Well, we can't have people getting all lost and ending up dead around here. That wouldn't be proper," and he smiled broadly revealing a full set of teeth.

The water was a Godsend and they drank it down, spilling as much as they swallowed. They didn't realise how thirsty they were until they took a few sips, then they couldn't stop.

"Steady on," advised Bill. "You might make yourself sick if you have too much. We've got plenty. With that they stopped. Three horses were tied up under a grove of trees. "Whose riding with me?"

Rudolph thought it might be best is Nina rode behind Bill and suggested and he climbed onto Scotty's horse as they set off. Neither of them had ridden before and they didn't like it. It was bumpy and uncomfortable and Rudolph asked Scotty, who'd said nothing to this point, "How far to the house?"

In a thick accent Scotty said, "A wee under three hours."

"Three hours," Rudolph said in alarm.

"Aye. Not long," Scotty replied

Rudolph looked at Nina who appeared very uncomfortable but there was little they could do but hold on.

Bill realised their plight and told them both, "Just relax and let your bodies move with the horses, it'll be easier for you both."

They didn't answer but followed his advice and discovered that it worked very well.

They both marvelled at the amazing landscape in this part of Australia. It was a wonderful country and full of wildlife, screeching birds, kangaroos and even a huge lizard of some kind which Bill told them was a goanna.

They reached the homestead just as the heat started to harass them again. A woman came to the door upon hearing the horses and called out, "What the Devil brought you home so soon…" But then she saw the two strangers. "Never mind, I'll set some places for lunch," and she went inside.

"Seems you've had unexpected guests before," Rudolph gleaned from Jane's reaction.

"Oh yes, you'd be surprised," he said as he expertly slid off his horse.

He graciously helped Nina down, grasping her around the waist and gently placing her on the grass. She blushed. Rudolph's landing wasn't so elegant, and he fell on his bottom which Paddy thought was most amusing.

"Come on, we'll wash up before we eat," and he took them around to a basin outside the house. He dunked his hat in first and filled it with water then tipped the whole thing over his face before washing his hands up to his elbows. "Come on, dive in, it's time to eat."

The other two did the same leaving the basin brown with dust and dirt and who knows what else. Rudolph and Nina washed up, drying their hands on their clothing as did Bill, Paddy and Scotty.

They all walked back around to the front of the homestead, a wooden boarded building with a veranda and a pitched roof.

Bill led them inside, along a short hallway, into a kitchen where Jane was gathering extra plates. He then showed them to the dining room where they all sat to eat lunch.

Jane brought the plates in and placed them in front of the men and Nina, smiling. She left briefly and returned with a huge pot of stew.

"Here's your roo from yesterday. I wish you could snag a rabbit or something. I'm getting a bit sick of roo."

"Well, the roos are easier to shoot, and they don't hide under the ground when they see you," said Bill, causing the other men to laugh.

"Yeah, well, I'll make you gut a few and you'll soon change your mind," Jane declared. "So, aren't you going to introduce me to these fine folks Bill or have you forgotten your manners," and she took her seat.

"I was about to do so darling", he said smiling. "This is Rudolph Fischer and his wife Nina," then he turned to them and said, "and this is my wife, Jane."

She was indeed beautiful. She wore a light dress and short sleeved blouse, much cooler for the conditions. Her hair was long and straight, blonde and she had steel blue eyes, "Welcome to our home but before we can eat, Bill, will you say grace please."

Rudolph and Nina watch the little ceremony, captivated at witnessing firsthand, the way of life in 1873, Australia. The short prayer of thanks ended and Bill said, "Beauty Jane, looks good." He filled everyone's plates with Kangaroo stew, a mix of meat, vegetables and broth and some homemade bread to mop it up.

Rudolph tried the meat as Nina watched. It was strong in flavour and a little tough. He wondered what it might be like if it were not stewed, like rubber perhaps, not that these people would know what rubber was, but he liked it and nodded, "Very good. Very good."

"Thank you," Jane replied.

Nina tasted it too and agreed that it was lovely although she wasn't sure if she believed it or was just plain hungry.

After the meal and the conversation Jane said, "You're welcome to stay the night. Tomorrow, if you feel up to it, you can get back to the road and head for Melbourne but if I were you, I'd stay an extra day and take the Cobb and Co coach into the city. You'll be there much faster and in slightly better comfort, but I can't guarantee it," which resulted in a chuckle again. "It passes here every week."

Rudolph smiled and simply said thank you again and ate his meal. He listened to the conversational exchanges between his hosts and was intrigued by the way they talked and the issues that confronted them. Simple things like clearing rocks from the new cattle yards, mucking out stables, checking the stock dam. As someone who studied languages and people, this was truly incredible to witness.

The rest of the day involved chores which Rudolph helped the men with and he enjoyed it. A bit of strenuous labour wasn't something he was used to, and he felt it as the day wore on.

The men planned to head back out onto the property the next day to check on the cattle and to maybe find the cattle thieves that had been seen on the property. They invited Rudolph and he eagerly accepted but wasn't too keen on riding again. Nina would remain at the homestead with Jane, as was the way of the time. Jane seemed more independent a woman than one might expect in this era, which was refreshing as far as Nina was concerned.

The evening meal was the same as lunch followed by cups of tea. Paddy and Scotty retired to the staff quarters after the meal and Rudolph and Nina spent the rest of the evening chatting with Bill and Jane. They all very much enjoyed each other's company which surprised Rudolph given the vast differences between them, not that their hosts would be at all aware of it.

The evening went quickly and soon it was time for bed. Rudolph and Nina were shown to a guest bedroom where they settled into a small, springy bed, nothing like the comforts of home. These people went to bed early but that didn't stop Rudolph and Nina from falling asleep. They were quite exhausted after their recent adventures.

The next day, Rudolph rode out with the others as planned which gave Nina a chance to talk woman to woman for the first time in a long while. She enjoyed the opportunity and was delighted by Jane's openness and her obvious intelligence.

As the day wore on Nina came to realise how simple life was here. No electricity or running water, no Internet or television and no virtual reality cineplex, just work and sleep. It was, in a way, quite relaxing but she wondered how long she could last before boredom took over but then, there was always something that needed to be done it seemed.

The men returned around dusk and the evening routine went the same as the night before with discussions about the day just spent.

Next day, Nina and Rudolph said goodbye to Jane as the men took them to the road, a good mile or two from the homestead. There they waited for the Cobb and Co Coach. As they didn't have any local currency, Bill gave them some coin for the fare which they promised to repay. He didn't ask why they only had Austro-Hungarian Gulden, but then people came from all over, so it may not have been that odd.

After a long while the coach arrived and Bill waved to the driver to stop.

Rudolph and Nina said thank you and goodbye to the men that had saved them, paid the driver and boarded the coach.

There were two other passengers on board as the coach set off. Rudolph and Nina waved to Bill, Paddy and Scotty as they disappeared in the dust kicked up by the horses and headed for Melbourne. From there they hoped to find a way to board a ship and get to England and ultimately Austria. How long that might take was anyone's guess.

Rudolph practically hugged his cargo all the way, knowing it's delivery to the Hitler family was essential to guarantee freedom from Nazi tyranny but right now all those things seemed so far away.

Chapter 25 – Xillinium

Janina Zielinski took her seat at the table with the IG Committee members in the meeting room, noting the absence of Kelly Antoniadis.

Janina had been in the facility hospital for a few weeks recovering from the damage inflicted by the Nazis during her incarceration; broken ribs, a broken wrist, burns, but other than that it was mainly welts and bruises that were still quite yellow as her body went through its repair processes. The psychological effect, well that might take longer to overcome.

Jean Claude Pinet spoke first as usual, "What do we know about the Fischers?"

"Not very much I'm afraid," answered Gabrielle Fawcett. "The software we installed to scrub the logs is very efficient. We simply don't know where they ended up."

"If they ended up anywhere," Davis Brigalow added which prompted a few nods of agreement.

"Perhaps I could look through archival material and see if their names come up," Sunil Patel offered.

"If you wish, but it's like looking for a needle in a haystack," Pinet told him. "I would imagine that they would have left word for us as we trained them to do and we have heard nothing. I think they were extinguished by the Nazi vortex interrupting ours."

The issue was discussed at length but in the end, it was agreed that the Fischers' were 'end of mission', meaning they had perished or been erased from existence. There was no hope of recovery. Still Sunil Patel would scour the records to see if he could find anything

"Our next order of business is the Nazi device that enables them to go forward in time," Pinet announced. "Janina, Klaus Haas said something peculiar as we left, he mentioned Xillinium, what did he mean?"

Janina turned to Jean Claude and winced as her ribs objected.

"Clearly, he was giving us information. It must be some kind of mineral that makes the device work." Then she smiled at Jean Claude, "Please tell me you didn't give their device back without making a copy?"

"Of course we didn't. We took that thing apart, digitised every component and every circuit, we even kept the software." Janina laughed and Pinet added, "You didn't think the Nazis were the only ones who could keep a straight face when they lie did you," Pinet told her.

"I could hug you," Janina said.

"So, we have a device but no way to make it work. What is Xillinium and can we trust this Haas character," Anastasia Kuznetsov asked.

Janina shifted and winced again to answer Kuznetsov, "He took a big risk offering that information, but you're right, it could be a ruse. I don't know much about him, but I think he was genuine."

"Why do you think that" Kuznetsov asked.

"The Nazis are dumb but they're not stupid. Haas appears to have the trust of Pfeiffer and probably told him he was feeding us false information."

"Maybe he did," Hamid Kanumbra suggested.

Janina nodded. "Maybe, but it was a dangerous thing to do, even in jest. They could very easily have arrested him there and then and are now interrogating him to within an inch of his life. No, I think he played a clever game of reverse psychology and gave us data right in front of them and they didn't even know it."

"Ok, let's assume for a moment that you're right, how do we find this stuff," Pinet asked.

"I suspect that it's not called Xillinium which means if the Nazis looked into it, his telling them it's a fake mineral would check out," Janina explained. "But I do think the answer may be in there somewhere."

"You mean like an anagram or something," Luciana Gonzales asked.

"Maybe."

"So, how do we figure it out," Pinet asked.

"Well, we could sit here for hours carving it up or we could run it through some software and see what pops up," Janina suggested.

"As long as we do so offline, that should be fine," Pinet agreed.

Their offline computer was engaged for the task and the word fed into the search engine. The best result they could glean was a similar word, illinium, an old word which referred to chemical element 61. The modern interpretation of it was known as promethium one of the rarest elements on Earth and radioactive.

The most interesting discovery was that if you bombarded promethium with uranium-235 it created promethium-147, which was essentially a fission product and just the kind of thing you might need in a time travel device. Best of all, promethium-147 could easily be found in atomic batteries, electronic components, and even luminous paint.

Jean Claude Pinet fell back in his chair and exhaled heavily, "I can't believe it was that easy, Haas actually gave us something."

"It would appear he did," Janina agreed.

"Right then, we must harvest some of this stuff and then figure out how to use it in the device we've created. That shouldn't be difficult," he laughed.

"Yeah, simple," added Davis Brigalow.

Sadly, the task proved much more difficult than anyone imagined. They had no trouble finding promethium-147 and harvesting reasonable quantities of it, but it was difficult to purify and then they didn't know how exactly to deposit it into the device.

It was looking like a lost cause, and they were beginning to become concerned that the Nazis were already infiltrating various time zones to strengthen their position while the IG committee blundered through this one issue.

The fact that the Nazis hadn't made another attempt on any of the IG committee members lives was also curious. They now knew all their names and could easily zip back and dispose of them at any time, but nothing had happened. They all agreed that the Nazis, having got their device back, probably felt that they need not do anything because they could undo anything that the committee did and then go home again.

The other probability was their intense arrogance, or they just enjoyed making the committee members suffer as they waited for the inevitable. Whatever the reason, it was giving the committee time to find the answer they desperately needed.

Scientists and physicists worked tirelessly to figure out the problem to no avail. Meantime, Sunil Patel came up with nothing in his search for the Fischers through the historical records. It was becoming increasingly likely that they'd vanished which added one more grave concern to the committee's long list of problems, they'd also lost their trump card, the war trophy that guaranteed victory.

At the next sitting of the IG committee, Jean Claude Pinet announced that the odds of solving the Promethium-147 problem in the short term might be out of reach and that it was time, again, to find a new plan.

The news came as a massive disappointment to everyone and the potential for finding a new plan that had any chance of working was probably as easy as solving the promethium problem.

One idea that was put forward was that of a direct assault on Hitler at his home in 1889, which meant killing him as an infant. The idea was heavily debated and many believed that the Nazis might not expect it given their level of over-confidence.

The same problem always plagued them though; the Nazis were always nearby and always on guard. They didn't know how many in any timeline, but they decided that they had to try, with a full-scale assault.

Janina's expertise from 2337 had enabled modifications to the IG machine which now gave them the capacity to keep their vortex open into the past for up to five minutes, more than enough time to send through a taskforce.

After consulting with the UN Security Council, it was decided to send an assault team of twenty, deposit them on the street in front of the Hitler home and eliminate the future Nazi leader.

The plan would see most wait in the street to hold back the Nazis they knew would be there, a chosen few would breach the home and hunt down the family, killing them all. It was barbaric but the countless lives that would be saved and a future without the Nazi threat were indeed worth the loss of a few innocent people.

Once again, the committee faced the prospect of finding volunteers who were willing to live out their lives, should they survive, in a very different world. Even though it was believed the committee would ultimately find a way to go forward in time, that would be dependent on the existence of the IG machine and, prior to 2147 it didn't, so sending anyone to a time before that year meant they could never be retrieved.

They were forced to negotiate with the Russian President, Dimitri Chadov, through Anastasia Kuznetsov. This time Chadov didn't play games. He'd had plenty of time to consider the ramifications for Russia should the Nazis invade his country in the 2300s and that didn't sit well with him. He found the volunteers they desired and had them transferred to the control of the UN Security Council.

They were transported to Cern posing as tourists, businessmen and women, newlyweds, whatever threw the Nazis off the scent. They gathered at the IG facility where they were briefed on their mission by Anastasia Kuznetsov.

None of them balked at the prospect, which Jean Claude Pinet admired. They were truly brave but then he thought that Chadov must have made certain guarantees for their families as inspiration. It made sense. Then again, their love for their country might have achieved the same thing.

Once again, the IG machine was fired up and a vortex established connecting 2215 to 1889. The Spetsnaz operatives walked into the void one by one, only to emerge on the Austrian street where the Hitler family should be. It was night and it was dark, which aided them considerably. Their leader made a hand signal and fifteen of the soldiers found cover in side streets and behind walls, covering the front and back of the Hitler apartment building.

At the same time the five remaining Spetsnaz moved to the main door of the building. They used a small silent charge to blow the door. While the explosion was muffled, the slamming of the door against the wall wasn't and the bang probably woke someone.

The soldiers moved into the building, along a hall when someone appeared holding a lantern. A double tap to the head saw them fall instantly, an old man as it turned out. The soldiers went from room to room, killing anyone they came across, most still very much asleep. The ground floor was cleared, and the operatives moved up the staircase to the second floor and started their next sweep. So far there had been no sounds from outside to indicate the Nazis were onto them, which seemed odd. They certainly expected a firefight by this time of the operation.

They pressed on and, room by room, assassinated the occupants. They were looking for a room with a baby but so far, nothing. Once again, a resident emerged, alerted to creaking of the floorboards perhaps. She too was gunned down with a double tap to the head.

The Spetsnaz cleared the second floor and moved up the stairs to the top floor. The street continued to be quiet. The same room by room approach was taken, with the sleepers killed off silently. Still no sign of the Hitler apartment.

There was only one more room to check and, as the Spetsnaz approached, they saw a glow emanating from under the door, a bright white light, too bright to be a lantern or a fire. The lead soldier burst in, not concerned at making a noise and was immediately brought down by a volley of shots from an automatic weapon which tore huge holes in the apartment wall. The remaining four Spetsnaz returned fire and killed one of the mystery shooters. They managed to get into the room just as the bright light faded.

What they saw completely and utterly overwhelmed them; the silhouettes of several figures encased in light. Clearly, they were soldiers but also civilians. Two were adults with two older children and the female adult was holding a baby. They had found the Hitlers!

The Spetsnaz fired into the void, but the light extinguished suddenly and they didn't know if they'd hit anyone. The room was full of smoke from the firefight and as they looked around, investigating the apartment, they found clear evidence that this was the right place. There were letters addressed to Alois Hitler, some personal belongings and in one room, a crib. They were in the right place, but the Hitler's were gone.

The Spetsnaz soldiers had no idea of what they witnessed but they were intelligent enough to realise that the Nazis had saved the Hitlers. The operation was a failure.

As advised, they left before the authorities arrived, separated and vacated the area quickly and quietly. The leader had time later to write a report and deposit it with a bank in Paris, to be retrieved by the IG committee in 2215 so they knew what had happened, but he had a feeling they would already have been aware given that nothing would have changed in the history books.

Most of the Spetsnaz made their way home to Russia, their dead comrade, left to become the lone cause of a mass murder, stripped of all future reference materials and weapons.

Jean Claude Pinet sat with his head in his hands as he read the Spetsnaz leader's report then turned to the committee members. "The Nazis took Hitler through a vortex. We know not where."

"What?" "How?" "Are you serious," were some of the remarks.

Janina Zielinski then said, "They have not only worked out how to move backwards and forwards in time, but they are also no longer need the machine to go forward prior to 2147. This is bad, very very bad!"

"You don't say," added Davis Brigalow.

"What do we do now," Zhang Jie wondered.

"I really don't know," Pinet said, "We have exhausted our last option."

"Where do you think the Hitlers are now," asked Luciana Gonzales to no one in particular.

Janina was the only one to put up an idea, "2337!"

Jean Claude Pinet then had a thought, "Well, I still have strong memories of Hitler and the Nazis in WW2 and the Holocaust, so we know they take him back. The question is when?"

Just then they were interrupted by a team of physicists, all with beaming smiles.

"What is it," Pinet asked them.

"We've solved the Promethium-147 problem," they announced.

Chapter 26 – Haas

Klaus Haas exhaled a heavy sigh of relief as Ernst Pfeiffer's jet lifted off from Cern, headed back to Berlin. While he considered Ernst a friend, he knew that the Nazis would always come first, so one step out of line and he too would meet the same fate as his predecessor, regardless of status. He needed to maintain Pfeiffer's trust.

He drove back to the IG facility, passed through security and took the elevator to the most secure floor in the complex where the IG machine was housed. He went into his office, sat down, and poured himself a stiff drink and gulped it down in one swallow. As he did, there was a knock on the door. "Enter," he called. Three white coated scientists walked in, the last one closing the door behind him. "What can I help you with gentlemen," Haas asked them.

The apparent leader of the group hesitated then said, "You took a very big risk with your remark to Pinet. Xillinium? I almost burst out laughing."

"I know, but it worked in our favour. Pfeiffer thought it was a great joke that I fed them false data," Haas explained.

"But of course, you didn't. Did you." the first man asked.

"Whatever do you mean?"

"You know what I'm suggesting. Xillinium? It's not real but it was a clue. Yes? Something to help them," Asked the first scientist.

Haas smiled but gave away nothing, "I did what needed to be done."

"What if Pfeiffer checks?"

"He'll find nothing. Xillinium, illinium, he'll only find dead ends. Besides, he's not that patient. After five minutes reading all the gibberish, he'll give up if he even bothers at all," Haas explained.

"For your sake I hope so," then the scientist bit the bullet and asked, "Why? Why have you turned against your friend? We had no idea that you felt this way."

"How do you know we are friends," Haas asked feeling astonished and wary at the same time.

"It's so obvious, he trusts you implicitly. Only a friend would be like that," The man replied.

Haas didn't bother to hide the fact. "It's not about our friendship, Pfeiffer has always been a bully, I just went along with him. When he told me of his plan to bring the Hitler family here, to save them from our friends in 2215, I had to act. The past should stay in the past."

"That's it? You have an issue with manipulating history through the time machine? If that's the case, you're in the wrong job," the scientist suggested.

"I have an issue with Hitler being taken out of his world, thrust into ours and the calamity that might cause," Haas announced with some venom.

"You mean a paradox? Something that might cause us all to be wiped out of existence," asked another of the scientists.

Haas laughed, "What can I say, I'm a pragmatist."

The scientists all smiled. "I doubt that a philosophical approach to this is going to keep you in good favour for long Klaus," the lead man suggested.

"Probably not, but this will." Hass tapped on his tablet and said, "Security to my office."

The scientists looked stunned, "What are you doing?"

"I'm handing the Nazis their traitors. Pfeiffer always believed there was someone here who was feeding information to the past, helping our enemies so I took it upon myself to find them, and here you are. Three of you in fact," and he smiled broadly.

"You bastard!"

Haas stood revealing a small handgun and pointed it at the scientists, "You made one very grave error, you assumed that what I did made me an ally of yours. It only made you surface, much sooner than I anticipated but I knew that you would come to me at some point. It was too easy really."

"But the information you fed them; we know what it is and we can tell Pfeiffer. You are a traitor too," said the man.

"That's true, but you were getting clumsy. Pfeiffer was putting two and two together. He knew that some things just didn't add up. As dumb as he is, he's not a fool. I will dispel his doubts, thanks to you," Haas told the trio.

The scorn on the faces of the three men was palpable as the lead man spoke again, "Your plan is flawed. We will most certainly take you down with us!"

"You can't do that if you're dead. You tried to attack me, and I had no choice but to defend myself," and he shot the second man.

"No, wait," cried the third but Haas shot him down too.

The leader of the now dead scientists said, "I hope you know what you're doing."

"Of course. I'm making certain that all suspicion is removed from the IG facility. Your deaths ensure it," and he shot the speaker of the group who crumpled to the floor.

Haas then roughed up his hair, pistol whipped himself, gashing his face, pushed over his desk and dropped the weapon before slumping in his chair just as security burst in.

The SS soldiers balked at the sight of the dead men, then looked at Haas.

"They are traitors. I tried to have them arrested but they panicked and attacked. I had no choice," Haas announced.

"Of course, Professor," said the SS leader. "Are you ok?"

"Yes yes. They were too slow. Get them out of here."

"Yes Professor," The officer tapped his communicator and called for more men to remove the bodies. "Is there anything else we can do for you Professor?"

"No, thank you," Haas said.

"Very good Professor," said the officer but then he added, "You will need to be debriefed, and a report sent to Reich Headquarters in Berlin.

"Of course. I understand. Whenever you're ready," he said, knowing that would probably be the case.

"I'll let you know. the sooner the better," the officer told him.

More men arrived and collected the dead scientists followed by a cleaning crew who mopped up the blood from the carpet. They cleared up every mark like nothing had happened, much to Haas's relief. No forensic examination so no chance they'd spot his ruse.

The debrief was as Haas expected. He explained that he was approached by the trio who thought that he was against the Reich after they heard him feed *false* information to Jean Claude Pinet. He explained that it was a part of his plan to flush them out and when they realised his plan, they tried to kill him, so he shot them. A simple story that had a lot of merit which was easy to sell.

When the session ended the SS officer said that it was only a formality and the report would reflect that he had done a great service to the Reich in flushing out enemy spies. They would even recommend that he be given an Iron Cross for bravery. He smiled at the irony. Haas knew that Pfeiffer needed his pound of flesh and he gave that to him. It also meant that he could carry on the work of the Underground without suspicion from Pfeiffer or anyone else for that matter. All his staff would believe him a true Nazi and would be careful not to cross him, and Pfeiffer would think his great friend a hero.

Back in his office, Haas could still smell the residue from discharging his weapon. He tried not to think about what he'd done. He'd never killed anyone before and didn't know if he had the nerve to do so, but in the heat of the moment, it proved an easy task. It was only now that he was starting to deal with his act and he didn't like the feeling. He expected not to sleep very well for a good long while.

Just then his communicator chimed through an encrypted channel. It was Pfeiffer. "Hello, my friend," Haas said.

"Klaus, you old devil, you found the traitors!" Pfeiffer announced.

"Yes. That appears to be the case."

"Appears? My men have found much to back up your suspicions. how did you do it?" Pfeiffer asked, clearly excited by his friend's act of bravery.

"Well," he hesitated as he strained to think of a simple explanation, "I just flushed them out."

"Come on Klaus, I want details," Pfeiffer urged.

Haas really didn't want to tell the story again, but this was Ernst Pfeiffer, you didn't say no to him. "Well, you recall me referring to Xillinium when Pinet and Zielinski were headed back into the vortex. That was a ruse."

"I remember you saying something to them, but I didn't understand," Pfeiffer said.

"It was aimed at confusing Pinet, that was just for fun but with all the scientists and physicians watching, I knew it might motivate someone to approach me. I hoped it would make them think I was...sympathetic to their cause. I just didn't expect it to happen so quickly," Haas explained.

"So, there is no Xillinium," Pfeiffer asked.

"Of course not, I made it up," Haas declared hoping that would be enough to extinguish any further inquiry from Pfeiffer about the mystery compound.

"Very clever my friend, and quite brave. If they'd realised you were playing them, you might be the dead one."

"Oh, I doubt that. They may have just let it slide, but thankfully, they didn't" Haas added.

"Yes indeed. Well done. You came through as you promised Klaus. You will receive the Iron Cross for this," Pfeiffer announced.

"That really isn't necessary," Haas said feeling somewhat guilty at being honoured for murder.

"Nonsense! You have put the Reich ahead of yourself and at great risk, I will not take 'no' for an answer. In fact, we will have the ceremony here in Berlin and I will pin it to you myself," Pfeiffer declared.

Haas said nothing for a moment.

"Are you there Klaus?"

"Yes Ernst, I am sorry. It's all been a little overwhelming," Haas said.

"Of course it has. You have never killed before. It will take some getting used to. That's what makes it all the braver. You had to, not only fight your emotions, but there were also three of them. Incredible, truly incredible," Pfeiffer suggested with much cheer in his voice.

"Well, they didn't know until I pulled the gun."

"Of course not. The perfect trap!"

"The plan was to have them arrested, but they attacked. I had no choice," Haas added knowing it was a lie.

"You did what needed to be done. If they killed you, they may well have claimed that you were the mole and where would we be now," Pfeiffer said in his friend's defence, "Besides, you saved us a lot of bother. The threat has been nullified. All is well, eh?"

"Yes Ernst. That's true," Haas told him. "Forgive me though, I'm still trying to process everything."

"Of course, I understand. You will be fine, I guarantee," Pfeiffer said. "And in a few days, we will fly you to Berlin and celebrate a true hero of the Reich. Thank you, my friend," and Pfeiffer cut the commlink.

Haas exhaled heavily. Pfeiffer bought the whole story and believed the threat had been removed. Haas knew he was very much alone, a pawn between the Reich and his own staff working on the IG machine for the Nazis cause.

Any way he looked at it, he had painted himself into an unenviable corner by killing potential allies, but what choice was there? They might have been close once, but Pfeiffer wanted blood and he would have killed his friend had the traitors not been identified. Haas convinced himself it was an act of self-preservation. For now, that justified his decision but deep down he hated himself.

He tried to push the experience to the back of his mind but a few days later, as promised, Pfeiffer's personal jet landed at Cern and Haas was picked up and flown to Berlin. A motorcade took him from Tegel Spaceport which Haas thought a bit of an over-statement but then, as he approached the Reichstag building, he saw a huge crowd assembled in the square, literally thousands of people. The limousine pulled up in front of a military Guard of Honour and as he alighted the vehicle they snapped to attention!

He walked along the rows of jet-black uniforms as the crowds cheered and jostled to catch a glimpse of the Nazi hero. Haas didn't know if it was real or staged but then decided that nothing the Nazis did was by chance, so this was probably a rent a crowd and would be recorded and telecast all over the world.

He was met at the end of the row of guards by the Fuhrer, Ernst Pfeiffer who gave him a traditional Nazi salute and ushered him up the stairs to a podium which was dwarfed by the imposing entrance of columns and glass.

The people screamed and clapped, and Pfeiffer allowed them to continue for at least a minute before waving them to be silent, which they did in an instant.

"I stand before you a very proud man because it is true patriotism that brings us all together today." The crowd cheered and Pfeiffer subdued them again, "Bravery is not something you know you have until you need it and today, we salute a truly brave man. He is not a soldier. He had seen no combat, but his act was no less brave."

Haas stood there, his legs quivering as the adrenaline surged through his body.

Pfeiffer continued, "Not only did this man uncover a dangerous enemy in our midst, but he also eliminated the threat with no thought for his own safety," the crowd cheered again and Pfeiffer simply added, "I give you a true hero of the Reich. Professor Klaus Haas!"

Ernst Pfeiffer then picked up a small velvet box from the lectern, opened it and took out the 'Iron Cross'. He then turned to Haas and pinned it on the lapel of his suit and saluted Nazi style as the crescendo of voices cried "Sieg Heil!"

Haas returned the salute as Pfeiffer urged him to acknowledge the crowd. He turned and saluted the people who seemed to really adore him and he smiled, feeling momentarily proud. The chanting continued for a few minutes before Pfeiffer urged people to calm down then said, "I have one more surprise for you today," he announced.

The crowd was silent as Pfeiffer spoke, "While our hero was otherwise indisposed, I arranged for his staff and my SS to do something in his honour and in the honour of the Reich."

Pfeiffer gestured to someone at his rear and the main doors of the Reichstag opened. A man and a woman holding a baby and two young children aged around four or five emerged. Pfeiffer urged them to join him. As they timidly stood beside Pfeiffer, he took the baby from the woman and turned back to the crowd,

"My friends, it is with great delight I share with you this glorious moment for the Reich! You are witness to history in the making because at this very moment," he paused for effect, knowing that everything was being recorded and would be seen on all networks of the free World. "Using the Infinity Generator, we have been able to go back to 1889, to the Austrian village of Braunau am Inn and rescue this family from those who would do harm to them and to the greatest man who would ever live then and now," Pfeiffer held the baby high so the crowd could see...

"I present to you The Fuhrer, Adolf Hitler! He is alive!"

Chapter 27 – Austria or bust

The city of Melbourne in the colony of Victoria in 1873 was a thriving place. With around a quarter of a million people, it had a larger population than Sydney, mainly brought about by the gold rush which had endured for around twenty years but was showing signs of fading.

The structure of the city was taking shape with the Supreme Court building; Government House and the Queen Victoria Market having been established as well as large banks and hotels on the main street of the city centre and high-end townhouses for the wealthy. Beyond that most people lived in cottages.

The first thing that Rudolph and Nina Fischer did on arrival in the city was to visit a bank and attempt to change their useless currency for the local coin. Melbourne had only established a mint to standardise local currency the year before, but it would be another 37 years before there was a truly national currency system, so for the Fischers, like everyone else, negotiating an exchange into a system of gold coins known as sovereigns and half sovereigns was necessary. One sovereign was equal to one pound in the British currency. Sadly, the currency exchange they negotiated didn't work out very favourably and they were left with barely enough to get by. They would need to find work.

As luck would have it, Victoria had passed the Education Act in 1872, and schooling was now deemed compulsory. With that, many new schools were established and they needed teachers. The Fischers found work easily as it turned out. Educational programs were very basic, focussed primarily on the three doctrines of reading, writing and arithmetic. The Fischers had no problems in that regard given their academic backgrounds. If anything, they found it too simple and uninspiring, but it was made up for by their delight at experiencing the lives of the colonial folk of the era.

Sadly, their income was barely enough to meet their rent and food leaving little. Their plan was to save enough to gain two tickets for sea passage to England and from there they would cross to Europe and complete their mission in Austria, but the circumstances made it clear it would take years to achieve. They became frustrated.

"How will we ever get there," Nina asked her husband.

"Patience Nina, that's what it will take," he explained then added, "You have to remember that our mission isn't time sensitive in real terms."

"How can you say that we were to deposit this…" she hesitated to describe what they possessed, "thing in Braunau am Inn, before the Hitlers moved in. We cannot do that now I fear."

"No, we can't but we can still achieve our mission. We'll just have to think of another way," Rudolph explained.

Nina frowned, "With the Nazis watching over them? Doubtful! In fact, suicidal!"

"Well, we can't change the way things turned out. It's already too late even if we could teleport there now. The Hitlers are already in residence, but Adolf won't be born for another sixteen years, we have plenty of time."

"But Jean Claude and the rest of the committee will think we failed. We didn't stick to the timeline," she said.

"You must look at it like this Nina, we are in the 'present' which means the future hasn't happened yet, so it doesn't matter how long it takes us, as long as it's done. Do you understand?" Nina looked confused. "The events of today dictate what the future will be like so essentially the future has not been set, correct?" Nina nodded. "So, we do the job now or in 16 years, it really doesn't matter, as long as it's done."

"But you forget the reason we were sent back to this particular year, to precede the arrival of the Hitlers at their residence, so the weapon, or whatever it is, will lay in wait for Hitler's birth without drawing attention. We cannot do that now," Nina argued.

Rudolph saw how frustrated she was. "I know, but we can't do anything about that. We have no choice but to do it the hard way. We must risk the Nazis being there when we arrive."

"And how do we deposit this thing without them noticing?"

"I'll think of something. There's always a way Nina," Rudolph said, smiling but Nina wasn't convinced.

They'd hidden the package in a recess within the pantry where they believed it would be safe. Petty theft was rife in Melbourne with many a pick pocket on the prowl so keeping the artefact on their person was hardly wise. Break and enter crimes weren't uncommon either so either way they were taking a risk.

Then, one day after they returned home from school, their worst nightmare unfolded before their eyes. Their cottage had been broken into, their pantry emptied of all its food, their savings also gone and to their horror, the package containing the one thing that would rid the World of the Nazis was gone too. They searched the entire cottage; the grounds and the streets, anywhere, hoping it was discarded when it was seen as valueless, but they found nothing. The weapon was gone.

"Would the thieves even know what they were looking at," Nina asked.

"They wouldn't even have a clue as to why we would have it or what we want to do with it, even if they did know what it was. Frankly, it's useless to them, totally valueless," Rudolph suggested.

"So, what will they do with it?"

"I expect they'll just throw it away if they open it up and see it," Rudolph said. "What would you do?"

"Probably just that," Nina answered. "So how do we find it?"

"I really don't know."

"Should we report the robbery," Nina asked.

"And tell them what? We have a future weapon that has been stolen, if it shows up can you please give it back?"

"You know that's not what it is Rudolph," Nina added.

"Of course, but how do we explain it? They're not likely to see reason should it show up. They'll have preconceived ideas and who knows how they'll react if we claim ownership," Rudolph said.

"So, we report the robbery but don't mention the weapon. It might lead to something," Nina said hopefully.

"Maybe. OK, we report the robbery, tell them what was stolen, minus the WW2 trophy and hope it just turns up."

At this time in Melbourne there were too few police to deal with the burgeoning population, so their details were noted but the officer told them there was little hope of them getting their money back and that the food was probably already eaten. They left realising the artefact was probably lost forever too and so was any hope of returning to Europe anytime soon.

That evening Rudolph and Nina sat in silence feeling miserable about how things had turned out for them. They were on the wrong side of the planet in an era when travel took months and sometimes years and they had lost the one thing they were sworn to protect and deliver. Then Rudolph's eyes brightened, "I have an idea!"

"What," Nina asked.

"We catch the thieves ourselves," he announced.

Nina looked at him doubtfully, "However will we do that?"

"We were robbed while we were at work, yes?" He didn't wait for her to reply. "That suggests to me that they knew we were out and probably check homes regularly. I think, if we restock the pantry and leave a few coins visible, they will strike again. We, or at least I, just must wait."

"It's a longshot," Nina suggested.

"True, but do you have a better idea?"

Nina shook her head.

"So, we should give it a try. What have we got to lose," Rudolph asked.

"Nothing I suppose," Nina replied and she reluctantly agreed to the plan.

When they next had enough money to buy food, they stocked up the pantry, making it as obvious as possible that they had much to take inside. As planned, Rudolph left a few coins in the open for any prying eyes at the window. The next day they set off for work as usual, but Rudolph wasn't going to the school. Nina would report him ill.

Once they were out of sight of the home, he quickly took station in a side street where he could keep an eager eye on the front of the cottage. He spent most of the day watching but nothing happened. The next day he tried again to no avail. After three days he was thinking it was a fool's errand, and he knew he couldn't stay away from work any longer without raising suspicion.

The next day, he upped the ante by leaving the front window of the cottage open, surely an invitation that any thief would not ignore. He watched nervously as people passed by, mostly women going about their daily tasks but then two youths came calling. They hesitated as they looked upon the cottage clearly noticing the opportunity presenting itself. They spoke briefly. Looked around to make sure there was no-one watching and then slipped through the front gate. Before

Rudolph could blink, one had boosted the smaller of the pair up and into the open window.

"Got you," Rudolph said to himself.

He walked around the corner like any other passer-by as the boy in the yard watched him. He even doffed his hat at the young lad who was clearly a street urchin. His clothes were practically rags and his white skin was barely visible under layers of dirt. The child ignored him when he realised that Rudolph was no threat.

When the boy turned his back Rudolph turned and rushed through the gate tackling the child to the ground, knocking the wind out of the poor fellow as his weight came down fully on the skinny child's frame. Rudolph felt terrible but he also knew how wily these street urchins could be based on conversations he'd had with his students, so he sat on top of the boy, waiting for him to catch his breath. When he did, the boy let fly with expletives that even Rudolph hadn't heard before.

"Settle down. I only want to talk then you can go, I promise."

The boy looked at him, not sure what to believe. Being street wise, he wasn't going to be duped so easily.

"Look, I'm not interested in having you arrested or prosecuted, I need your help," Rudolph explained.

"My elp," the boy replied, "It'll cost ya!"

Rudolph smiled. "I'm sure it will and you will be paid if you give me what I want."

The boy looked him over, "Awright, now git off me!"

"You won't run away," Rudolph asked.

"Course not," the boy yelled trying to attract the attention of his partner in crime.

"I know about your friend. He's probably having a good feed while you wait outside." This made the boy frown.

"Willy," the boy yelled and another dirty face appeared at the window, cheeks bulging as he chewed.

"Gord! RUN," Willy yelled as he jumped out the window, but the older boy didn't move. Willy was about to sprint off when he noticed his friend was standing firm, "What are you doing Davey?"

"Ah Davey, is it," Rudolph said. "I'm Rudy, nice to meet you Davey." Then he looked to the younger boy, "You too Willy. Listen, I have a problem and I hope you can help me. I'll pay for good information of course."

With that, Willy cancelled his escape attempt and slowly walked over to his friend, "We're listenin."

Rudolph smiled, "Can we do this inside? I'll make you something to eat."

Davey and Willy looked at each other and were up the steps and inside in a flash.

Rudolph fed the duo, being careful not to spook them. He knew this was probably his one and only chance to find the artefact. "So, boys, as I said, I need your help. I've lost something and I'm hoping you can help me find it."

"What is it," Willy asked.

"It's a case and inside that is a bag. It's very special to me and my wife and we desperately need to get it back."

"What's in the bag," Davey asked.

"Ah, well. It's complicated," Rudolph said clumsily.

"Is it valuable," Willy wondered.

"Well, no not really."

"So why do you care," Davey asked.

"It has personal value. Not monetary value. Does that make sense," Rudolph asked.

"We're not stupid," Willy said.

"Of course. Sorry. Anyway, we were robbed and the case was taken. I don't care about the money or the food, but I do care about the case. Can you help me," Rudolph asked, hoping against hope.

The boys looked at each other, "Five sovereigns," one said.

"What," Rudolph asked a little confused.

"Money, five sovereigns for our trouble," Davy said.

"Oh, yes, of course, but how do I know you will come through for me," Rudolph asked.

"If you was robbed then it was our gang that done it," Willy explained. "This is our turf!"

"I see, well that's great. How does this work?"

"Money first," demanded Davey.

"Yes, of course. Well, there were the sovereigns on the…" Rudolph looked at the table near the window where he'd left the tempting coins, but they were gone. "Of course. I don't suppose they count as part of the payment?" The two boys feigned ignorance. "Very well, five sovereigns it is. I will need to go to the bank. I don't carry that kind of money around, for obvious reasons. Can I meet you somewhere?"

The arrangement was made to meet in a place that Rudolph knew to be an unsavoury part of the city, the northern suburbs, but he had little choice. These boys may well be faking it just to snatch some coin, but he had to risk it. He took the last of his reserves from the bank and ventured into the suburb of Collingwood, to the address given by Davey.

He knocked and the door opened. A heavy-set man with a bushy black beard and body odour that could have killed a horse ushered him inside, clearly expecting him. It was gloomy inside and he was led down a hall and into a sitting room where the boys waited with another man, a skinny man with stringy, slimy hair who smiled, revealing a few useless teeth. "Well, here he is boys, just like you said."

Rudolph gulped, "Yes, hello, I have your money as promised. Do you know where my container is?"

The man smiled insincerely, "You talking about this," as he held up a case.

"Yes!! That's it, oh thank you," and Rudolph reached for the case.

"Not so fast. The finder's fee first!"

"Oh of course," and Rudolph fumbled in his pocket taking out five shiny gold coins and handed them over, then held his hand out to collect his artefact.

"Not so fast. What is this thing anyway? Looks useless, all dirty and burnt up and what's this glass box it's in?"

"You looked at it," Rudolph asked.

"Of course. Can't see how it's got sentimental value. It's as filthy as Willy here," the man said.

"Oi," cried Willy as Davey laughed which resulted in a whack across the back of the skull from the man.

"So, what is it," the man asked again.

Rudolph realised he couldn't get it back without some kind of explanation. "OK, you'll find this hard to believe but I'm from the future, the year 2215 to be precise and that's an artefact captured by Russian soldiers at the end of World War Two in 1945. With it we are going to stop the Nazis and stop a holocaust! Oh, and the box isn't glass, it's high tensile Perspex with a newly developed clear lead lining."

The boys gazed at Rudolph, their faces blanked by confusion. The man glared at the Perspex box then looked up at Rudolph, "Ten more sovereigns and it's yours."

As the remark sank in Rudolph smiled. He'd suddenly had an idea, "I think I can do much better than that."

Chapter 28 – The Hitlers

Alois Hitler stood at the window of his Berlin apartment, looking around the room and out at the wonders of the future. The flying machines that made no sound. The speed of horseless vehicles on roads and boats on the river and the strange shiny screen on the wall that showed moving pictures. It all mesmerised him.

He felt out of place in 2337, his rotund frame and big, round, near bald head and handlebar moustache at odds with modern society. He was still in shock at having been snatched out of his home with his family in 1889 to emerge in the Germany of the future.

It had been explained that people from the 2200s were sent back to eliminate his son Adolf and that couldn't be allowed. It was also explained that his son's destiny was to become the leader of a great Nazi Reich which would last a thousand years and he had to be protected, something that the future Nazis went to some lengths to prove.

Alois, unfamiliar with computer technology, barely grasped the basics of browsing, but was able to read much about the loss by Austria and Germany in World War One, the impossible conditions of the Treaty of Versailles and the rise of the Nazi Party with his son leading the nation to another war. The Nazis of 2337 had, quite deliberately, redacted all references to the atrocities endorsed by Hitler and his power base, pitching Hitler as a saviour of the World.

Even though Adolf was in 2337 here and now, the fact that the data existed meant he would be returned to the past at some future time, a point that his father didn't really grasp. Frankly he was getting frustrated and just wanted to go home.

The saving of Hitler from the insurgents created a problem for the Nazis, Alois had to die on January 3rd, 1903. The passing of his father had a profound effect on young Adolf, and the Nazis were now concerned that the dramatic change in circumstances would alter the course of Hitler's development.

Ernst Pfeiffer, the Nazi leader of 2337 consulted experts in psychology and psychiatry to find answers. Pfeiffer's advisors were adamant that Adolf Hitler shouldn't be kept in the future for too long, but Pfeiffer wasn't convinced and wanted experts to argue the pros and cons of Hitler being raised in 2337 and reinstalled at the right time in the past.

Pfeiffer strongly believed Hitler faced grave danger in his own time and having him in the future was the safest solution for the sake of the Reich.

A hastily arranged round table sat before Pfeiffer in the Reichstag to offer advice and candour in the matter. The delegates were told of the rescue of the Hitlers from a squad of assassins in 1889 and how, had they not saved the family, the Nazis would have been doomed.

Then the question of keeping them in 2337 was raised and several delegates shifted uncomfortably in their seats. It was clearly a disturbing paradox that required immediate action.

Pfeiffer addressed them, making his point very clear, "The Fuhrer must be allowed to grow and develop through his childhood to guarantee the future of the Reich, but I fear that sending him back to his time too soon will be dangerous. So, gentlemen, how do we achieve this?"

The first speaker cleared his throat, "Sir, he needs to be reinstalled into his natural environment immediately!"

Pfeiffer saw red, "You make him sound like an endangered animal! We rescued him, all of them, from certain death; sending them back now will put them right back in it!"

"The first man spoke again, "We realise that, but it is essential that Adolf Hitler be brought up in his own environs. To become the man, he was and will be!"

"I disagree," said the next man. "Having them here ensures their safety. We cannot send them back now."

A third man then spoke, "I cannot agree. Keeping the family, Adolf himself, here could seal the fate of the Nazi regime through time."

"How," Pfeiffer asked.

"What if he has an accident here and is killed, what happens then," the delegate asked.

Pfeiffer ignored the remark then said, "What if we did keep him here, groom him, as it were, to become the Fuhrer and reinstall him at the most opportune time?"

"It would not work," came another contributor. "He would not have the same emotional responses to world events. If he grew up here, he would only read about whatever the world might have become without his influence, and it would be continually altered the longer he was absent. When he went back, he would likely be an outsider, unable to take his place in German politics."

The arguments went on and on, debating the potential positives and negatives of keeping the Hitlers in 2337 against sending them back. The more it went on the more Pfeiffer grew impatient.

Yet another delegate spoke up, "And how do you replicate the tragedies in his life, the death of his father, the loss of his mother and siblings? He must experience these things in Austria in the early years of his life. I already fear that bringing them here has disrupted the timeline enough to have adverse consequences."

"How so," Pfeiffer asked.

"Alois for example," said the man, "he has now seen the future. He knows of things he should never have been able to learn. It may be enough to change him, enable him to want to be a bigger part of his son's legacy. He may not die in 1903, what then? It's anyone's guess!"

Pfeiffer rubbed his chin trying to process the information as the delegates chatted amongst themselves, comparing their thoughts, some arguing.

At the end of the table sat a small, weedy looking man with a sickly complexion who had said nothing so far, he waited for the discussion to calm before he spoke. He stood so that everyone, including Pfeiffer, recognised he had the floor.

"We must take them all back immediately but first we must remove the threat to the family."

Before anyone could interject, he raised his hand to halt comment then continued, "We send a task force to 1889 to kill the oppressors, then we reinstall the Hitlers. We maintain vigil on them for as long as necessary AND future proof any place that Adolf Hitler will be in his life regardless and we do this without interfering in their affairs."

He looked around as the delegates listened. "And if need be, we kill Alois at the exact moment it's supposed to happen, if necessary."

Many gasped at the idea but others nodded as the man continued, "This is the only solution. We have saved him yes, but we may have also changed him through his father and mother being here, in 2337. This must be corrected so the natural state of history is maintained. It will take manpower and dedication, but it is the only way, and we must do so immediately."

The man sat and a short silence enveloped the room until Pfeiffer reacted, "At last, some logic. This idea I like. Do we all agree?" He'd been told as much by almost everyone else but somehow this man got through to him on terms that Pfeiffer connected with.

After a few mumbles and a few more moments of silence there were no objections.

"Good. It will be done," Pfeiffer announced. He didn't bother to thank anyone as he turned to his aid. "Make it so!"

He then watched as the delegates left, discussing the plan as they departed. The room cleared except for Pfeiffer, his SS guards and the man at the end of the table who convinced him to send Hitler back.

The man didn't mince words with his delivery of the solution, and he didn't hold back now. "You are a very stubborn man Ernst, to the point of being incredibly stupid!"

Pfeiffer was shocked by the insult, "How dare you!"

But before Pfeiffer could continue the man interrupted, "Please Ernst, allow me the indulgence of saying what is true, you can kill me after that if you wish."

Pfeiffer raised his hands in resignation while he gritted his teeth in anger but said nothing.

"Thank you," said the man. "The Reich is here because of Hitler, but you have jeopardised it all through an act of self-indulgence."

"What? How can you say that?"

"You never needed to bring the Hitlers here. You had to meet the man, even as an infant. You solidify your reputation and your position in this time through such an act. I thought holding Hitler up to the crowd a brilliant touch, but you did it all for yourself," said the man.

"You have me at a disadvantage, I don't know your name or your qualifications," Pfeiffer said.

"Forgive me Ernst, I am Johann Steinbrenner, a distant descendant of Adolf Hitler! As far as qualifications are concerned, I am a chemistry tutor at Berlin University and a devout supporter of the Reich."

Ernst Pfeiffer's jaw dropped and it took him a moment to gather his thoughts, "You're a Hitler?"

The man smiled. "Yes and no. I am a descendant through his sister's blood line but that's irrelevant. Chances are I would still exist with or without Adolf but having his entire family wiped out in 1889 would see me vanish I suspect. That's why I took the opportunity to be here."

Pfeiffer snatched upon the revelation, "So, I did the right thing saving the family!"

"Yes, of course but bringing them here? That was a serious mistake."

"What else could I have done?"

"Clearly you were aware of the threat. You could have simply intercepted it and not disrupted the family, but you decided to bring them here, into a future they cannot possibly understand.

Alois never knew what his son would become, now he does. What if he hates the idea? What if he wants his son to be someone else? What if it inspires him to be his son's right-hand man? Did any of that cross your mind," Steinbrenner asked.

Pfeiffer, while angry that he'd been put on the spot, was already nodding in agreement, "You know Johann, not many people get the better of me. You are brave."

"True but as a descendant of the Hitler family, I also suspect that protects me so I can afford to call you foolish."

"I'm not very forgiving either so you best be careful," Pfeiffer reminded him.

"Of course. I've said my piece and you are doing something about it. For that I am grateful," Johann paused then added, "But if you must, you will kill Alois. Adolf must experience the loss. That is critical in his development."

"You have already made that clear," Pfeiffer replied.

"Yes, but you said yourself you are stubborn, so I fear you might balk at the idea if it came to the critical moment," Johann suggested.

"You need not fear that. I will issue the order if it becomes necessary."

"Good. That's all I can ask," and Steinbrenner stood to leave.

"Wait Johann," Pfeiffer said, "You clearly have a vested interest in what is going on, why don't you work for us? I cannot find enough people with your...commitment or such a connection for that matter. I need an advisor, someone I can trust, what say you?"

Johann smiled, "Let me think about it."

"I'm not a patient man, Johann," Pfeiffer repeated. "Don't take too long with your answer and I expect it to be yes!" Pfeiffer urged.

Steinbrenner smiled, offered the Nazi salute, and left.

Klaus Haas heard his personal tablet vibrating under a pile of papers on his desk at the IG Facility. Despite paper being a rarely used commodity these days, he preferred the tactile joy of writing with a pen rather than tapping onto a touch screen or dictating his remarks and ideas into the cloud.

He'd been studying them furiously when the call came in. He dug the tablet out of the paper pile and looked at the screen, "Good afternoon my friend. I hope all is well?"

"Yes Klaus," Pfeiffer said. "I am bringing someone new in, someone to help us."

"Oh? Who," Haas asked.

"Johann Steinbrenner, do you know him?"

"Um, only by reputation, Berlin University if I'm not mistaken. We have crossed paths once or twice but that is all," Haas suggested.

"Well then, you will see much more of him I think, he is going to assist us with the Hitlers," Pfeiffer said. "He has convinced me that we must return them to 1889 immediately.

"That seems wise," Haas agreed.

"Yes. I will send him to you with the Hitlers, please follow his advice on the matter. We must reseat the Hitlers to make certain that their history remains intact," Pfeiffer explained.

"Very well. I will do everything I can to make sure they are delivered safely," Haas suggested.

"I expect nothing less Klaus," and Pfeiffer cut the connection.

Klaus Haas sat for a moment and pondered the possibilities. Could he kill Hitler when they were back at the IG facility? No, there would be too much security and no doubt the Hitlers would be returning with a task force of protectors. He would have to leave that job to the IG committee in 2215.

Of course, killing the infant Hitler would immediately distort space and time and he might well be safe after the act. It was something to consider, after all he killed the other scientists in cold blood when he had to, this would be the same, wouldn't it? But as he considered the idea he began to shake.

The killing of his colleagues was to save him from his own execution should he have failed to reveal the spies in the IG facility but killing Hitler? That was way out of his league. He decided to leave it to history.

He looked over the papers on his desk. They were covered in random calculations and concepts, easily destroyed when he had to.

He had indeed been successful in achieving two-way travel through the Infinity Generator, enabling time travellers to return and it got him to wondering if it were possible to also open two-time vortices simultaneously to two different time destinations. He'd been playing around with the idea for some time, writing down random thoughts and doing the calculations, sometimes waking in the middle of the night with an idea. The page he looked at was one he wrote down at around 2am before he dropped off back to sleep. He'd given it a passing glance as he shoved it in his satchel and hurried off to work but now it attracted his attention again.

As he looked, the figures whirred around in his head and like a bolt from the blue, something clicked. He was about to cry out *Eureka* but thought better of it, should it attract the wrong kind of attention. He had his answer and all it would take was to write the software. The existing hardware system was flexible enough to create multiple wormholes if the machine was programmed to do it. He couldn't believe it would be so easy, but the calculations didn't lie.

Haas smiled. He now had the capacity to send the Hitlers home to 1889 and, at the very same moment, send a message to 2215 and no-one would be the wiser.

He opened an encrypted private channel on his computer and began sequencing the software he would require. He worked on it for the entire day and most of the night and after 17 hours without moving from his seat, it was done.

He ran a series of simulations, trying everything to break the code but it stood up, much to his surprise. *Nothing ever works first time*, he thought then he allowed himself to laugh.

He then slipped into the IG transfer room and loaded the software into the IG Quantum computers, making sure that the data was well hidden and accessible only to him.

Haas felt excited. The Hitlers would go home and the message he sent to 2215 would tell Jean Claude Pinet exactly what he and his committee needed to know. It was the perfect solution.

Chapter 29 – Levelling the playing field

The scientists and engineers left the IG Committee meeting, all smiles. They had cracked the puzzle of two-way time travel; thanks to the hint they received from Klaus Haas.

Promethium-147 did indeed give them the basis for developing what they required and now they had a fully functional device retro fitted to the IG machine that would enable return travel from the past and the capacity to travel forward and return to the present. Jean Claude Pinet was delighted, knowing that they were no longer at a disadvantage with the Nazis of 2337.

This war being fought in different centuries, he believed, was turning slightly in their favour but that didn't resolve the remaining issues, where was Hitler and where were the Fischers? Without the precious cargo the Fischers held, the chance of eliminating Hitler became incredibly difficult. As of now, getting Hitler within a bull's roar of the weapon was unlikely. The thought immediately wiped the smile off Pinet's face.

"Do we have any more information on the whereabouts of Rudolph and Nina Fischer?" No-one answered. "We have to find them!"

"It's likely they don't exist and the Russian artefact went with them, dissipated into time and space," Janina Zielinski suggested.

Pinet frowned. "I don't accept that and I won't accept it until we've checked every conceivable possibility!"

"The trouble is we've lost the logs," Zhang Jie said, "Our need to hide things from the future has come back to haunt us."

Pinet nodded and then asked, "Are we being too technical about this?"

"What do you mean," Luciana Gonzales asked.

"I mean, we're looking for data errors, mistakes in the telemetry or assuming the disruption to the vortex caused a rift. What if it was something else, something we've overlooked," Pinet declared.

"Like what," came a few simultaneous voices.

"I don't know, a simple mistake, a moment of confusion, a mental lapse perhaps," Pinet told them before huffing in frustration.

"Like entering data in kilometres instead of miles," Davis Brigalow declared.

"Exactly," Pinet replied.

"It reminds me of the end of WW1, when the Australians occupied territory once held by the Germans," Brigalow added, "They were met with suspicion from some of the people in the liberated towns."

"Why," Pinet asked.

Brigalow smiled. "Because the villagers thought they were from the Austrian Army. They thought the Aussies were enemy soldiers. It took some fast talking to sort it out."

Pinet laughed, "I would have liked to have seen that exchange."

Then Muhammad Galal jumped to his feet. "That's it! We sent them to the wrong place!"

There was a collective, "What?"

"Think about it. We were sending them back to 1873 Austria, right? Is it a stretch to think that they were dumped in Australia instead? I think not," he said.

Everyone sat dumbfounded for a few moments before Hamid Kanumbra asked, "How do we prove it?"

"We ask the technician who entered the coordinates," answered Pinet.

To deposit someone or something to a designated point in the past, the IG machine required targeting data, including longitude and latitude which was combined with time declination, right ascension data and the distance the Earth had moved forward or moved backwards as the case may be to allow for variation in space time.

The complexities of time travel notwithstanding; it was conceivable that a simple input error could land someone in a totally different country while depositing them into the correct era. While the correlation between Australia and Austria was not nearly similar in terms of their respective coordinates, would a technician be aware of that?

But the question remained, how could someone get confused by the town of Braunau am Inn with a town in Australia? It didn't stack up.

The technician in charge of entering the data was tracked down and Pinet asked him straight, "Did you feed in the correct coordinates when we delivered the Fischers?"

"Yes, of course," he answered.

"Are you sure," Pinet urged.

"Very sure," came the reply.

Then Brigalow asked, "How are you with navigation?"

The man looked surprised. "Well, I know what it is but if I was told to navigate a ship, I'd be clueless."

"OK, so where did you get the data for the jump," Pinet asked.

"I looked it up," said the technician.

"Do you have any notes," Pinet urged.

The man remained silent knowing that they were never to keep any data that could compromise them if it could somehow be found in the future.

"It's ok," Pinet reassured him. "I know everyone keeps notes."

"Yes, I kept my notes, but I intend to destroy them," the man assured Pinet.

"May we see them, we have an idea that you can assist us with," Pinet said trying not to spook the fellow.

"Of course. I'll get them," said the man and he hurried off.

Pinet nodded at a guard to follow, just in case the man decided this was going to get him into trouble and destroy the data instead. They soon returned, the information intact.

"Show us the notes please," Pinet asked.

The technician flicked through a notepad looking for the coordinates. "Ah, here it is. 37.5 degrees south, 143.8 degrees east and -20 degrees 14 minutes 48 seconds declination and +238 degrees 13 minutes 31 seconds right ascension" he said, smiling broadly.

Everyone sat clueless for a moment, then Zhang Jie asked the man, "You do realise those are coordinates for the Southern Hemisphere, don't you?"

"No, no, I checked," the man assured Jie.

"May I see," Pinet asked as the man handed over his notepad. "What are the coordinates of Braunau am Inn," he asked to no one in particular.

It took a few moments to find the information, "In terms of latitude and longitude, 48.25 degrees north, 13.04 degrees east," Jie said.

Everyone looked at the technician who was turning a deep facial red, "I don't know how?"

"It's ok, you are not in trouble, it was a mistake," Pinet assured him.

"Like a nine point nine on the cataclysmic scale mistake," Brigalow added, drawing a few smirks despite the situation.

Pinet ignored them and asked the technician another question, "How did you decide on these coordinates? We were specific about the target, Braunau am Inn."

The man's face was roasting now. "Um, I didn't write it down, I looked up the data and saw a town and, well entered that information."

"What town," asked Pinet, frustrated.

"I can't recall, I'm sorry," the scientist said as he bowed his head in shame.

"Can we cross check the coordinates," Pinet asked.

"On it," Jie said. They were all still working off the grid and he tapped the touch screen of the offline computer and waited a few seconds. "It's Ballarat! Victoria, Australia."

Everyone looked at the technician who simply said, "I knew it started with a B."

Pinet shook his head. "You're dismissed," he said as the man sheepishly slipped away.

"So, they are probably in 1873 Australia, somewhere near Ballarat? What was happening then," Jie asked.

"Colonial Australia? Convicts from the UK, new settlers from all over including Germany and even China. The gold rush was in full swing too," Brigalow said. "It was a truly multicultural environment back them. They'll probably blend in to be honest."

"That's good," Pinet said. "So, if you were the Fischers, what would you do?"

"Find a way home," Jie said.

"Exactly," Pinet said. "Check shipping records, passenger manifests, census records too, anything you can find from 1873 to 1889. We might get lucky."

"Assuming they used their real names," Brigalow announced.

"Let's hope they did," Pinet said as he rubbed his temples.

Everyone took turns scouring the offline records which proved to be time consuming and tedious. Again, they dared not risk any online activity which would be recorded on drives and in the cloud, easy fodder for the Nazis in 2337.

Initially there seemed to be nothing of substance to discover and they were all losing hope when Sunil Patel noticed something from a newspaper archive.

"Look at this! It appears our intrepid time travellers got mixed up with a criminal element. It says here that a Rudolph Fischer is suspected of laundering money for someone named Albert Clarence! It couldn't be him, could it?"

"Let me see," Pinet demanded, practically pushing Patel out of his seat. "Hmm? I suppose it's possible. They could be trying to raise money for passage. This would be the fastest way."

"But crime," Patel added.

"Why not? They have no-one to answer to, no allegiance to the people or the era. That might give them licence to act outside their normal limits," Pinet suggested then added, "Keep following this path, see where it leads. Find out about this Albert Clarence too."

Meanwhile, Anastasia Kuznetsov had another potential hit. "There's a Victorian Census which shows R and N Fischer living in Collingwood in 1881.

"Surely they didn't stay there that long," she suggested.

"Maybe they did," said Pinet. "If they were saving for a journey, it would take time."

"Or they ended up in jail, if Sunil's theory is correct," she said.

"Worth checking," Pinet added.

Further scouring of the records found that a Rudolph Fischer was sentenced to the minimum 3 years and 6 months in prison in 1882 for petty larceny, but they still couldn't connect this man with the time travelling couple and frankly, they couldn't imagine that an academic like him would go down such a path. Perhaps they were desperate, knowing how imperative their mission was.

Dead end after dead end frustrated their search until they discovered a shipping manifest dated 1885, the SS Chusan. The ship was a regular traveller between Australia, Singapore and England, a P&O steamship that also used sail power.

"It says here there were two passengers who left Melbourne in 1885 headed for London, R and N Fischer," Sunil Patel announced.

"It has to be them," Pinet agreed.

Over time they found more bits of information that slowly pieced together a story that seemed plausible, if not likely despite several years of nothing. Newspaper articles involving criminal activity, prison records, ties to Albert Clarence who mysteriously disappeared in 1885 around the same time as the Fischers left Melbourne and further, records of a couple by that name arriving in London eight months later. That made sense given the shipping of the era. A trip of that distance would indeed take that long. From there, they vanished from the records.

Jean Claude Pinet aired his thoughts, "Let's assume the Fischers did travel to London with the artefact. They would then have to cross the channel and make their way to Austria, yes?" Everyone nodded. "So, they're trying to complete the mission!"

"But that was, what? 335 years ago," Luciana Gonzales revealed. "We should be aware of their success by now, shouldn't we?"

"True," Pinet said. "But what if Hitler isn't there. We know he was taken away by Pfeiffer. Perhaps that very act changes the time continuum until he returns."

"Wait a minute," Brigalow interrupted. "So, the past can't be the past until the future sends Hitler back to that time?"

"That seems to be the case, "Pinet added.

"If they return him, "Brigalow added.

"They have to," Jie suggested. "If they don't send him back there will be no Nazis and they'll disappear anyway and we know that hasn't happened...yet."

"I think the to and fro between now, the future, and the past is complicating the plan we're trying to execute, perhaps even blocking it somehow," Pinet explained.

"So, what do we do now," asked Muhammad Galal.

"We wait," answered Pinet.

"For what exactly," asked Brigalow.

"For Hitler to surface and hope the Fischers come through," Pinet declared.

For the next few days everyone hung by tenterhooks, scouring historical data for some kind of clue about where and when Hitler reappeared in the past.

Pinet assumed it would be around the same place and time that the family was grabbed by the Nazis, 1889, but it was also possible that the future Nazis kept him longer and would reinstall him later, when he was older.

Pinet also wondered if that would be wise given Hitler's childhood. He needed to experience certain things, many emotionally traumatic, to turn into the dictator he became. Pinet doubted that the Nazis could replicate that in a controlled environment.

Jean Claude was working late in his office as usual, trying to figure out the space time complexities they were experiencing with two of the IG physicians when he heard shouting from the transfer room. He ran into the chamber as the IG machine lit up bright as day. He didn't need to alert the guards who were already pointing their weapons at the vortex expecting a Nazi assault team but instead a small canister dropped out of the void and bounced a few meters across the floor stopping at Pinet's feet. The vortex immediately closed.

Everyone cleared the room expecting the device to detonate but after fifteen minutes, nothing happened. A Hit-Man robot was sent in to inspect the item and again, nothing happened.

Pinet looked at the cylinder from the safety of the blast shield then entered the room, bent over and picked up the tube-like canister. It was small, light, and quite cold, probably some kind of alloy or aluminium.

He noticed it had a simple slip-on lid, which he popped off. Inside there was a piece of paper which he extracted.

The writing, in English, simply said, *Hitler returned to Braunau am Inn, November 23rd, 1889.*

Chapter 30 – The delivery

As Rudolph and Nina Fischer stepped onto the dock at Portsmouth, they breathed a sigh of relief. Their long sea journey was over. At least the part they'd dreaded. Being at sea for so long hadn't been at all enjoyable, particularly when the ocean grew heavy.

Being from 2215 where sub orbital air travel enabled journeys like the one they just did to be completed in a matter of hours, they weren't prepared for the slow, crude sea voyage they had just completed; the tedium and the seasickness never abating. So, it was with a great deal of happiness that they stood on solid ground.

The journey had one benefit though; it gave them an opportunity to formulate a plan to return to Austria and deposit their cargo. Rudolph wasn't proud of himself, but he also had no choice when it came to negotiating a deal for the return of the artefact that had found its way into the hands of criminals. They held it for ransom but Rudolph, unable to come up with the money offered an alternative option, to work with them and make them rich beyond their wildest dreams.

The offer was met with scepticism at first, but when Rudolph explained how he could achieve it the syndicate found the offer enticing. The deal was done and Rudolph knew it would mean burning valuable time before they could consider leaving. It might even require him to commit some distasteful acts, but he had little choice.

After a few years he did succeed in making the syndicate a fortune through gaming houses, high end robberies and white-collar crime which were outside of anything his criminal contacts could ever have contemplated but Rudolph didn't predict that they would turn on him, once they'd learned everything he knew. When their activities drew the suspicion of the law, Rudolph was the scapegoat and was arrested, convicted and served a prison sentence. His position as a teacher somehow worked in his favour and he was given the minimum sentence.

Nina, on the other hand, stayed out of trouble, saving everything she could in a bank account that had no connection to Rudolph. They were just about ready to leave Australia when he was captured and they had to delay the journey until his release, three and a half arduous years later.

Upon his release in 1885, Rudolph took his revenge on the syndicate, killing their leader, Albert Clarence. The syndicate leader posed as a petty thief, using street urchins to do his dirty work but he was only one of many who operated a criminal network in the suburbs of Melbourne.

Disposing of Clarence's body was easy and he knew that suspicion would not fall on him when it simply looked like Clarence had disappeared with a great amount of cash. Rudolph simply called it compensation for hard time served. It seemed that he'd learned much during his prison time.

Rudolph and Nina gained passage to England and left Melbourne at the very first opportunity. Eight months later they set foot on English soil. Now they had to get to Austria.

After a few days' rest, they convinced a fisherman to give them passage to Calais and paid him handsomely to remain silent. It would be easier to just slip into Europe rather than leave a paper trail.

They landed on the beach and walked into Calais where they found an Inn and stayed a couple of days. Crossing the channel was easy but now they had to find their way across the length of France and Germany to get to Braunau am Inn on the western border of Austria, around 1000 kilometres in total.

Crossing France wasn't overly complicated, much of it they did using rail. Changing trains in Paris for a crossing into Germany also proved routine. When they reached Salzburg, they only had another 60 kilometres to travel to Braunau am Inn. The roads in Europe in 1886 were of dirt and not an easy journey but they negotiated a fare and managed to get most of the way to Braunau am Inn, finding a hotel to stay the night.

While they were both able to speak fluent German, they found the local dialect a little challenging at first but in time they overcame it. Rudolph's work with the criminal element taught him about patience and planning and so, he and Nina didn't even consider looking for the Hitler home for many weeks while they settled into a cottage they rented.

Both assumed that the Nazis were already watching over the Hitlers. That would mean they would need to tread carefully when inspecting the Hitler apartment building at Salzburger Vorstadt 15.

Age was an advantage, both now being well into their fifties. The Nazis might not suspect an older couple of subversion, more likely they would be expecting a military incursion; that's what Rudolph hoped anyway.

One Sunday they took a stroll along Saltburger Vorstadt, walking slowly and chatting about the weather. They spied the apartment building but didn't pay it any extra attention. As they walked, they saw two men who, while initially seeming quite normal, loitered too much and were out of place.

Rudolph could tell that one of them at least was carrying, his hand hidden under the jacket and there was that steely gaze Rudolph had learned on the streets in Melbourne. Clearly the Nazis were here. Rudolph bid the fellow a 'guten tag' and smiled but was ignored.

They walked on, planning not to return to the street for many more weeks. Too many visits in too short a time would illicit suspicion. Better to be deliberate in managing their time, of which they had plenty.

Over the next few months, they became a part of the fabric of Braunau am Inn, making friends, attending the theatre, festivals, fairs and celebrations.

As historians now living a world they only ever read about in books, they felt incredibly fortunate. It was a dream come true and despite the problems they'd had during the mission to date, they now felt very much at home and ready to complete the task.

On their next sojourn to the street, they rounded a blind corner and literally ran into a couple coming the other way. The woman spilled her groceries, which tumbled in all directions. Rudolph and the woman's husband scrambled to catch the vegetables as they rolled around everywhere, looking rather comical and the woman laughed, as did Nina.

"I'm so sorry," cried Rudolph.

"That's quite all right," the other man said.

It took a while to collect all the goods to the amusement of Nina and the man's wife. It was Nina who broke the ice, although the comical scene had probably done that for them already, "Hello, I'm Nina Fischer and this is my husband, Rudolph."

The woman smiled. "I'm Heidi Hofer and my husband is Zlatko."

The men shook hands before Zlatko said, "We are new to Braunau. How long have you lived here?"

"Only about six months ourselves," Rudolph answered, "What brings you here?"

"I am a customs inspector," Zlatko said, "and Heidi is a housewife. We're hoping for children soon." This made Heidi blush. "What of you? Why the move to Braunau?"

Rudolph and Nina hadn't missed Zlatko's comment about his line of work and immediately thought of Alois Hitler. They had also anticipated they would face the question of their being in

Braunau at some stage and concocted a simple story that they had used already on occasion. "Oh, we were both teachers in Vienna, but needed a change, so here we are."

"A noble profession indeed," Zlatko said. "Where do you teach now?"

"To be honest we are on a sabbatical, so nowhere for the time being," Rudolph explained, "and to be honest, I'm not sure I would like to return to the classroom. I feel like a change."

"What about you Nina," Heidi asked, "will you teach again?"

"I don't know yet. We worked hard for many years, never had children, so I don't need to go back but I worry about boredom too."

The remark made Heidi and Zlatko laugh, "Well you've come to the right place, I think. Long cold winters indoors can have that effect," Zlatko added.

Rudolph took advantage of the topic of conversation, "So, Customs, what's that like?"

"Oh, it has its moments depending on where you're situated. Being on the German border isn't too bad though. We're all much the same so it's rare we have a major problem," Zlatko explained.

"How many people do you need then," Rudolph wondered being careful not to appear too nosey.

"There are 12 of us here now, working various shifts, mainly rail freight. Perhaps I can investigate a job for you Rudolph," Zlatko suggested.

Rudolph couldn't believe the suggestion and the possibilities it created. "That would certainly interest me. It's not an area I'm familiar with but I could learn."

"Believe me, it's not that difficult. Checking of manifests, looking for contraband, very easy," said Zlatko.

"Your offer is most generous and yet you don't know me," Rudolph added.

"Oh, that's part of the craft, being a good judge of character. You seem to be down to earth, honest people. I can tell," Zlatko said with a wink.

Then Nina said, "Perhaps we should formalise our friendship with dinner. Would you like to join us?"

Heidi smiled widely. "Oh yes, but please, come to our house. As you can see, we have plenty to offer. It would be my great pleasure to cook for you both."

"And believe me, Heidi is an incredible cook," Zlatko announces with some pride.

"That sounds wonderful. When," Nina asked.

"Tomorrow night?"

Nina smiled, "Perfect. Where should we go?"

"Oh, just across the road," Zlatko said pointing to his building. "Salzburger Vorstadt 15 apartment 4. We just moved in," Zlatko said.

Rudolph almost choked when he heard the address but hid it well. "Very good, shall we make it 6 o'clock?"

"Yes," Heidi said. "I can't wait."

"Neither can we," Nina replied, "See you tomorrow."

"Yes, goodbye," Zlatko said and shook Rudolph's hand again and the couples parted.

When Rudolph and Nina got around the corner and out of sight Rudolph said, "Can you believe that?!"

"No. Pure chance indeed," Nina added.

"It gets us inside the building and very close to the Hitlers. We should be able to find somewhere to hide the object and deposit it during a future visit, so this friendship is one we need to keep," Rudolph said.

"That shouldn't be too difficult. They seem like very nice people and, if he gets you that job, all the better," Nina added.

"Won't that be a coup," Rudolph said, laughing a little. Nina simply smiled and nodded.

The next evening Rudolph and Nina walked to the address on Salzburger Vorstadt pretending not to notice the loitering Nazis who certainly noticed them but didn't interfere with their arrival.

They entered the main door and followed a corridor checking doors for number 4, which was at the back half of the building on the ground floor. Rudolph knocked and the door open within seconds and they were met with the beaming smile of Heidi. "Welcome, welcome. Please come in."

Rudolph and Nina stepped inside handing over a bottle of wine for the occasion. The apartment was small but roomy enough for a couple in their twenties.

Despite the sizeable age gap, the four of them got along extremely well. As promised, Heidi was an excellent cook, serving up Rindsuppe (Beef soup) followed Fasan (Pheasant) and finished off with Tirolerkuchen (Hazelnut and chocolate coffee cake).

"I have to confess I didn't make the cake," Heidi said, "I bought it at the patisserie."

"But she could have," Zlatko added with pride.

"I'm sure," Rudolph said and he didn't doubt it either.

After dinner the two couples sat in the living room and talked, getting to know each other better. Rudolph and Nina had to be on guard. While they knew Austria well and could relate to a great many things through their study of history, they had to avoid obvious blunders that might alert their hosts to any oddity like words from the future that didn't exist yet, or mentioning events that were historical to them but hadn't yet manifested in the lives of Zlatko and Heidi. It was harder work than they anticipated.

"Oh, I almost forgot," said Zlatko, "I talked to my supervisor about you. He would like to meet and discuss a job!"

"Really." Rudolph said.

"Yes, he thinks you would be perfect. What was it he said? Mature and yet untainted," Zlatko laughed.

"Well, he's right about that," Rudolph replied knowing it was a lie and remembering his dirty deeds in Australia.

"He told me you should come down to talk whenever you like, he's there most days. His name is Alois," Again Rudolph almost choked on his wine and couldn't hide it this time. "Are you ok." Zlatko asked.

"Yes, my apologies, went down the wrong way," Rudolph said quickly before recovering. "So, Alois you say? What's he like?"

"He's a little too serious if you ask me but he's been in the business for a long time."

"That's understandable," Rudolph said although he knew better. "I will visit him next week. Please tell him thank you."

"I will, oh and he lives in an apartment upstairs with his family. That's how we attained this place. He recommended us," Zlatko told them.

"Well, he sounds like a well-connected man," Nina suggested.

"Oh yes, that's true."

The rest of the evening went well, and the couples parted with a promise by Nina to return the favour soon.

As they walked home Nina asked, "Did you see where we could put the object?"

"Not really, but I'm sure we'll get another chance," he told her.

"Perhaps you can befriend Alois," she added.

"That's not in the least funny," Rudolph said and Nina laughed.

The following week Rudolph visited the Customs Office to meet with Alois Hitler. He was shown to an office where a burly, bald man sat studying some paperwork. The man glanced up at Rudolph and stood.

"Guten Tag. I'm Alois Hitler, you must be Randolph,"

"Rudolph sir," he said as they shook hands

"Ah, Rudolph! Sit, sit," Alois said gruffly. "So, you're looking for a job, ja?"

"Yes, I am," Rudolph said feeling suddenly very nervous.

"Gut, sehr gut," Alois said, "When can you start?"

Chapter 31 – The Conglomeration

It was now 2217 and the IG Committee had so far failed to accomplish their allotted United Nations mission. Counting all the tests and missions they had conducted, there were upwards of fifty people from the current era who had been sent to various places in history to affect the killing of Adolf Hitler but to date, their missions had failed outright, mostly because the Nazis of 2337 had intercepted their attempts.

Moreover, those attempts forced the Nazis to send back a great many people to various times to protect Hitler and his family and guard their future and past homes and localities making it impossible for the IG Committee to stage any further attempts. The last big move against Hitler failed when the Nazis snatched him from his home in 1889 and briefly took the family to 2337, returning them when the threat was gone.

Now, their one great hope lay in the hands of a civilian couple who they had sent back to 1873 who were deposited to Australia instead of Austria by a blundering technician. The couple surfaced in historical documents and were traced back to England in 1886 but that's all the committee knew. Would the Fischer's complete the mission, or had they somehow been discovered, lost or died? No-one knew for certain.

There was also the constant fear of a Nazi incursion to kill all the members of the IG committee, something that still hung over their heads. They knew it was only a matter of time but for now Ernst Pfeiffer, the future Nazi leader, was toying with them, making them suffer the stress of waiting for the axe to fall.

As much as they tried, they couldn't come up with another feasible plan to eliminate the Nazi dictator and the weapon that would seal Hitler's fate, an artefact attained by the Russians in World War Two that seemed to have been lost in time. Their only solid fact was a message from a Nazi in 2337, Klaus Haas indicating the return to Austria of the Hitlers in 1889, but the information was useless without the Fischers.

In the end they could only hope that there would be a sudden change in the written history to show that the Fischer's had succeeded however every day when Jean Claude Pinet woke he remembered the Holocaust was still real and that the Nazi leader was still in the history books.

With their IG machine now capable of return travel from the past or the future, at least to the origin of the IG machine, work was being focussed on some kind of mobile device to enable a two-way wormhole to be created further back than that, to recover those who had been sent back further should they wish to return. It seemed only right but it was probably a long way off in terms of development.

Pinet knew the Nazis of 2337 had achieved such a breakthrough with the snatching of the Hitlers in 1889, but their technical abilities were clearly far more advanced. Reports from the Spetsnaz who attempted the killing of Hitler then were sketchy but the fact that certain things in the past had happened with no consequences in the current era made it clear that Hitler was taken out of his timeline at some stage. Pinet shook his head wondering where it all went wrong.

The rest of the committee members arrived in dribs and drabs for their next brainstorming session, none of them looking particularly enthusiastic, including Janina Zielinski, an IG operator who had escaped the Nazis of the future when her subversion became impossible to hide.

As they assessed options again the building shook as the unmistakable rumble of the IG machine's power banks spooled up. The white light of a time vortex brightened along the corridors. UN Marines on guard, stood at alert with guns aimed at the vortex but before they could react to the likely invading force, they were killed by an unseen enemy who seemed to have infiltrated the entire building, leaving the facility defenceless.

Jean Claude stood as Nazi soldiers burst into the room forcing him and the other IG delegates to their knees with hands behind their heads. Seconds later Ernst Pfeiffer walked into the room beaming a smile so broad it threatened to split his ears.

"Hello again Jean Claude. Lovely to see you." Pinet didn't answer. "No words Jean Claude? I wonder why. Perhaps the fact that you and your friends are about to die. I told you your time would come and now it is here!"

Despite the inevitable, Pinet had one question, "How did you kill our men?"

"I suppose it doesn't matter if you know, you'll take it to your grave," and Pfeiffer snapped his fingers and a few seconds later a contingent of Nazi Marines materialised around Pinet and the others. "Stealth suits. Something new. Pretty clever if I do say so."

"What about our robots, how did you stop them," Pinet wondered, not expecting any latitude from Pfeiffer but if he could keep him boasting it might buy time. Not that he anticipated a rescue.

"In the end it was simple, we hacked their drives. They are just computers after all. We shut them down with a wireless signal," Pfeiffer admitted. "They are useless to you and, in the future as it turns out. Too easy to hack. Is there anything else you want to know before we finish you?"

"Yes. Again, I wonder how you can hope to hold this place. You were forced back last time."

"That's true but we've been working on some new ideas. We can now open multiple wormholes at the same time, so we've sent troops all over this world. It's only a matter of time," Pfeiffer declared.

Pinet was left hanging and took the bait, "A matter of time for what?"

"We will take out all the current world leaders and military leaders. From there we will start a global war. This era will destroy itself."

"And perhaps you along with it. How do you know you won't disrupt your own time," Pinet asked.

"Because we know who to save and who to kill. Like I said, we've done our homework this time," Pfeiffer boasted, "By the time we're done, your world will be a wasteland, and we will rise from the ashes."

"Sounds like the same kind of rhetoric you Nazis are famous for, all hiss and vinegar," Pinet replied but it only elicited another smile.

"Insults won't change the fact that what I have told you is happening as we speak, but you need not take my word for it; I'm sure it's on television already! Would you like to watch," but Jean Claude said nothing this time. "Very well," Pfeiffer declared then turned to the Marines. "Kill them. Kill them all." He looked back to the IG Chairman. "Goodbye Jean Claude."

As Klaus Haas kept the wormholes open in the modified transfer room of the IG facility in 2337, hundreds of soldiers walked freely through the vortices and back to 2215 to carry out their respective missions. He had revealed his multi vortex technology to Pfeiffer to reinforce his solidarity with the Reich and been given much more freedom as a reward.

He had gained total trust with Pfeiffer, which was what he wanted, needed in fact. He knew turning over the data would probably give Pfeiffer a significant advantage in the fight against the people of 2215, but it was a risk he was willing to take.

As the last of the soldiers disappeared into the void, Johann Steinbrenner walked into the chamber, "Hello Klaus," he said.

Klaus Haas looked around and smile. "Hello old friend. Good to see you."

"You too. All goes well I see," Steinbrenner said.

"Yes. Your ability to convince Pfeiffer to send Hitler back was impressive. I didn't think he would go for it."

"It was easier than I expected," Steinbrenner declared. "He's not very bright and bought the whole story, even the part about me being a descendant of Hitler's sister."

"That was a nice touch. You weren't worried he would check?"

"Not really, he wanted to believe me. That's how soft minds work," Steinbrenner declared.

"Very true," Haas said with a smile.

"So have we heard from your friend Pinet?"

Klaus Haas pulled a small metal canister from his pocket. "Read it for yourself," and he tossed the message to Steinbrenner, who popped the lid off the container and extracted a note,

"Ah, so they're aware of where Hitler is and claim to have a weapon to dispose of him. That's good news," Steinbrenner said but was interrupted as a single Nazi soldier entered the transfer room.

Klaus Haas smiled when he saw the soldier, "You know what to do?" The man nodded. "Very well, it's safe to walk on in. You will emerge in the hallway."

The soldier nodded again and without a word, disappeared into the vortex.

Steinbrenner looked at Haas, "What now?"

"We do this," and Haas shut down the IG computers, literally closing all the time windows and stranding Pfeiffer and his entire army in 2215. "That should give them something to think about."

"Indeed," Steinbrenner said.

"Now we message Pinet before the purge, a week ahead should do it," he said as he rebooted the quantum computers and tapped in the data. His colleagues didn't quite know what was happening but given they weren't privy to the entire plan; they didn't consider that it was the beginning of a coup.

A single vortex opened, and Haas tossed another canister into the void. "There. That should do the trick," he said.

"What does it say Klaus?" Steinbrenner asked.

"What Pinet needs to know," Haas said.

Steinbrenner smiled.

Rudolph and Nina Fischer had spent weeks getting to know Heidi and Zlatko and visited their home multiple times. The Nazi observers had become so used to their comings and goings they didn't pay them any attention.

Rudolph had spent a great deal of time and effort scouting the building for a secure place to hide the weapon that would see the demise of Adolf Hitler, and thus the entire Nazi Third Reich and ultimately negate the Holocaust of WWII and the Nazis of 2337 by default. It was a simple case of putting it somewhere close to the Hitler apartment and waiting for the infant to be born. Rudolph didn't really understand what would happen next, but he didn't need to know. He assumed it would just activate but he didn't know how.

On this their latest visit he excused himself to use the bathroom, and, having brought the box with him, snuck out of the apartment and climbed the stairs to the top floor where he knew the Hitler residence to be. Having been at work for Alois Hitler at Customs for some months now, he hoped it wouldn't be a surprise if Alois happened across him knowing that Rudolph and Zlatko were friends. He walked up the hallway towards the Hitler front door and spied a manhole in the ceiling. He was thinking of a way to climb up and through it to empty the item above the Hitler residence when a voice startled him.

"Vas is Das?"

He spun around and saw Alois standing at the end of the hall with two other men...Nazis.

"Oh! Hello Alois. It's me, Rudolph."

"I know who it is. What are you doing at my front door?"

Rudolph had concocted a cover story for just this situation but at the critical moment sheer terror had caused it to evaporate from his mind. "Um. Well. You see..."

But before he could utter another word, he heard a whiff of compressed air followed by a sting in his chest. He looked down and saw blood pulsing from a small wound as pain erupted inside. He collapsed to the floor and exhaled for the last time as his precious cargo dropped onto the floor.

Alois walked over and picked up the box and was about to examine the contents but as soon as he touched it, he felt it vibrate and it became hot, so he dropped it. One of the other Nazi guards picked it up and stashed it in a carry case.

Jean Claude Pinet sat in his office as usual when Zhang Jie burst in. "We have something!"

"What?"

"A newspaper story from 1886 in Braunau am Inn, a murder. The victim was a man named Rudolph Fischer and there were three more victims including Nina Fischer. The article suggests he was caught up in a robbery gone bad."

"Good God! What about the artefact," Pinet asked.

"No mention of it!"

"We have to assume the Nazis have it," Pinet suggested, "DAMN!!"

"Very likely," added Jie.

Pinet paused, thinking about the news, a pang of regret tightening up inside him, but he shook it off for the time being. "Do we have dates or times?"

Jie smiled, "We have both!"

"Brilliant," answered Pinet, somewhat relieved, "If we time this right…" but he didn't finish the sentence.

"Indeed," said Jie knowingly. "And with the information Haas sent us we can stop the attack next week too."

"We might not have to worry about that." He grabbed a com cylinder, wrote a note and stuffed it inside. He then spooled up the machine and tossed the message into the void.

As Captain John Williams and his contingent gathered for their mission to alter history by winning the Battle of Fromelles in 1916 a new wormhole briefly manifested itself and a cylinder emerged plopping into the mud at his feet. He opened it and saw a message inside. He read it and gasped loudly, "Jesus!"

"What is it skipper," asked one of his men.

"We're to stand down immediately, the attack is off!"

The men looked dismayed at the news then someone asked, "What are we supposed to do with these things," gesturing towards the HIT Men, their robot allies.

"We are to wait for further instructions," Captain Williams said.

"Well, they best hurry it up, we can't hide these things for very long," said another man to which Williams simply nodded.

As Rudolph Fischer inspected the manhole in the hall ceiling, he was startled by a voice with a German accent, "Fischer! Get down now!"

He didn't know who it was, but he followed the directive instantly, falling spread eagled on the floorboards just as Alois Hitler turned into the hall with his two bodyguards.

Before another word could be uttered, three silenced rounds zipped over Fischer's head and felled the trio. The two Nazis were dead before they hit the floor while Alois Hitler was wounded by a precision shot. He screamed in pain.

Rudolph lay for a moment then the voice said, "Give me the box!"

"What?!"

"Give me the box. Now!"

"But the mission? I must complete the mission," Fischer announced.

"Jean Claude has changed the mission. Now give me the box!" the assassin announced.

Fischer recognised Pinet's name and relaxed a little. "OK, here," and he handed the package over to a seemingly invisible figure who snatched it and headed for a rear window. "Wait, what about us?"

"Someone will be in touch. For now, go home and stay out of sight. You don't want to be here when the bodies are discovered." And the figure literally vanished.

As Captain John Williams waited for further instructions a messenger rode up on a pushbike as the battle raged ahead of them. "Captain Williams," cried the despatch rider.

"Yes?"

"This is for you," and the rider handed over a satchel. "Didn't think you'd be exactly where they told me to go, but here you are! First time that's ever happened," he laughed.

"Thank you private," Williams said.

"What is it anyway," asked the Private.

"I have no idea," Williams replied.

He opened the satchel and found a Perspex box. Within it something old and dirty, he couldn't make it out in the dark. He also found a note, *Recommence attack immediately.* As he read through the instructions his eyes widened. When he finished reading, he destroyed the message then addressed his men, "OK, it's back on but the plan had changed. Listen up!"

Ernst Pfeiffer was furious.

"Get us reconnected immediately!" he screamed.

The disruption caused the Nazi marines to balk on the order to shoot the prisoners. Pfeiffer was too distracted to reinforce the order as he ranted and raved at the technicians who had not yet completed the task of programming the computers for a return trip to 2337. He was so loud that Jean Claude Pinet could hear him screaming from the meeting room and smiled.

Pfeiffer burst back into the room and marched up to Pinet, grabbing him by the throat with one hand and began crushing. "What have you done?"

Pinet couldn't reply until Pfeiffer let go. He coughed as he tried to regain his breath. "I have done nothing Ernst, maybe your idiot Nazi technicians couldn't add up."

Pfeiffer punched him in the nose which broke and bled profusely. "You will pay!"

Pinet smiled again and looked Pfeiffer in the face, blood drizzling into his mouth and staining his white teeth. "You idiot. You think this was us? Your arrogance may well be your undoing after all," and he spat a glob of blood on Pfeiffer's face.

"SHOOT THEM NOW," Pfeiffer screamed in a rage.

As the Nazi Marines raised their weapons everyone screamed, "No! Please no" but there was little they could do. Seconds morphed into what felt like hours as their fate was sealed.

Jean Claude closed his eyes waiting for his body to be torn apart by gunfire but after a few seconds passed, nothing happened. He opened his eyes and saw Pfeiffer, the Nazis, and everyone who came through the wormhole from 2337 writhing on the floor, their bodies quite literally evaporating molecule by molecule.

"What's happening," Pfeiffer demanded, his voice sounding hollow and distant, as if he were down a deep tunnel.

Jean Claude Pinet walked over to him and watched as Pfeiffer disintegrated and said, "You lost!"

Pfeiffer's face revealed alarm followed by utter defeat and a few seconds later he and the entire Nazi force were gone, disappearing from this time to who knew where. Pinet suddenly had another episode of mixed memories, changes in history that he'd never known before.

Captain John Williams, under new orders from Jean Claude Pinet didn't attack the Germans at Fromelles. He was ordered to retreat and work his task force around the battle to a quiet sector on the line.

Their objective was a railway station. They entered the Allied trenches ignoring shouts and cries from the British soldiers and jumped into no-man's land. The HIT Men fired a series of volleys onto the German strong points, destroying their machine gun nests and blockhouses with ease. They then targeted artillery and reserve lines. The Germans on the front line didn't know what to do. Their means of defending the line had been obliterated. The Australian task force, protected by their robotic companions, advanced. There was little fire from the enemy line and what was coming was dealt with via precise return fire from the HIT Men.

As the task force reached the German wire, the HIT Men swept it aside like it was a cobweb, creating a huge gap in the line. The soldiers in the Allied trenches saw the opening and charged!

The Germans, realising they were about to be over-run, panicked and retreated, opening even more gaps in the line. The British took the trenches while the task force moved into the support lines, eliminating resistance, as pitiful as it was. They continued to forge forward, breaking out of the communications saps and emerged behind the lines as a group of German surrendered.

Captain Williams approached them.

"Where's the railway station?" The German looked dumbfounded but another soldier who understood English said, "That way." He pointed. "Find the road and it's about a mile north."

"Thank you," Williams said. "Let's move men."

The Germans looked at the HIT Men in complete amazement and muttered between themselves.

The task force rushed out of the trenches, amongst Germans who were retreating, but when the Germans in the back sections of the line saw the robots, they too surrendered.

Captain Williams and his men found the road and sprinted for the railway station. They could hear a train whistle and knew the train was leaving. They had to intercept. The HIT Men were ordered to rush ahead and did so at inhuman pace. It would mean leaving the task force exposed but it didn't matter at this point, besides, the Germans here didn't realise the soldiers were an enemy unit and thought they were just trying to get to the train. Some even laughed at them and flung a few insults and jibes at the Australians. In the darkness, their uniforms were difficult to see, which was a blessing.

They sprinted as fast as they could and saw a billow of steam, which suggested the train was about to move but it soon became clear that it wasn't going anywhere. HIT Men had it surrounded while one held its driver at gunpoint.

Members of the 16th Bavarian Reserve Infantry Regiment on board the train poured everything they had into the robotic attackers to no avail. Their Mauser bullets just glanced off, doing no damage. The gunfire continued as the Australians arrived and Williams ordered that no-one fire back.

The Australians took defensive positions, anticipating that more Germans would be attracted to the frenzy and waited for an attack, but no-one came. It seemed the English onslaught was keeping them busy down the road.

On the train the Germans realised that there was no incoming fire and stopped shooting. Captain Williams called out, "We order you to surrender. There's no need for anyone to die here tonight!"

The remark was met with a fusillade of gunfire. When that died away, he tried again. "We have you surrounded. You cannot escape, throw down your weapons and step off the train. You will be treated with honour."

Another fusillade erupted but much less intensely this time. When it stopped, Williams said nothing. He decided to let the Germans think about their situation. It took a while but eventually a white handkerchief attached to a rifle muzzle appeared through a carriage window. Williams said, "Stay alert men!" Then he called, "Exit the train slowly. Bring your weapons and toss them on the ground and line up along the side of the train single file. hands on heads!" He repeated the order three times.

The response was slow but eventually Bavarian Guard soldiers emerged. They looked at the HIT Men with obvious alarm but did as they were told.

Williams also knew that there would probably be Nazis from the future amongst them and that they might try something but exactly what he couldn't be sure. He was surprised that nothing had happened yet, but it was possible that this eventuality hadn't been made apparent to them for some reason. Williams was in the same position but gleaned that the fact that he was getting some data meant the UN was ahead of the game for a change.

The HIT Men were on ready alert and could detect changes in body heat and even read mood signatures from the captives. Most were showing signs of fear or resignation, but a few were clearly demonstrating defiance. Until they tried to rebel, it couldn't be ascertained whether they were Pfeiffer's men or genuine Bavarians.

It didn't take long to find out, one of them raise a weapon but before he could fire, a single shot from the nearest robot put him down. Williams was surprised to see that the man fired a Mauser and not something from the future. Another tried and he too failed. They were clearly outgunned and the rest, five in all, tossed their guns and raised their arms.

Williams separated them from the other captives and examined their uniforms. While they were dressed in WW1 Bavarian garb, there was something different about them, the fabric was cleaner and better tailored. They weren't of this time; he was certain of that.

"Anyone else," Williams asked but no one moved. Without really needing to, he addressed the HIT Men via wireless, "Watch them closely. if anyone moves, kill them!"

For now, the battle behind them had quelled and Allied soldiers appeared, but they left Williams and his contingent to deal with the Bavarians. It was also clear that they didn't want to go near the robot soldiers, the Allies as dismayed by them as the Germans.

Williams turned his attention back to the captives. "I'm looking for one of your men. A corporal, his name is Adolf Hitler. Please step forward."

Everyone watched in anticipation, but no one moved. "I repeat. Adolf Hitler, step forward immediately!"

Again nothing.

"Perhaps they don't speak English skipper," suggested one of the Australians.

"They know enough. Hitler doesn't speak English but many of them do. They'll tell him," Williams said. "I ask again. Adolf Hitler, step forward now!"

A few more seconds of silence and then a soldier stepped forward, hands raised. Williams knew it wasn't Hitler and then the man said, "Bitter. He is still on board the train. He is gravely unwell."

"Is he alone," Williams asked.

"Ja, he is," the soldier said.

"How long has he been unwell," Williams asked, hoping for a particular response.

"A few minutes," the man replied.

That was all Williams needed to know.

"Bring him out." No-one moved. "Bring him now NOW," Williams demanded.

Two Bavarians skittered into the train and worked their way through a carriage. Williams saw them lean over and struggle to lift the man inside and eventually got him moving. They helped him down the steps and brought him forward. He could barely stand as his condition clearly worsened when Williams approached, writhing in something akin to pain which was clearly something else. He was very white skinned, a gaunt looking fellow with a thin face, black hair and large moustache typical of the era.

"Are you Adolf Hitler," Williams asked.

He obviously didn't speak English, but he understood the questions and nodded. "Ich Bin (I am)."

That's all Williams needed to hear. He opened the satchel he'd received from the despatch rider, but he didn't open the wooden box and said to Hitler, "This is for you," and handed it over.

Hitler looked confused and someone translated for him. He limply reached out and took the box from Williams, his hand briefly brushing Williams's finger. He felt eerily cold. Hitler looked at Williams, fear rather than loathing in his eyes, and then he looked at the box, his body trembling as he did so, clearly confused. He then opened the box and looked closer. If he expected medical aid, he was very wrong.

What happened next would perhaps be a story that might be told for years and get exaggerated by its retelling.

Hitler fell to his knees and wept, the box falling to the ground and spilling its contents. Williams could see the box contained another box made of clear Perspex and inside that a few odd-looking items, dirty or rusty, he could not tell. They just looked like jagged pieces of metal. Despite his worsening condition Hitler looked at it curiously, picking it, up rotating it in his hands to try and understand the objects.

His curiosity got the better of him as he looked for an opening on the box. He found a small clip which he snapped open and prised the lid off. It did not give at first but in a few moments the lead seal tore and the air of 2215 mixed with that of 1916, and a puff of vapour vanished quickly in the cool night air. But then something else happened. The effect of opening the box had an immediate impact on Hitler, his body now prostrate, was convulsing.

"Was ist los (What is happening)?" he asked in clear panic, his voice oddly distant and echoing.

No-one said anything, there was nothing to say but as they watched, Hitler's head began to evaporate, disappearing in chunks like it was being erased by something supernatural. Then the rest of his body disintegrated like it was aspirin dropped in water. Hitler faded away at an accelerating rate, dissipating into the ether like a ghost and was suddenly not there at all.

Williams immediately felt weird, his memories became mixed, and his recollection of the Nazi leader faded. He knew Hitler was real but at the same time he also knew the man had somehow never existed. Similarly, his memories of studying the great battles of WW2 also faded away, the existence of the Third Reich, also evaporating from his memory. Everyone's memories were blurring into the non-existence of the man known as Adolf Hitler.

It was over. Hitler was no more! In fact, he never was.

Williams' only thought was that it might have been more humane to shoot him in the head, but when he looked at the other Germans, they too appeared confused and disoriented. Just as surprising, the Nazis of the future who were sent back to guard Hitler had also evaporated.

Then Williams, after collecting his thoughts, looked at the Perspex box that had spilled onto the soil where Hitler dropped it. It was empty. There was no sign of the contents inside or anywhere nearby.

Chapter 32 – The New World

The Vortex opened with its white light and Klaus Haas stepped into 2216 with a wide smile and was met by Jean Claude Pinet.

"Welcome Klaus."

"It's good to meet you at last Jean Claude."

"Indeed. I wasn't sure this day would ever come," Jean Claude confided.

"Me either, it was touch and go there for a while," Klaus added.

Stepping through the Vortex behind Klaus Haas was Johann Steinbrenner, who was greeted with the same enthusiasm.

Between the three of them they had concocted the plan that ultimately led to the Hitler Paradox which extinguished the Nazi leader from existence and ultimately made sure that the Nazi Party and its shadow groups through history never came to be and thus, the Holocaust and many other atrocities became just mixed memories in the minds of a handful of people in the world across two independent time frames.

"Your decision to act alone was a master stroke Jean Claude," suggested Klaus. "Working outside your committee was bold. I followed a similar approach until Johann came on board."

"We learned the hard way that having too many people 'in the know' was dangerous. The Nazis were able to stay one step ahead of us for a long time," Jean Claude said.

"So where are the other members of your committee, Jean Claude," Johann asked.

"Well, funny thing, after the Paradox was effected, it changed our timeline to a point where some of them didn't ever join the IG Committee. They were spread all over the world in a variety of roles, but they retained the memories of our success. It's not something I'll ever get used to I don't think," Pinet said.

Klaus Haas smiled, "I know what you mean. We too have had similar experiences."

Just then a third individual stepped into the transfer room from the Vortex, Janina Zielinski. Jean Claude was very pleased to see her, and she him.

"Hello Jean Claude."

"When you vanished like the Nazis, I feared the worst. It's good to know you are ok."

"It was the strangest thing. I'm with you one second and then without warning in 2337 like it was just an ordinary day, in a job I'd never had before with people I never knew," she explained. "Most disconcerting."

"I think we can all agree on that," Johann added.

The four moved out of the transfer room and walked down the corridor to the meeting room where some members of the committee were waiting. Those that had been disrupted by the change in the timeline joined the rest via teleconference.

Present were Davis Brigalow, Anastasia Kuznetsov, Luciana Gonzales, and Muhammad Galal. Their timelines didn't seem to have been affected by the paradox, but it was very different for others. Gabrielle Fawcett found herself at NASA, again, Zhang Jie was in China, a high-profile Government Official whose job was to liaise with the West, Hamid Kanumbra was a Human Rights advocate in Africa and Sunil Patel was an elected official with the Indian Opposition. All had to come to terms with their sudden upheaval because of the Paradox.

To confuse people more, there were members of the Committee that Pinet and the others had never met but they had memories of working with them for many years. One however stood out clearly, Kelly Antoniadis who, without the existence of the Nazis, had never been killed, a paradox because everyone knew her to be dead. It was truly bizarre and would be the subject of much study going forward, although Klaus Haas was already privy to the data which was available through the documented history of these recent events, another odd paradoxical effect.

The group talked openly about how they won the day and cleansed the Earth of hatred.

"I must congratulate you Klaus for having the mettle to contact us and share your knowledge. Without you, this scheme would have been doomed," Pinet announced.

"Thank you, Jean Claude," he replied. "But I had been Pfeiffer's friend for a long time until he was radicalised into the Nazis and rose through their ranks. I knew from the start that I wanted them gone and so, I got close to him when the time was right. He trusted me. In the end it was easy."

"I think not," Pinet said. "You took many risks. It's a pity there isn't any form of recognition for what you did."

"I didn't do it to be rewarded," Klaus said.

"Of course," Pinet added. "But if it's any consolation, you have my deepest gratitude."

Jean Claude then turned to Janina, "What of you? What have you been doing since you got thrust back home," Pinet asked.

"I have been helping Klaus perfect the mobile vortex unit, the one that enabled the Nazis to snatch the Hitlers. It enabled us to send the stealth operative to 1886 to collect the artefact then deposit it with a Bank in Paris until 1916," she explained, "A master stroke of engineering Klaus."

"Thank you, Janina. If we can mass produce, it then humanity will no longer need to live in one lifetime. People will be able to travel anywhere at any time and return. You could work in New York in 2337 and go home to your wife or husband in London in 1920 or wherever you chose to live. The future, the past and the present will effectively become one."

"Astounding Klaus," Pinet said. "It's truly miraculous."

The discussion continued, everyone keen to add their experiences to the mix, all with equally amazing stories.

Surprisingly the global population didn't alter much even though the First World War was shortened and there was never a Second World War. While around 100 million lives were saved as a consequence, the years that followed the WW2 era, 1939 to 1945, didn't suddenly see a global population explosion.

For a start there was no baby boom, there were most likely a significant number of changes in how relationships developed globally and family blood lines would have changed but it was impossible to know who, what and how things were different, but everyone agreed that one consequence was that some people who existed before, never came into being after the paradox and vice versa. Again, people struggled to wrap their minds around the concept. Nonetheless, the global population remained stable.

Rudolph and Nina Fischer lived out their lives in Austria in the late 1800s. They survived World War One and lived to see a world without a second war. With their future knowledge they dedicated their lives to education.

As for Ernst Pfeiffer, he didn't die because of the Paradox. He, like Janina, was thrust back to his time and became something of a political radical. He tried and failed to start a movement based on white supremacy and Nazism, but it gained no traction. His frustration erupted into violence and ultimately a life sentence for crimes against humanity.

Klaus Haas became a frequent time traveller as did Jean Claude, traversing the years from the 2200s to the 2300s and back many times, being careful to avoid crossing the time paradox limits. Eventually they were able to perfect a miniature, personal time vortex generator, which could be used anywhere, anytime. It, like the Internet, changed humanity forever. Time travel became as common as air travel. People visited long dead relatives, saw the future and the past while technology advanced much more quickly in all timelines.

One of the most interesting side effects of open time travel was the human response. There was concern that people might try to take advantage of the technology and deal with issues of the past that they felt might have disadvantaged them, but the opposite happened. By default, many wars simply didn't occur.

Time travel enabled people from all walks of life and all times to understand the bigger picture, to understand, not only themselves but where the World was headed and why. It also enabled quality of life to be of a high standard for everyone. Hate seemed to have also fallen victim to the Hitler Paradox.

To ensure that such travel didn't create complications, the United Nations appointed a Time Management Division to administer time travel and to avoid any catastrophic paradox events. While travel was easy and encouraged, there were rules that could never be broken, like visiting yourself at any place in time or visiting the same time frame more than once. All such situations simply would cause an individual to be erased. Time travel devices were strictly managed and retained all their data and thus, a paradox could not happen intentionally or by accident.

Tearing down the walls of history and opening doors to the future had, in the end, turned the World into a timeless community, one that most hoped would see humanity itself become selfless.

BUT it wasn't to last.

Chapter 33 – Epilogue

Dimitri Chadov, the Russian President, answered his private commlink, "Hello?"

The voice at the other end told him that the war trophy that the United Nations IG Committee needed had indeed been found and retrieved.

"Bring it to me immediately," Chadov demanded.

A few days later the item arrived in a specially made Perspex box. It had been long forgotten and looked like nothing more than a dirty, decrepit lump of junk that should have been thrown out a long time ago.

Chadov examined the contents of the box, frowning at its condition.

"Are we sure this is what they claim it to be," he asked.

"Da Comrade President, it is confirmed," explained the archaeologist who delivered the package.

"Tell me about it," Chadov urged the man.

The archaeologist, knowing that the question would indeed come up, had done his homework and began his explanation like he was giving a lecture to his university class,

"On April 30, 1945, Adolf Hitler died. It was 10 days after his 56th birthday. As you would be aware Comrade President Chadov, the Allies attacked Berlin from the west, we closed in from the East. The Germans had built strategic defences to stop us, realising that an attack on Berlin was imminent. We began that attack on April 16."

Chadov sat quietly and listened. He knew most of the story, but hearing about a great Russian victory from an esteemed Archaeologist intrigued him.

"We attacked on three fronts. From the east and the south, while shelling Berlin relentlessly. Another attack from the north crushed the German forces."

"What was Hitler doing while this was happening," Chadov asked.

"He was running the defence of Berlin from his bunker, but he had no control. In fact, he refused to believe that they were losing. Even when he was told there was no army to defend Berlin, he ordered non-existent battalions into battle."

"I see. Go on, please," Chadov urged.

"Our glorious Red Army encircled Berlin and commenced shelling the centre of the city. The dishevelled Germans were no match for us and over the course of a week, we broke through and finally took control of the battle," the archaeologist said.

"And Hitler," Chadov asked, knowing the answer, given the evidence that now confronted him.

"When he finally realised all was lost, he committed suicide. Our army took the city two days later."

"What happened after Hitler committed suicide," Chadov wondered. "There seems to be much confusion and speculation about this," he added.

"You would be aware Comrade President Chadov that Hitler married his mistress four hours before his death. He ventured outside only once, around 1.00am on April 30. At around 2.30am he addressed his staff and then retired to his quarters. Late on the morning of April 30, when the Red Army was within 500 meters of his bunker, Hitler met with General Helmuth Weilding, who oversaw the Berlin defence. He told Hitler that they were about to run out of ammunition and that Berlin would fall soon after."

"And then," Chadov asked, eager as a schoolboy listening to a bedtime story.

"Around 1pm he gave his staff permission to leave. Some did but many stayed with him. Around 2.30pm he and his wife, Eva Braun retired to his personal study. Many witnesses reported that around an hour later, they heard a loud gunshot. Heinz Ling, Hitler's valet, entered the study to what he described as the smell of burnt almonds. Hitler's adjutant, Otto Gunsche entered the study where he found two bodies on the sofa. Eva Braun was slumped over next to Hitler, she died because of cyanide poisoning. Hitler was face down on a table, a gunshot wound to his right temple. Gunsche announced Hitler's death to the remaining staff."

"I see, and what became of the bodies," Chadov asked.

"This is where there has been much speculation but according to Otto Gunsche, Hitler left written and verbal orders which were carried out. The bodies were carried upstairs via an emergency exit and into a garden behind the Reich Chancellery where they were doused in petrol and attempted to be burnt. I might add Comrade Chadov, that this did not go well. Several attempts failed but eventually they were able to ignite the bodies by stuffing them with paper. This was witnessed by several high-ranking Nazi officials and staff."

Chadov motioned for the man to continue.

"Joseph Stalin, upon hearing of Hitler's death demanded proof and ordered the body be found. On May 2, two days after Hitler's death, we took the Reich Chancellery, but it was two days later before the SMERSH Counter-espionage unit found his remains and those of Eva Braun and their two dogs in a shell crater. Even so, Comrade Stalin was not convinced and ordered the identity be proven and on May 11, dental work confirmed that Hitler was indeed dead."

"And you believe this," Chadov wondered.

"I do Comrade President; Hitler's body was also the subject of a post-mortem examination conducted by Soviet scientists. It is, without doubt, a fact that Hitler died in his bunker on April 30 as claimed by the Germans."

"I see," Chadov said as he again examined the content of the Perspex box. "So, tell me please, what I am looking at here."

"You are looking at Adolf Hitler's head sir, or part of it at least. That is Hitler! We kept his body and secretly buried it, moved it, and buried it again. The body was ultimately disposed of by the KGB. That information went to the grave with those members of the KGB, but his head was kept in a box by the Russian FSB."

Chadov stared at the shards of skull in the box, blackened and rusty from being burnt, buried and reburied over time. "And this will eliminate Hitler from history?"

"As I understand it sir, yes. If they take this back in time and get it close to Adolf Hitler it will create an irreversible paradox."

"How?"

"It's quite simple I believe. He cannot be in two places at once and therefore will cease to exist. His molecules will unravel and he will be erased."

"So, they simply need to deliver it to him in person and science, physics or whatever it is will do the rest," Chadov asked.

"Yes, Comrade President, that is the case," the archaeologist said.

Chadov pondered briefly then slapped his desk, making a loud bang.

"If it saves the lives of tens of thousands of our countrymen and eliminates the Nazis from history, it shall be done. We will deliver this to the IG committee immediately."

Chadov smiled, his great army of World War II may have won in 1945, but he would fire the shot that would eliminate the Motherland's greatest threat from existence.

As President Dimitri Chadov escorted the archaeologist out of his office and saw the Hitler artefact handed to his security detail for delivery to the UN, his encrypted Commlink chimed. He looked at the display and smiled again. "Hello comrade," he answered.

"Comrade President," said the voice in acknowledgement.

Chadov advised the caller, "You will be pleased to hear that we have found the artefact, it is being dispatched to the IG facility now."

"That is very good news," replied the caller.

"Now, do you have more good news for me comrade," Chadov asked.

The woman said, "I do Mister President, I have secured the complete blueprints, schematics, and detailed construction data for the Infinity Generator. Undetected of course."

"Wonderful! That is great news. You have done well. Your country is in your debt."

"Not at all Mister President, anything for the Motherland," replied the voice.

"With this we will now have the freedom to do the things that our forefathers could only have imagined," Chadov suggested.

"Indeed sir."

Then Chadov added, "You will stay in Cern, keep looking for opportunities and collect any new information and data that we will require. Once the Nazi threat is eliminated, we can begin."

"Yes, Mister President. I will fulfil my duty," the voice told him.

"I have no doubt. With your help we will re-establish the Union of Soviet Socialist Republics. We will become the one true Superpower," Chadov said.

He smiled once more as he gazed out his window over Moscow and imagined the possibilities where the CCCP would reign over a new future for all mankind under the hammer and sickle. Then he said,

"Godspeed Anastasia Kuznetsov!"

END.

From the author

Thank you for buying my book, The Hitler Paradox. I really hope you enjoyed it. Please leave a review wherever you purchased your copy of the book.

Here are some more of my publications, available through most online outlets and in bookstores.

All I See Is Mud

5 Irons Don't Float

Parallax

The #Covid19 Experience

The Terranian Enigma

http://andrewdunkley.com

Contact the author at alliseeismud@gmail.com